THE LIFE I'M IN

THE LIFE
I'M IN

SHARON G. FLAKE

Scholastic Press / New York

Library of Congress Cataloging-in-Publication Data available

ISBN 978-1-338-57317-6

1 2020

Printed in the U.S.A.   23

First edition, January 2021

Book design by Abby Dening and Elizabeth B. Parisi

To survivors everywhere

A BUS TO NOWHERE

CHAPTER 1

MAYBE I WAS born bad. Some people are, you know. I do bad things and bad things happen to me, no matter how hard I try to be good. Now my sister wants me gone. I don't know what I did this time exactly, 'cause I'm always doing something, she say. Like punching a teacher, making a girl set our classroom on fire. But I don't wanna go. I was born in this house, right in the living room. It's the only house I ever lived in. She don't care. Not no more. We leaving for Greyhound in a few hours.

Getting dressed in the dark, I leave my bonnet on. Then I walk over to the window to watch the sun come up. Every day it's another color. A different sun, seem like. Wish I was different. But the same old me still here doing the same old things I always done.

Zipping up my backpack, takes a while 'cause it's full. My sister JuJu would be mad about the things I snuck and put in here—gin, rum, that kind of stuff. I started to pack my coloring books and crayons, but I ain't done with those yet. JuJu said be ready first thing in the morning, but when I sit my backpack and suitcase out in the hall it's still dark, and her door is shut tight. Maybe she changed her mind. I changed my mind about some things, like calling Maleeka Madison, when I said I wouldn't never, ever speak to her no more in life. They kicked me out McClenton Middle because of her.

Maleeka ain't the same Maleeka she used to be. She don't walk the same. Don't even look the same. She got a fro now, wears lipstick, not gloss, foundation, and eyeliner. I seen her online with her new friends. She go to a school for smart kids now. I don't go to school at all.

I'm in bed lying down when I call her. "Maleeka."

"Char?"

"Don't hang up."

"I wouldn't do that, Char."

"Oh."

She ask what I been up to. I ain't talked to her since last year. I done plenty of things since then. Only, I can't think of nothing good to tell her. When the quiet gets too loud, I tell her why I called. "She don't want me no more. She putting me out the house. Can you ask your mother to talk to her?"

Maleeka know who I'm talking about. She asks if JuJu still throwing them parties, but don't wait for the answer. She could ask her mother to get on the phone, she says, if I want her to.

"You ask her. She might tell me no."

Maleeka used to always do what I told her. She knew I'd beat her ass if she didn't. This time she say I should talk to her mother myself. "This is really important. It should come from you."

I sit up, breathe in slow and easy, so I don't get mad. "Please, Maleeka." I say it in a nice and quiet voice, when I really wanna roll my eyes and scream.

At first, she say okay. Then just that quick she change her mind. "I always did what you told me, Char. But not this time."

I hit the wall with a pillow. "Just ask her! She your mother!"

"One, two . . ."

"Stop that."

"Three . . ."

"What you doing? Why you counting?"

4

"I'm giving you time to apologize."

"Huh?"

She see a counselor at school, she tells me. If people scream at her or she feels disrespected she supposed to count to five. "If they don't quiet down or apologize by then, end the call, walk away, get help, my counselor says."

She start counting again. I stop her when she get to four and a half, and apologize. I never do that. People apologize to me or else.

She'll get her mom, she says, if I still want. I tell her not to. Her mother wouldn't help me now anyhow. "How come nothing bad ever happens to you, Maleeka?"

"You know my dad died, Char. That's something bad. And my mother—" She yawns, then say how her mother ain't sad and depressed no more, or sewing to help her nerves. "She work for the cable company."

"Oh. Tell her I said hi."

"Last year she had breast cancer. She's in remission though."

I tell her I'm sorry to hear that. Out the blue, she tell me I'm smart. That maybe it's not all my fault that I act the way I do. "Both your parents died. You had it way worse than me."

I don't talk about my parents to nobody. Not even JuJu. I almost tell Maleeka that, then change my mind. It wasn't gonna come out so nice, I could tell. So, I go to my desk. Sit down to work on a picture I'm almost done coloring. We both quiet for so long, I get half the sky in my picture done.

"Where she sending you, Char?"

"To my grandparents."

"She could change her mind. You never know."

"You never know."

I put down the Lemon Drop Yellow crayon. Pick up a white

one. Lay my arm on my desk, then my head on my arm, and take my time filling in the clouds. A therapist said coloring would be good for me, a way to relax, calm myself down and chill. I do it 'cause I like it now, and I'm good at it. I don't tell nobody, but when I color, seem like my whole body getting a massage.

"Char?"

"Yeah, Maleeka."

"Have a nice trip."

"Thanks."

"You can text me, or call when you get there. But if you mean to me, Char, like you used to be—I won't give you no more chances."

She gone before I get to have my say. I sit seven crayons aside to color the butterfly, fifteen more for the flowers in the garden. I like soft, light colors, so my pictures always look like spring, happy.

"You too big to color," JuJu's girl friend told me once.

"Leave her alone," my sister yelled. "There's worse things she could be doing."

I never color outside the lines. I always take my time. 'Cause if you mess up, you gotta start all over again. And I hate starting over.

CHAPTER 2

THIS THE SECOND time JuJu brung me to the bus station this week. The first time ain't work out so well. I cried like a baby, got loud and said I wasn't going nowhere and she couldn't make me. Somebody got the police. My sister wasn't happy about that.

JuJu been my guardian four years now. She's twenty-seven. I'm sixteen. She carries papers on her that prove she's responsible for me. "See." She had 'em out by the time he got to us.

"Char," my sister said after he gave the papers back and said for me to have a nice trip. "Let's go."

"Home?"

She didn't answer.

I followed her out the station, up the sidewalk into the parking garage next door. All the way home she ain't say nothing to me. That night I was in my pajamas in my bed thinking I was home for good when she told me I still had to go. She sat down on the edge of my bed. "No more chances, Char. I'm done."

Now we back at the Greyhound bus station. I'm outside next to the bus standing beside my sister—hoping. She beside me telling the man who loads suitcases onto the bottom of the bus to be extra careful with mine. It's brand-new, expensive, she says to him. She don't mention that her old boyfriend stole it from Macy's.

"JuJu. Can I stay, please?"

She turn her back to me and start walking. By the time I

catch up to her, she's inside the station. I gotta run to keep up.

Seem like everybody in the city going someplace. They lined up ten deep at the ticket counter on the other side of the room. Lined up beside doors to take buses to Texas, New York, Boston, Philadelphia, New Mexico—anyplace you can name. They rushing through the station with food and kids, in wheelchairs, pushing carriages—yelling at people that get in their way. Some of 'em stare at me on their way by. Could be because of my hair. I done it myself. I got four shiny long black braids—two up front and two in back— that stop at my stomach, and a yellow bandanna tied on my head. It might be my eyelashes they checking out. JuJu say they look like caterpillars.

Parts of me jiggle and shake when I walk. But not 'cause I'm making 'em. I'm getting big all over—mainly up top and on the bottom. I got thick pretty legs now too.

By the time we stand still, I'm out of breath and we're in the middle of the station. When she lift her shades up, I see her eyes is still red, puffy. "Charlese Jones! Everything can't go your way."

"I know. I'm sorry. Don't holler." I look around to see who watching.

JuJu takes my hand, says she not used to me being like this, "Nice—sad all the time." She sits down in a row of black plastic chairs. I sit next to her. Her eyes blink a few times. I ain't sure if it's because she really don't want me to go, or maybe it's from the smoke always stinking up our house. When JuJu throw a party, they last two and three days. The one from Friday still going on at our house. All that smoke and weed. Drunken grown-ups everywhere. I ain't gonna miss that. But that don't mean I wanna go live with my grandparents.

"If you let me stay—"

"You can't."

"I was just gonna say I'll work for you for free."

She start digging around in her purse. "Why can't I find it?"

I pull at my shorts. Not that it do any good. They tight and small, the way I like. I bought 'em with my own money. I work JuJu's parties. Serve the drinks, make 'em sometimes too. People pay to get in. Pay extra for food and liquor. And they tip good. She didn't have to pay me, I told her yesterday. "Just let me stay. Please." She gave me half of what she cleared so far. I left my tip money home. For when I come back. 'Cause I'm coming back.

"Here." JuJu stick her hand out. "Read it. So, you remember—you brung all this on yourself."

The paper in her hand is folded small as a pack of Tic Tacs. It's yellow with lines. I don't take it fast enough, I guess. So, she drops it in my lap. I cross my legs. Some old dude near us smiles, likes how they look, I guess. The hair on his head is white as smoke. So is the hair sneaking out his ears. "Pervert," my sister say. He gets up and leaves. "Watch out for men like him." She always tells me that.

I open the letter. Ask if she wants me to read it out loud. I had to sometimes when teachers sent home bad reports about me.

"No, Char, you too old for that."

Dear Mis Saunders:
I apologiz for stealing your watch and bullyin Maleeka into setting your classroom on fire.
I was having a bad day.
Char

She never wrote back. Or treated me as good as she did Maleeka. That's why I got expelled.

I been to three different schools since they kicked me out Mc-Clenton Middle: a Catholic school, a charter school, and a white school in the suburbs where JuJu faked our address so I would get in. They all threw me out. The same thing gonna happen in Alabama, I told JuJu.

Looking her in the eyes, I tear up the note. Throw every single piece on the floor. JuJu tell me to clean it up. I don't. That was a practice copy, anyhow. There wasn't no mistakes in the one I mailed to Miss Saunders.

"See, Char. You admitted right there it was your fault."

I stand up.

She wanna know where I'm going.

I don't tell her.

I just start walking.

JuJu's right behind me. But she can't follow me everyplace, all the time, she been saying lately. I blew it running away, skipping school. If it wasn't for that she mighta let me stay.

They got two machines on the other side of the room. By the time I get there, I got my purse out my backpack and my wallet open. Four people in line ahead of me. JuJu is beside me when I ask how she found my letter. She says she was going through my drawers. Double-checking. Trying to make sure I didn't leave anything I might need later.

"I ain't need no letter."

"So, why'd you keep it?"

I put ten quarters in the machine. Press the Coke button. "I don't know. Guess I forgot about it."

The soda takes a roller coaster ride to the bottom. I rub the ice-cold bottle on my arm. Twist off the top. Sip and swallow. And ignore my sister with her hand out wanting me to share. "Miss Saunders coulda gave me another chance."

She look at me like I got two heads. "You had plenty of chances since you left McClenton Middle—a whole year's worth. And what you do? Cut class. Fight everybody that looked your way. Quit therapy."

I stopped therapy 'cause I don't need therapy. It's stupid. You sit around and talk about stuff you don't want to talk about—like my mother and father shot dead outside the chicken joint. So, I quit. Saved my sister all that money she was paying. Only, I ain't tell her I quit. I would take the bus downtown. Window-shop. Sit on benches and talk to people, grown-ups mostly. I get along better with them anyhow. I get along better with boys more than girls.

"Here." I hand JuJu what's left.

She take a swig, then another one, then finishes the bottle. "I called her."

"Called who?"

"Who you think—your old teacher. Miss Saunders."

Before I ask why she called a teacher that don't like me or her, JuJu bring up the time I ran away. She think I was with a boy. I wasn't. One of her regulars let me sleep on his couch for two whole weeks. I told him I ran away because of my sister and her parties. But it was everything, not one thing. JuJu ain't been herself since I got back.

"I didn't know what else to do, Char. So, I called her. I mean— she helped Maleeka. You said that. So, I thought—"

I stop. "She told you to throw me out, didn't she?"

JuJu got her arm through mine when she start walking. The exit door that lead you outside to my bus is halfway across the room. Her voice is quiet and calm when she brings up the bank teller job she's starting next week. It's the first real full-time job she ever had. The pay is low, but she can work with that, she told me the other day, long as they pay her way to school like they promised. She never cared about school or working for other people till I stayed out that night. The party that's going on at our house right now is the last one she plan to throw. She did it for me, she said, so I would have spending money.

Before I can stop myself, I put my arms around her neck and hold on tight. "What if it don't work out? Can I come back home then?"

"Call me when you get to a rest stop." She lifts my arms, then puts her glasses back on. "That way I'll know you safe."

She don't say good-bye, I love you, or nothing. Turning around to leave, she stops. "I almost forgot." She pulls a big envelope out her purse. Makes me promise I'll read what's in it, like I ain't done enough reading already. I take it anyhow. And shove it in my backpack. With my head up high, I leave her before she can leave me.

CHAPTER 3

THE BUS IS mostly full when I get on. But people still line up behind me with drinks and snacks in their hands. The driver's at his seat talking on the microphone. "Folks, this bus will be full in a little while. If you have things in the seat beside you, set them in your lap, on the floor. I need room for other passengers."

I look at the people behind me. "Don't nobody sit beside me," I say. "Or you'll be sorry." I walk a little ways, then stop, hoping to find the best seat. The man who liked my legs is on the sixth row with his finger pointed at the other side of the bus. He asks if that's somebody I know knocking on the window.

Sure is—and she crying.

I look straight ahead. Try to fix my mind on something else. It's hard though, 'cause all I can think about is home.

"Young lady!" The driver's coming up the aisle. "Can you hear? Take a seat. Any seat." He squeezes past me, pointing. "There's one. Another one on the last row."

"By the bathroom? No! I'm looking for an all-by-myself seat. 'Cause like I said. I don't wanna be bothered with nobody."

"And I told you—sit somewhere, anywhere. We're packed. Everybody has to share."

I walk some and stop. A woman with kids in a seat near my right elbow smiles. Her little girl is beside her turning pages in a book. A boy who look just like her is on the same row on the opposite side of the bus. He by the window—my favorite seat—sitting by hisself. He's like maybe five years old. Too big to suck his thumb, but he is. My grandmother put hot sauce on my thumb to break the habit.

"Miguel, por favor." Guess she's that boy's mom. Patting her lap, she smiles at me. Like I'm in a smiling mood. Miguel walks past me, then jumps on her lap.

"This is a full bus." The driver looks down at me. "Next time take your limousine if you don't wanna be bothered with people."

Before anybody get any ideas, I drop my backpack in the empty seat, sit down by the window, cover my head with my jacket.

"What's wrong with her, Mommy?" Miguel wants to know.

"Hush. She's sad."

When I bust out crying, it's got nothing to do with the driver or my sister. It's my mother and father. If they was alive, I'd be an A student, I bet. Still living at home—happy.

CHAPTER 4

I'M HUNGRY, STARVING, mad at everyone on this bus who got family sitting next to 'em that want them there . . . like the lady across from me, and the man and his wife sitting behind me. So, I try to make myself go to sleep. 'Cause when I get like this, bad things happen.

Soon as I close my eyes, I think about my sister back at the party and wonder if she missing me—even a little bit. I miss her already. I miss home and my bed, my mother massaging my scalp every Saturday night—Daddy telling me I was pretty.

Them tears start up again. So, I reach for my backpack. I got all kinds of things in here—snacks, my coloring books and crayons, drinks. I take out the first bottle I get to. Cover my head with my jean jacket again. Twist off the cap. Drink it down straight, no chaser.

I brought five minis with me: pineapple rum, lemon vodka, gin, and plain old whiskey. I took 'em right before JuJu put a new lock on the liquor cabinet last week. She said God told her to. That made me laugh. So does the rum after a little while. Guess that's why I call her. "Maleeka?"

"Char? Hey. How you doing? Sorry, I can't talk." She in a hurry, she says. Her mother put her in a summer camp for kids good at math and science, and this is the last week. "We built a robot." Right now, her team is on a bus to a university, to race robots with kids from all over the city who built robots too. "Real engineers are gonna pick the best winner."

"Oh."

"You gonna wish me good luck?"

I do like she asks. She's gone right after that. She don't even say bye.

My eyes close, and I pretend I'm back in my room sitting at my desk, coloring. My mother's downstairs cooking red beans and rice, her favorite. My dad's in the basement banging a hammer on something he wanna fix, but probably don't got the skills to fix. JuJu is somewhere partying, like she done when they was alive.

CHAPTER 5

THREE HOURS UP the road most people asleep except me. I'm staring out the window at cows—so many they cover the grass and hills like weeds. I never seen one in person before. The prettiest ones—light brown with white spots—was up the road, outside a barn that needed painting. For a minute, I think about not eating hamburgers no more.

The bus pull off the turnpike, rocking like a boat. Then it turns into a parking lot, passes Macy's and Penny's, Target and Burlington—then stops outside a pretzel shop. I smell the butter, count the people—six—who think we got space on here for them.

The driver opens the door. "There's plenty of seats, folks."

The first person on takes a seat behind the driver. He got blond hair, a bun, bleached-blond eyebrows, skin that spent too much time in the sun. But he's cute.

A girl with a purple Mohawk stares at the seat beside me on her way by. I close my eyes. People less likely to disturb you if they think you asleep. Only, I get disturbed anyhow.

"Excuse me."

It's a boy. I open my eyes.

"This seat taken?"

I look at the seat beside me. The one with my stuff on it. Then I get back to him—a boy so tall he got to hunch over so his head don't hit the ceiling. Plus—he cute. Maybe my age—sixteen. Wiping my lips with my tongue, I sit straight up. "Can't you see?" I turn and face the window like he ain't nobody when anyone can see he is fine, my type just like Caleb, the boy Maleeka stole from me. Which is why I got to play hard. Easy gets taken advantage of.

"It's the last seat left."

I fold my arms. Close my eyes again. Ignore this pretty-ass boy and all them bags he got: one hanging off his shoulder like a purse, one in his hand, a black suitcase with wheels on the floor between his legs.

"Hey, you! Sit down!" the driver says to him.

"I'm trying to but—"

"Driver, she won't let him have the seat." It's the man sitting behind me. He white, old with dark purple spots on his cheeks. "We pay for one seat each, girly. Pick up your things so the bus can leave."

I tell him to shut up. The driver stomps up the aisle like my father used to stomp up the steps with his belt, ready to beat us. Only he never beat us. He wanted to scare us into behaving, is all. It worked sometimes. When I'm a mom, I'll just use the belt.

He stops at the row in front of mine. I put my hand on my backpack in case he try to move it. "I retire tomorrow. This is my last trip." People clap. "Know what that means?"

"I don't care."

"That's exactly right. It means I don't care about anything either. And I will throw you off this bus in the middle of the highway if you cause any more trouble. Do you hear me, young lady?"

If I answered, I wouldn't say nothing nice. So, I keep quiet.

The driver got my backpack in his hand when I tell him to leave it alone. He drops it on the floor anyhow, just missing my feet.

I got my fist balled, ready to punch him in his big fat ugly stupid face, when I hear my sister say, "Why you always causing trouble, Char?"

I sit down. Not because of him but because of her. If I'm good, maybe she'll let me come home.

CHAPTER 6

YOU GOTTA LOOK out for yourself. JuJu say that all the time. Before our parents died, words like that never came out of her mouth. It was their job to take care of us, my father and mother would say. "Your job is to go to school. Get a good education." JuJu thought that way too, at first. Then they died. Three months later, she quit waking me up for school, making my breakfast. One day she walked in my room smoking weed. She lifted the shade up and sat at the foot of my bed. "You big enough to take care of some things for yourself." She swallowed the smoke. Blew it out when she couldn't keep it down no longer. "Want some?"

I never liked the smell of weed. So, I said no. Anyhow, Mom and Dad never smoked. They ain't let nobody smoke in the house, either. I sat up and pointed my finger at her. "JuJu. You gonna get in trouble."

"You not a baby. And even if you was, who got time for you to learn to walk. If we don't run—we gonna get ran over." She shoved the blunt my way.

I pulled the blanket over my head.

"I dropped out of school yesterday." She was in community college, her first year. It took Mom three years to talk her into going. Before then, JuJu worked at the corner store and the gas station 'cross town. She never got enough hours, she said, or could afford to get the nice things she wanted. She was taking things back then too, only Mom and Dad didn't know it.

"We need money, Char. We down to three eggs and one piece of chicken."

"Don't steal. Mom won't like it."

I remember her saying we might have to do things Mom and Dad never had to. She brought up the rent, electric, and water. All past due. Our cable was already turned off.

I came out from under the covers crying. She put the blunt between my lips. "Try it."

One puff was enough. I ain't never done it since.

JuJu walked across the room with that blunt stuck between her lips. "I make the rules." She was almost out the door. "Here's the first one. Don't tell nobody what go on in this house."

The parties JuJu threw, plus the clothes she stole and sold, been good business. We ain't had nothing turned off since she started. Plus, the rent is always paid three months ahead. She take that job with the bank and she might end up homeless, I told her. "Maybe," she said, like she ain't care one way or the other. "But I gotta do something different—otherwise nothing's gonna change."

Truant officers came by our place on the regular. People complained that our grass was too high and called the city. A neighbor— Miss Kim we think—reported me to Children and Family Services. They made a wellness visit once. But never came back again. Maybe JuJu is tired of living that way. Could be Miss Saunders is making her change, or told her she was better off without me. She that type of person.

CHAPTER 7

HOW THEY SLEEP on this cold bus, I don't know. The windows is steamed up, sweating, from heat outside and the cold in here. A girl wearing a pink blanket like a shawl sneezes her way back to the bathroom. The lady across from us got her sweater spread over her legs, a quilt on her kids.

JuJu said I would be cold. But what did she expect me to do? Dress like a grandma? "Bus driver—" Before I say he need to turn off the air, he pick the microphone up. He knows it's cold. He apologizes for that. But a warm bus can make a driver drowsy, he say. "And I want to get everyone where they're going alive."

I got goose bumps on my legs and arms, I tell him. I got my arm in one sleeve when I say, "You could turn it off if you wanted to."

I head up front, leaning with the bus. Stopping, I hold on to a rail so I don't fall. That old dude looking me up and down, smiling. Men always do. It used to make me uncomfortable. Especially at JuJu's parties. My father's old fatigue jacket helped some. I wore it while I served beer and drinks or dumped ashtray or collected money for fried chicken dinners. But men got X-ray vision Clark Kent–style. They see me, through me, anyhow. So, I expect it—them looking at me like the last beer at the party. Guess being cute gonna come in handy when I'm in Alabama.

The bus go too fast on the curve. "Woo—" Old man grabs my

waist after I almost fall in his lap. He likes the shorts I'm wearing, he says. My top too. I push his hand away and stand up.

The driver watches me through the mirror. He got a big belly like my dad. Skin as brown as Maleeka's. "You all right?" he ask.

I pull at my shorts, not that it do any good. "Yeah."

"You sure?"

I almost tell him I can take care of myself. "I'm fine" is what comes out.

I quit walking when I get to the yellow line painted on the floor so people don't get too close to the driver. "It's really cold back there." I fasten my jacket. "Some of us ain't bring blankets."

He beeps the horn to keep a truck full of sheep from running into us. "Okay, but you guys are never happy. Ten minutes from now someone else will ask for air." He beeps again. "Can't anybody drive?" His eyes find mine again. "And you—sit down."

The bus still think it's a boat. On my way to my chair, I got to hold on to seats on both sides of the aisle. Twice, I look over my shoulder at him. His eyes is on the road, not me. "Bus driver. Do you got kids?" I hear someone say.

"Two. Girls . . . twins, twenty years old next month. They gave me these gray hairs. God should have gave me boys. They're easier."

My dad said stuff like that.

Back in my seat, I stare out the window at trees every shade of green in the crayon box. The driver gives us the name of the creek on our right. He says Native Americans named it, but he can't pronounce it like he should. "I won't try." It's lazy today—quiet—'cause there's no wind, he tells us. "But if y'all look closely, you can see where it overflowed last winter and wiped out three farms." People stand in the aisle for a better look. If you woke and got a window, you stare out—not saying a word. One person died in that flood, the driver says. I think about the cows, sheep too. Who look out for them when the water gets high?

It's quiet again when I check out the boy beside me. There's a name tattooed on the back of his neck. Jason. Hope that's his name. Not his boyfriend's. Otherwise, I'm screwed. So I don't think too hard about him or his dumb neck, I grab my backpack. And finally do what my sister asked. It's out my purse when I see she wrote a note to me on the outside of the envelope. My legs is on the seat, folded, when I start to read.

Dear Char,

The letter inside is from Miss Saunders. I know u hate her but read it anyhow. And not just 1 time, but as many times as it take 4 u 2 c that some people in this world care abt u and me. I woulda had you read it at the station. But I knew you would tear it up right in front of me. It came a year ago. But I was too mad at her to pass it on. She ain't as bad as people think, Char. I know that now. After you came back from running away, she called me. Asked if we could meet 4 chicken and waffles at Mr. Dan's on Fifth. Her treat. She asked about you. But mostly she wanted to check up on me. Who done that since Momma and Daddy died? Nobody. I was 23 when they passed. Too old to need a mother, I guess people thought. Miss Saunders ain't never had kids of her own. But she been giving me good advice.

It's your choice to read her letter or not. But quit being mad at her, me, and everybody else 'cause that won't bring Momma & Daddy back or make things right 4u at school.

JuJu chose her . . . over me. She on Miss Saunders's side now, not mine. I keep reading, stopping at the part where JuJu says she's passing Miss Saunders phone number on to me, in case I might want to call her. Then I open the envelope. Shake out the letter. And rip it up.

The bus is humming, extra quiet, when I make up my mind not to go to Alabama. My grandparents is good people, but they family. And JuJu done showed me you can't trust family neither. You got to look out for yourself. Take care of yourself the best way you know how. 'Cause nobody else will.

Miguel pulls his thumb out his mouth. "Don't be sad."

I lie. "I ain't sad. Go to sleep, okay?"

The boy next to me sits up. "What?"

I am tired of people all up in my business. "You gay?" I ask. "'Cause you look gay."

His legs cross at the knees and ankles. "All day every day—proud too." He pulls a jacket out his backpack the color of peas and covers his head with it.

I'm crying by the time the man behind me stands up. "You okay? Driver—"

"Everybody leave me alone!"

Jason or whatever his name is waves a tissue my way. "Here. I was crying before I boarded the bus. I saw my ex-boyfriend on the way here."

I take the tissue. Then blow my nose and wish I was dead. Miguel's mother offers me apple juice. I shake my head no. The boy next to me steps on my foot on his way to the bathroom. Miguel's mom gets in his seat. "Shhh. Shhh. It's okay. Sometimes you just need a mother."

She rubbing my back when I tell her that my mother and father are dead.

She says, I know. Or I thought so. Something like that. Then she hugs me—tight—like she my momma, daddy, and JuJu wrapped in one. I don't know what she saying when she talks that Spanish in my ear, all calm and quiet, but I like it.

CHAPTER 8

"WHAT'S YOUR NAME?" He back in his seat.

I got my eyes on a booger under the window next to me. Miguel came to visit and left it there, I think.

He say he can't sleep no more, so he might as well talk to me. He's skinny. With wrists small as Miguel's seem like. And lashes longer than mine. I ain't notice his shirt before—lemon yellow with a polo player on it. His loafers is doubled stitched at the sole.

His name is WK. The initials stand for his real name, he tells me. The one his mother gave him to get back at his father, only he hardly uses it because it sounds like a payback name. I wanna laugh. I don't 'cause I didn't come on the bus to chat it up with nobody.

"Ill." It's Miguel. "What's that stink?"

"Pigs." It's the man behind me.

All of a sudden, the whole bus stink like a Porta Potty got dumped on it. Miguel and his sister run up and down the aisles, snorting like pigs. A lot of people, even me, hold their noses. WK pull out a can of Right Guard and sprays. Then he squirt sanitizer on his hands like he touched them pigs.

I take out my coloring book and crayons. He get the hint and start talking to Miguel's momma. Her name is Mrs. Rodriguez. She takes bubble gum out her pocket and gives it to her kids on their way by. WK moves on. Two rows back, he talking to purple Mohawk girl, who tells him she's on her way to Arizona. He is too, he says.

I heard of that place. Dry heat. Sand and coyotes. My fourth-grade teacher showed it to us on a map. She told the class she was gonna retire there one day. I said, "Maybe I can go there and be a teacher."

"Teacher?" Mrs. Gamble smiled. "Charlese, I hadn't realized you aspired to that?"

I asked what aspired meant. Everyone laughed but her.

While WK walking up front, I dig around in my backpack for the piece of paper I wrote that word on. "Aspire. To attend to, go after, to make happen," the definition says. I found it myself. Researched it at the library last Monday. Didn't even ask a librarian for help 'cause they think you stupid sometimes too, you know. *I aspire to a few things.* That's the sentence I wrote beside the word. The kids at school would laugh if they saw it. I would too, six months back. But things with me is changing too—not just for JuJu. I aspire to be somebody people like.

WK talk a lot. Now he up front with the driver. And the whole bus can hear him. "I had surgery." Why he lifts his shirt, I do not know, 'cause how can a man drive and stare at your cut-up belly at the same time? The driver tells him that too. "My brother was on dialysis ten years. My parents said I was too young to give him my kidney until last March after he almost died." He holds on to a pole to keep steady. "I had two—so why not?" He lets his shirt drop.

That boy still talking about kidneys when he sit back down next to me. Do I know how many black people die because family members and friends won't give one up? he asks me.

"I'm taking both of mine with me when I die." I put away my word.

"Organ donations—"

"I want to be buried with everything I was born with."

"What good would that do you?"

"My body ain't the 7-Eleven where you can get what you need whenever you need it."

He's quiet. The whole bus is. Guess they didn't like what I said.

He takes a bottle of water out one of his bags. I ask if he's gonna drink it all.

"Duh, yeah."

"Well, can I get a sip?"

It's one of them small ones. After I open it, I pour some in my mouth and swallow. Then dribble water onto that tissue he gave me and hand him the bottle. "Thanks." I got one eye closed while I'm rubbing away that booger. When I drop the tissue on the floor, I tell WK that it's okay. They hire people to clean up after we gone. He like Caleb. He picks it up, including the letter I tore up. Then gets back to talking about kidneys. To get him to change the subject, I ask who Jason is.

"Nobody." He lift his shirt, traces scars with his finger. Doctors cut him from the middle of his back to his navel.

"It hurt?"

"My brother had it worse. At the dialysis center, they stick horse needles in your arm," he says, "and pump chemicals in you to get the bad stuff out your blood. They're killing you and fixing you at the same time," he whispers.

I ask if his parents made him give up that kidney. He swear it was his idea. What would I give up for JuJu? Not a kidney, I know that.

He wanna know if I got a boyfriend.

"No."

"A girlfriend?"

"No."

"Both?"

I laugh a long time. "Nope."

He gets back to his favorite subject—him. Tells me he's headed to Atlanta because they do a lot of movies there.

"I thought you were going to—"

"Yeah, I go there first to speak at churches, the NAACP, and community centers about kidney donations. Then I go to Atlanta. My sister's boyfriend's family lives there. They say I can stay a while . . . attend cyber school." I should memorize his face, he say, 'cause one day I'll see it everywhere.

His nose is long, crooked in the middle. He got big round eyes that remind me of girl eyes, now that I think about it. They sad and soft and sexy-looking at the same time. There's a dimple in his chin, and a cross earring dangling from his ear.

"I hate when a boy is prettier than me."

Out of the blue he say, "I loved him. But—"

"Everybody can't get with pretty, you know." I'm thinking about Caleb. He was cute. I'm cute. Why he ain't want me?

WK kisses my cheek. "Don't worry. It'll be okay."

"What?"

"Whatever made you so sad and mad."

"No, it won't."

He take my hand and puts it on his scar. "There's worse things that could happen to you. Your boyfriend could break up with you at the hospital the day after you had surgery to help your brother."

"Wow."

"Then dump you two more times after that."

"Dang." I look at him. "You still love him."

"I know. But I shouldn't." His boyfriend's new bae is a junior in college. "A 3-D copy of me."

"I don't understand."

"It's like when you buy jeans. If they fit well, make you look amazing, you get the exact same pair in another color." That's what his boyfriend did, he say. "Got me in another color—white." He twists the ring on his left middle finger. "Like he could ever replace me."

He blinks, fanning hisself like he might cry. I tell him he better not. Then I go into my backpack. "You play?" I pull out a pack of cards. He ask if I can play Tonk. I play it all, Blackjack, Poker, 500, Joker's Wild, Spades, slots. Sometimes, I had to deal—when JuJu ain't trust nobody else in the room.

I break open a new deck and shuffle. "My sister kicked me out, sent me away. But I'm not going where she sending me."

He rubs his hands after he sanitizes 'em. I let him cut the cards before I deal. "You got a knife?" he asks me.

"No."

"You should. People crazy, you know. I wouldn't want to hear about you on the news."

I am the type to end up on the eleven o'clock news. The twins' mother said that once, and it's true. Girls like me always do.

June 29, 8 p.m.

CHAPTER 9

THE BUS IS empty when I wake up, parked at a rest stop. The building where you eat and buy food is right in front. I stay in my seat wondering why nobody woke me up or asked me to go inside with 'em.

Getting off, I see the Jacksonville, Florida, bus. I got an aunt there. We almost ended up living with her. But she lost a baby she was carrying, and my grandmother said, "Let her sit in her sorrow for a while." Guess she never got over being sad 'cause she never came for me or JuJu.

Soon as I get inside, I'm sad too. 'Cause everybody got somebody to be with except me.

Mrs. Rodriguez and the kids found a table by the front window. She got a red plastic tablecloth, food on pink paper plates, napkins on her children's laps.

The farmer and his wife eating white pizza with forks.

WK don't notice me. He too busy up in bun boy's face.

Amish men in straw hats, people wearing family reunion T-shirts, Indians, and white people in cowboy boots eat and laugh at tables in the middle of the room with people who look like they belong with them.

I wish I was home.

Passing a rack of magazines they let you have for free, I run to the bathroom. Soon as I get to the handicap stall, I take out a bottle and pour the whole thing in my mouth. It burn like fire going down. So does the bourbon.

Bourbon on ice was Mr. Bobbie's main drink. He let me make it for him at JuJu's parties, but not while I was staying with him. For breakfast he made me eggs every day, scrambled—almost as good as Dad's. Mr. Bobbie wouldn't let me cook or clean for him 'cause I was a kid, he kept saying, and he was letting me stay 'cause he was afraid I might end up someplace worse. Before I left, he put a fifty in my hand. If I ever came back to his house, he would call the police, he told me. Every once in a while, I call him. He don't never answer. He said he wouldn't. "'Cause you is a child, and I am a grown man, and we got nothing in common. Remember that, Char—you got nothing in common with grown-ass men no matter what they tell you."

That wasn't true exactly. He played checkers and liked old movies, same as me and Dad. He is good at baking brownies, like Mom. Except he puts nuts in 'em, and she never did. I would live with him, if I could.

It don't take long for me to feel the liquor. To feel warm and happy. To hear music when there ain't none playing. Snapping my fingers, I move my hips, dance out the stall and give that purple Mohawk girl the finger. I got my butt parked on a sink when I call Mr. Bobbie. I want him to tell me what to do—go home to my sister, take the bus to Alabama, or find my own place like I'm planning. He used to have voice mail. I think he disconnected it because of me.

My sister bought me this phone. It don't do nothing but take calls and let you make calls. I used to have one that cost eight hundred dollars. It did everything except fly. JuJu took it from me, gave me this. That was my punishment for running away, she told me. "And for getting kicked out of school again."

I try Mr. Bobbie one last time—hoping. He don't pick up. I got nobody else to call but Maleeka. But all she seem to do now is talk about herself. So, I find another stall and drink the last bottle. Laughing, I dial *her* number. "Miss Saunders. You still ugly?"

"Charlese Jones, is this you?"

"You know it is." I pee my shorts some, I'm laughing so hard.

She ain't never quiet. Right now, she is. So, I wait for her to hang up on me.

"It's good to hear from you."

I don't ever remember her being nice to me. She always yelled, "Charlese, stop cutting in the girls' room! Charlese Jones, quit kissing in the hall!"

"I know it's been a difficult transition since leaving McClenton."

I guess teachers treat you better once they know you not coming back.

She bring up the three schools I went to, the time I ran away. How McClenton teachers and students posted flyers, asking people to call JuJu if they knew where I was.

"I ain't run away."

"Your sister told me—"

"I knew where I was. *She* ain't know where I was, that's all. And what you doing talking to her about me anyhow? I don't go to your school no more."

The room start to spin. I lean my forehead against the door and close my eyes.

"How are you, Charlese?"

Drunk, I want to say. Then I sit down on the floor, scoot over to the toilet. With my hands wrapped around the bowl, I stare at the water and wonder when I'm gonna throw up. "Miss Saunders."

"Yes, Charlese."

I gag. "I gotta go."

She tells me that she is glad I called. That I can call her anytime—day or night. "It may not seem like it right now, Charlese, but your life won't always be like this."

I almost miss the toilet when I throw up.

CHAPTER 10

HE THE FIRST person I see when I step out the bathroom. "You got any gum? I need some real bad."

"No, but we can go buy some." It's the old dude from the bus. "I'll buy you anything you want."

I could use a pack of cigarettes. "Anything?" Just that quick I change my mind. "Naw." I stick my hand out. "I just want a piece of gum or a mint. You got any of those?"

He licking his lips like they taste sweet or something. Says he might have a few mints after all. Like magic, he pull one out his shirt pocket. It's red, cinnamon, the kind I like. His hand is all sweaty and warm when I take it. "Thanks."

I can call him Wilbert, he says. When he lean in close to whisper in my ear, I laugh. His breath smell like beef jerky. He covers his top lip with his hand after I say that. "Let's go for a little walk."

Miguel's mother waves at me from across the room. He turn his back to her. "What ya say?" He pull out his wallet. It's an old man's wallet—fat, brown; split in places. "Twenty dollars okay?"

I laugh out loud and say I'm worth way more than that.

Mrs. Rodriguez stands up. "Charlese."

"Okay, thirty." He looking outside at the lot where trucks park. "In ten minutes, we can be back on the bus."

I need to sit down, I say. He tell me there are tables with umbrellas outdoors. That if I come with him, everything will be okay. Staring at his old man feet, I say, "I don't like your shoes."

"What?" He staring at 'em too.

"Look. The heels are run over." I burp.

JuJu said you can tell a man by his shoes. The cheap ones don't bother to keep 'em polished or maintained. They say they gonna tip, but they don't. They claim they want extra sides with that meal but try to get 'em for less than you charging.

My eyes hurt when I look up at him. "Go away."

Miguel's mother got her hands on her hips like my mother used to do when I was taking too long to get in the house after the street-lights came on.

"She wants me."

"But—"

"I changed my mind! I can change my mind, you know!" I'm loud. JuJu say you gotta be if you trying to save yourself or stop what got started even if you started it and changed your mind midstream.

He looking around. Clearing his throat. "Lower your voice." His wallet slides back in his pants pocket but don't go in as easy as it came out. "Maybe later."

On my way out the building, I see him walk up to that purple-haired girl from our bus.

CHAPTER 11

THE MAN IN the seat behind me don't like me. But he don't know me. He knows I'm drunk though. Guess the whole bus does. Mrs. Rodriguez whispers when she say for him not to judge me too harshly. Life is hard for kids today, I hear her say. "The world is loco."

He don't agree. He think the driver shoulda kicked me off the bus. Did I do something to him? I don't remember nothing except falling asleep with my head on WK's shoulder and him covering my legs with his jacket. How long I slept like that? It was light when I got on the bus. Won't be long before the moon is out.

WK wipes drool off my bottom lip with his thumb. "You always this nice to everybody?" I ask.

"I guess."

Nice get you beat down at the schools I went to, I say. With my head in his lap, I tell him about Maleeka. How people bullied her. Made her do whatever they wanted. I don't tell him it was me who done it most of the time.

He reach in his bag to hand me a bottle of water. "You need to stay hydrated when you drink too much alcohol," he says. I swallow the whole thing down at one time. Next, he gives me bubble gum. "For that stank breath."

We laugh.

I close my eyes. Try to remember what happened after that old man hit on me. I left the building, I know that. Came on the bus and sat on the floor. WK says I threw up outside the bus. He rubbing my ear and asking if I want another hole in it. No, I got three in each one already, plus one in my nose.

"I do piercings." His tongue slides out. "I did my tongue but—"

I laugh while he tells me his tongue swelled up and turned blue when he pierced it. The doctor had to take the tongue ring out and drain the pus. He did his boyfriend's tongue at the same time and the same thing happened 'cause the needle he used was rusted, it turned out. "Maybe he left you because of that."

He laughs. Then gets serious. "Don't be out here, drunk girl, or something bad is gonna happen to you."

"I know."

He makes fish lips and snaps his fingers. "And I'm too pretty to fight."

"I know," I say, and I mean it.

On my way back to sleep, I hear Miguel ask his mother when he'll be able to come over and color with me. I promised him and his sister they could. I know what page we'll color and everything. But I'm not up to it right now. On my way to sleep, I ask WK about the boy he was with inside.

"His name is Blaine. I'll tell you about him later."

"Hey." I sit up, stretching my arms in the air. "What I miss?" I know I missed something because bun boy was sitting up front behind the driver. Now, he three rows away from us, still on the opposite side of the bus.

WK blows his breath in my face. "How does it smell? I brushed my tongue in the bathroom while you were asleep. Do you realize how long you slept?" He don't let me answer. "Three hours, girl. We stopped again. Look."

"At what?"

"Empty seats."

My stomach burns and bubbles. I promise myself not to drink no more. "Did you kiss him or do something worse?"

He smacks my hand. "Girl, no." He swear all they did was talk. "It's too soon for me to do anything else." He pull his jacket to straighten out wrinkles. "I keep myself a boo. But that's not always a good thing, you know."

"I know."

If I see him hugging that boy or sitting too close to him, "Come get me," he says.

"Yeah, right."

"I'm serious."

"Okay."

"Because I have other things on my mind. Starting my own nonprofit. Giving presentations around the country to get people on the transplant list. Acting. Most guys my age don't understand that." He stands up. "And I am tired of trying to make them." He holds on to the luggage rack on his way to that boy. "I'll be right back. It's just a little visit."

Miguel makes a little visit too. Soon as WK leave he's in his seat, then in my lap. He put his thumb in his mouth and hums. I squeeze him tight and tell him a story about crayons who act like people. The man behind us is surprised at how good a job I do. I ain't. I would babysit at JuJu's parties, find books in the trash and save 'em—just in case. When I got kids, I'ma already know what to do with 'em.

I ask Miguel what name he wants to give the red crayon. He

says Rita. That's his mom's name. He names the black crayon Sky. When I ask why, he point out the window. "Because that's the color it is sometime."

If Mrs. Rodriguez was a different kind of mother, she wouldn't let me be with her kid. Miguel stays as long as he want. His mom reads to his sister. When Miguel gets enough of me, his mother takes his seat. She don't give me no speech. But she do let me know if I drink anymore for the rest of the trip, she won't let them visit with me no more. Her fingers find my chin. She turn my face toward hers. She know I am not a happy girl, she say. "But things will get better." Them Miss Saunders's words. "Trust." She points to the roof of the bus, but I know what she mean.

CHAPTER 12

SHE'S ON THE last row of the bus when I get to the bathroom. My stomach feels queasy. I think I might throw up—again. That's why I'm back here. I go inside the bathroom, gag, rinse out my mouth with sink water, and walk out. She sitting with a baby in her lap. Guess she got on while I was sleeping. She the one sleeping now.

I get close enough to smell her baby's baby-sweet breath. "Hey." She hold on to my finger. I tickle the palm of her hand. "You strong, huh? Pretty. What's your name?" She got chubby legs and feet. A strong, hard kick. Her hands shake like rattles when she laugh. If I was her mother, I couldn't sleep on no bus. Somebody might run off with her.

It's hard to know what all she got in her, some black for sure, maybe a little white mixed with Chinese or Japanese or Filipino— something beautiful anyhow. It shows in the shape of her eyes. Wish I had 'em—light gray with brown highlights. She my favorite color in the crayon box—Raw Sienna.

They both got thick dark hair. Her mother's is extra long, real. Their skin don't match though. Her momma's skin is white, but not white-people white exactly. For a minute I wonder why there ain't different shades of white crayons in a box.

Before I ran away, I promised myself I'd have a baby if I didn't get back in school or have nothing better to do. Lifting the pacifier off her green blanket, I slide it between her lips. She sucking it like a bottle when her mother's eyes open.

"Sorry. I—"

She looks at me, then the front of the bus, then me again. She let out a yawn and stares down at the baby. "It's okay. People play with her all the time. I don't mind." Another yawn and her eyes close and stay shut. "You don't want one. They're so much work, you wouldn't believe."

I ask how old she is.

"Old, old."

It's a lie. She my age I bet—could be younger. She been through some things too, worse than me I bet. It show on her skin like lint on carpet. And that foundation she wearing don't hide what she trying to hide anyhow—dark circles under her eyes, a cut on her right cheek.

She asks where I'm going.

"Nowhere."

She laughs. Sits up. Finds him before I do. I don't know if he coming for me or the bathroom. Real quick—I let her know what happened at the rest stop. His hand is on the bathroom door when he smile and wink at us. She lifts her top, flashes him, and asks, "How much?"

Licking his lips, he look up front. And tells her he got twenty for her if she meet him in the bathroom after everybody goes to sleep.

She puts her hand out. "I'll take it."

He repeat what he said.

"Driver!" she yells.

I stand up. "Driver!"

He pulling out money faster than a cop taking out his gun. Dollar bills rain on us. I pick 'em up, divide 'em up. Once he back in his seat she says, "When you can, make 'em pay for being jerks."

CHAPTER 13

IT'S RAINING. SEEM like the windows is crying it's pouring so hard. The driver says it won't last. I'm back in my seat all by myself, so I hope it do. Crying while it rains reminds me of home. Coloring does too. So, that's what I do: cry and color with my jacket hanging over my head. I don't know what started it. Maybe it's because of what that girl April said. "Those kids are lucky. She seems like a good mother." She was talking about Mrs. Rodriguez. Which made me think about my JuJu. She the only mother I got now. And when your mother don't want you—whether she birthed you or not—it make you feel real bad—hopeless.

CHAPTER 14

I GOT A job. I get ten dollars to make sure WK leave this bus without swapping spit with that dude. Staying put next to me would be cheaper, I told him. He walked off again anyhow—smiling. Guess I'm the kissing police now.

When his elbow lift off the armrest and he lean Blaine's way—I stand up and yell, "Hey! I'm watching you." Everybody else is too for a minute. I crack myself up and do the same thing three more times mostly 'cause I'm bored. It works. He change seats. I was hoping he would come back to me. He in a seat on my side of the bus right across from that boy. Who don't know it won't last all that long?

"Look." It's the farmer behind me. "Right there." His finger taps the glass. "Won't see many now that the sun is down. Lucky there's a full moon."

It's the most cows I seen at one time. The farmer says there's seventy, maybe eighty out there. For a while he tells me about his farm. His grandson names the cows, which he say ain't good to do.

"Because one day he's gonna find them gone, right?"

"Off to slaughter."

"Slaughter?"

"Jeepers. You must know what that word means. What do they teach you—"

His wife stops him from saying all of what he thinks. That's good 'cause I don't want to hear it anyhow. What he know about me, my school, or what I know? Nothing—just like I don't know nothing about running no farm or milking cows. I do know it ain't right how they treat them poor old cows. They look dirty and sad, bored and worn down. Just like some people. Thinking on it some more, I ask, "How do milk turn white anyhow? Grass is green."

He talks like he a science teacher. Says something about proteins and intestines, chlorophyll. Fifteen minutes later he still explaining. Blah, blah, blah. I quit listening. When I say he should shut up, he gets mad. I get on my knees in the chair and face him. "I'm only saying what other people won't."

His wife smiles. "Dear, leave the child alone."

"She's interested in cows and farming, what harm does it do to educate her?"

"I'm not dumb."

He kind of apologizes, but not really. I take my seat, pull a magazine out my backpack. It's my sister's. She used to only read magazines about movie stars and cheaters. Now she buy this kind with articles on how to get ahead, talk better, do better, want more. Guess Miss Saunders told her to. "I read, you know. See." I hang my arms over the headrest and poke the actress's cheek on the cover.

"I never liked her." He hits the magazine. "Just a troublemaker."

"Shhh." It's his wife.

"Why do I have to be quiet? Tell her to be quiet."

The driver asks if the people in the back can please be respectful of others. She's already seated. Flipping pages, I find the recipe section. It's the Thanksgiving issue even though Thanksgiving was a long time ago. Where's the macaroni and cheese? I wonder. The hog maws and chitlins; fatback in the greens? My mother made her food like that. Now JuJu does. Once, Miss Saunders said that kind of food was unhealthy. She was wrong though. Wrong about a lot of things. When I'm married, my kids are gonna eat like I do. "Hey." I knock on the window. "Mister. You got kids . . . grandkids?"

He holds up three fingers. "Why?"

"I just wondered."

"Oh."

"Any of them like me? You know—with some black in 'em."

"Jesus. What kind of person is she?"

"I think she means biracial, dear."

I can tell without seeing that his neck is red. "No."

"Oh."

He asks why I want to know. No real reason. I think about that baby in the back. "One day you just might have one."

"Have what?"

"A grandchild like me."

"Jesus Christ."

"Maybe not the same color, but black just the same."

He stands up, sits down, knocks his knees or something against my chair. His wife tell him to be still and watch his blood pressure.

I put away the magazine. Pull out my coloring book. I like princesses, 'cause my father used to call me his little princess. I find a page and start with the crown. It's got thirty stones in it. So, I take out thirty crayons. I color the way some people paint their nails—slow and careful—perfect. It's the only thing I do right.

CHAPTER 15

THAT BABY AND her momma sitting beside me when I wake up. April say she don't got the hang of being a real mother yet.

"I couldn't get Cricket to stop crying. I walked her up and down the aisle a long time. I sat down beside you and she shut up." She hands her to me. "I think she likes you." She cut her eyes at a woman walking up the aisle.

"Hey, girl," I say. "You been bad while I was asleep? Don't be bad." Cricket drools a lot. I wipe her lips with my jacket collar. "No!" I say when she try to eat it. "This ain't food." She kicking her legs, wiggling her whole body. April closes her eyes, asks if I got anything to eat.

"Take what you want out my backpack. I got more than enough."

She goes in my bag, holds up a bag of corn chips. "This?"

"Sure."

"And these." She got two Mounds bars in her hand now.

There's honey-coated peanuts in there too, I tell her. Peanut butter crackers. Guess she don't need to hear that twice. Out everything comes. Dumped in her lap. She pick out what she want, pulls back the wrapper on a Lunchable, and makes a double-decker ham-and-cheese cracker sandwich. Crumbs fly when she telling me Cricket drink a lot and she didn't know how much babies ate, so she ain't have enough Similac or money when she started the trip. She kisses Cricket on the forehead. Slides a piece of ham into her own mouth, chews, and leans Cricket's way, then sticks her tongue out like a spoon. There's a tiny bit of smashed-up food on it—a dot. Cricket used to eating this way, I guess. She open her mouth wide, and before I know it, the spoon goes in and she chewing—or trying to.

Mrs. Rodriguez says Cricket too young for that kind of food. April grab her bag off the floor and puts all them snacks in it. She talk about running out of baby food, being down to the last scoop of Similac in the can. "I borrowed some from a woman on the last bus."

It's the farmer who says, "Jesus—young people."

I got my fist balled when his wife stands up. "Does anyone have Similac on this bus?"

It ain't her business, but I'm glad she asked. I didn't even think about it. "Yeah," I say, "we need milk. A baby got to have milk."

The driver says the next stop is in a couple hours. Cricket's already frowning and kicking—with her mouth wide like a baby bird's. April looks at Mrs. Rodriguez, chomps down on a cracker this time, sticks the spoon in her baby's mouth.

Cricket smacks her lips, moves her mouth, gags while she swallowing. Then we hear it. The biggest belch ever, plus a fart. Poop fills up her diaper. Warms my leg.

"You got more diapers, right?" I ask.

"One."

"Bus driver!" I hand Cricket over to her mother. "Can't we stop somewhere, please? It's an emergency."

The old man who wanted to get with me says that once the bus stops I ought to be left behind 'cause since I got on they haven't had much peace. I'm not sure who claps, but a few people do.

"Screw y'all." I raise my voice louder. "Y'all probably the ones sitting up in church talking about God, but okay with letting a baby go hungry."

The driver got his eyes on me, not the road. "See what kind of life I been having as a driver, folks. Selfish people who make it hard on everyone else."

I ain't figure him to say that. But I keep standing. For once, I'm quiet though. 'Cause JuJu said you gotta know when to shut up sometimes and let what you already said marinate.

Twenty minutes later the bus pulls into a rest stop. "Jesus!" It's the man behind me. "This kid gets whatever she wants."

I hear his wife say, "The baby . . . needs milk. And Pampers."

A woman standing up front is holding dollars in her hand. "I can spare three bucks."

Mrs. Rodriguez opens her purse and dumps change into a hat. She speaking English and Spanish when she walk the aisles asking people to give what they can.

The bus door opens. Mrs. Rodriguez puts Miguel's baseball cap in April's lap. "For me?" She tears up.

"You and me," Mrs. Rodriguez says, "we go inside and get what you need."

Her children stay balled up asleep in their seat. I hold on to Cricket. The man behind me asks his wife if April will give them back what she don't spend.

"Bus driver," I say once April gets off. "Would you like to hold the baby?"

"I will retire in a few hours if y'all don't get me fired first. So, no, I do not want to hold a baby. But someone can give me a Tylenol."

CHAPTER 16

TRUTH OR DARE. April came up with the game. We four sitting in back the bus playing it—no feeling people up or taking off clothes though.

Three of us are on the aisle seats on the last two rows. The baby is on my lap. I'm across from WK. April and that purse of hers is on the floor facing the front of the bus. She always got to see what's ahead of her, she says.

WK looking at Blaine but pointing to me. "How old were you when you first kissed?"

I lay Cricket over my shoulder and burp her. "Ten. After school in the playground with Caleb. I made him."

Everyone laughs.

"April, you next," I say. "How many girls you kissed?"

She don't kiss and tell, she say. So, she take the dare. It must be a lot of 'em, that's all I can say. I dare her to kiss that girl up front with the purple hair. April take her time getting there. Almost everybody else is asleep. We cracking up when she lean over that girl, kissing the top of her head. Purple girl don't even know it happened. She never moved or woke up. But that stupid driver sees everything. So, he calls April over. Lowers his voice. Looks through his mirror at us while he talking. "Yes, sir," we hear her say. "No, sir, I don't want to be kicked off." She runs our way laughing. Saying this is the most fun she had in a long time. Then she get back to playing and watching. I ask what she looking for. Why she stare at people so hard? She smiles, turns her head, watching Mrs. Rodriguez on her way by. "No reason," she say. But I know that's a lie.

For the next hour we talk more than play. Find out all kinds of things about each other. WK is in the gifted program, runs track, the 400 and 200, still wears his old boyfriend's ring. Blaine goes to private school, never had a boyfriend—spent last summer in France with his aunt.

"Why you riding on this thing?" I ask.

He like to travel. Got this plan to visit every state, even Hawaii, by the time he's twenty-three. I ask how many states he been to already. "Twenty-five, including Puerto Rico." Last summer he biked sixteen hundred miles to raise money for kids with leukemia.

WK bats his eyes. "You want company the next time you go to France?"

Blaine picks his eyebrows a lot. "I don't think my aunt would mind."

WK jumps up, walks over, and fist-bumps me, then accidentally knocks April's purse off her lap. He get down on his knees in a hurry to pick up lip gloss, a silver earring, pens, her phone, and a bottle of pills that she snatch out his hands quick as she can. Putting her things away, she tells us some of the places she been—Mexico, San Diego, LA, Atlanta, DC, Erie, and Ohio. I ask which place she liked the best. She give us a fake smile. The kind where the bottom and top row of your teeth meet, but your eyes don't seem to be having the same good time as your mouth. "I was really little. I don't remember much." She wanna work on a cruise ship and travel the whole world, she says. I look at Cricket but don't ask what she plan to do with her.

My phone rings. It's my sister. She said to call her from every rest stop. I woulda, but she'd ask a bunch of questions I can't answer. Like, what time should my grandparents pick me up? Who did I meet on the bus? Did I do like she said and tell the driver about the man who tried to hit on me? She knew it would happen. It always do. But you can't snitch every time somebody try to take advantage of you. You got to learn to stand up for yourself, 'cause sometimes all you got is you. Maleeka finally learned that. She got me to thank for it. "Right, Cricket?" I lift her high in the air and laugh when spit drips on my nose like syrup.

WK ends up on Blaine's lap. "Truth or dare, Char. How old were you when you first had sex? And don't lie."

Blaine's face turns red.

I take the dare 'cause who would believe I never did nothing like that ever? Nobody—not that old dude up front or the kids at school. So, when they say I have to chew and swallow ten sheets of wet toilet paper from that grimy, nasty-ass bathroom, I do it. But I don't like it.

CHAPTER 17

SHE GONE WHEN I wake up. So is Cricket. WK is back in his seat, like he never left in the first place. "Where she at?" I stand up.

"April? She's in the bathroom." He unwraps an orange Tootsie Roll, sticks it in his mouth. "I bet she's on drugs. Popping pills."

Mrs. Rodriguez looks back. "Maybe we should tell the driver." Her daughter is awake sitting sideways in her lap—kicking her legs. "Forty-five minutes is a long time to be in there."

I don't mean to run—but I do. I don't mean to bang on the door like I'm the police and she stole something—but I do anyhow. All I can think about is them TV shows I watch. Sometimes girls flush the baby down the commode.

"April!" I got my lips near the crack of the door. "You can give me Cricket. I'm up now. And it's extra tight in there, I know it. You can't hardly wash your hands—let alone do your business holding a baby." I'm thinking 'bout that pretty baby splashing in the water or already drowned. It happens a lot, on the news anyhow. "April!" I use both fists this time.

The driver don't sound happy when he get on the intercom. He asks if someone is sick. The farmer says there's a drug addict on board and she shooting up.

For the first time, the driver swears. When he reach for his phone to call the police, the bathroom door opens. Seem like every eye on the bus is on April. "What?" The door slams behind her. "Can't a girl change?" She walked in wearing jeans and came out in black tights. Her top is different too, a crop top like mine, long sleeves.

I sit down beside her in the last row. "I'll take her." I stick my arms out.

She holding tight to Cricket like I'll kidnap her if she don't. We stay that way awhile. Not talking. Looking straight ahead. Yawning. I whisper, "This my favorite part."

"What is?"

"A full moon night with the clearest sky ever."

She ask if I ever been on a boat. I ain't. Because if I had been, she say, I wouldn't think this little old piece of sky was anything much.

April lays Cricket facedown on her lap. It take a lot of digging through her purse, but she find what she looking for. A Gucci wallet, probably fake. She opens it. "See?" It's a picture of a ship on the ocean late at night, under a sea of stars. The next picture is way different.

"That you?"

"Three years old at home . . . the day before Christmas."

She take out more pictures. Holds 'em in her hands like a deck of cards. Shows 'em to me one at a time. Her sitting on a dock by a river. Her riding high on some boy's shoulders with him walking barefooted up the street. I don't ask if that's the father. I stop her at the last picture though. She on a blanket in a alley smoking blunts with a bunch of other kids. They dirty. Look like they stink. I ask how long she was homeless. She rolls up her sleeves.

I point to the tattoos on her right arm where there's a whole row of numbers, one after the other, from her shoulder way past her elbow. None the same font or size. "You do that?"

"With an eraser."

Six is the number of kids in her family, she says. Three is how many years they lived in a van after their parents lost the house. Her dad is a veteran. He got that PTSD, she say. Her mom's a diabetic, and medicine costs a lot. Doctors cost more. "Sometimes you lose your house trying to pay the bills. Lose your job when you take too much time off because your husband is sick—crazy in the head."

I trace the number four. It's puffed up like all the numbers she tattooed on herself. "What's that stand for?"

"That's how many years I lived on the street by myself." She goes down the row of numbers. "This is how many foster homes I've been in—seventeen." She chokes up when she gets to one. "It only takes one person"—she clears her throat—"to help you set things straight." She pinches Cricket's chin. "That's gonna be my aunt Helen. Cricket's going to live with her."

April bend down to kiss Cricket on the forehead. She'll pay her aunt to take care of her. Send her clothes from around the world. "I'll help my family too."

"Are they still—"

Her folks live in California someplace. Her sisters and brothers are in foster care somewhere. "I used to write them when I could." She's thinking about her family, home. You can tell by her eyes.

"April?"

"One day you'll see."

"See what?"

"How good you had it with your sister."

I sit up. Put my feet on the floor. "A sister can try to be your mother, but she can't never be your mother, not really."

"Go home, Char. Bad things happen if you out here too long."

CHAPTER 18

"PEOPLE—" THE DRIVER'S voice cracks over the intercom. "This is the final rest stop until we part company and some of you change buses or go home to your families—thank God."

Before I know it, Miguel and his sister squeezing past WK to sit on my lap. "That breath." I pull Miguel's thumb out his mouth and cover his lips with my hand. He covers mine too. "Guess both our breath stink, huh?" I plant a big kiss on his right cheek—his sister gets one on the nose. "You!" It's the driver. "I'd like to see you for a minute."

WK clowns me on my way up there. Says the driver think he's my father.

I step over the yellow line. "What?"

He don't answer. He let me stand there while he pull into a tight space, then turn off the engine. "Here's the plan." He puts on the brake. Gets off the bus before me and everybody else. "Mrs. Rodriguez will escort you wherever you need to go—to the bathroom, for a drink of water—no stores whatsoever. She says she has food for you."

I say it's against the law what he's doing. He asks if I want him to call the police. "There's a station up the road."

Most people on the bus still sleeping. One or two come off, look my way and shake their heads. When I ask the driver why he's doing this to me, he says, "Passengers talk. Some like to take pictures. Underage drinking is against the law, you know."

WK gets off the bus with Blaine. "You okay, Char?"

I think about the police. About me being drunk on the bus. What if they arrest me, call JuJu, or keep me from getting back on? "I'm cool."

Them two walk away holding hands. Mrs. Rodriguez's kids hold my hands after they hop off the bus. "Come along, Char," their mother says.

April come off last, sweetening the air on her way by.

"Who got Cricket?" My eyes go from one bus window to the next, then back to her.

"Some man and his wife said they'll watch her."

"I woulda done it if you asked."

She walks past me, past the rest stop and the lamps that light up the dark. Taking off her heels, she walks through the grass, then runs over gravel, stopping when she get to the trucks parked in the lot across the way. It's full of eighteen-wheelers—with pictures of food on 'em—hamburgers and fries, bottles of milk, crackers, and vegetables. Men, like cows, stand around waiting.

CHAPTER 19

WE ALL AT the same table. The one by the front window. I picked it 'cause you can see the truck stop from here. I made up my mind. If April take too long, I'm gonna find her. WK ask if I'm crazy. Says there must be twenty trucks over there, so ain't no way to know which one she's in. Then for the first time he say something mean. "Maybe she's the kind of mother that needs to stay gone."

I'm being mean too when I look at his hand lying on top of Blaine's and say, "Thought you were staying away from boys."

"Away from boyfriends. Not friends who are boys who are cute and can kiss." He winks, then asks Blaine to be nice and buy him a latte with extra cream from the coffee shop. "I need to go to the boys' room."

They both gone by the time Mrs. Rodriguez gets to her feet. "Char, sit their snacks and drinks out, please. I'll take them to wash their hands."

I point to myself. "Me?"

"You."

"But we don't got time."

"Thank you very much."

The drinks is on the table when the farmer walk in holding Cricket. Before the door shuts behind him and his wife, I'm in front of 'em with my arms stuck out. "I'll take her."

"No, you won't." He walks past me. "You see a police officer? A guard?" Cricket's head is lying on his shoulder. His hand is on her bum and back. "They have to have one. Where's the driver? He'll know." His head goes left to right too many times to count.

"Dear. It's not our business," his wife says, catching up to him.

He turns around so fast she bumps into him. "She left her! In the bathroom. On the floor. Like trash."

"Cricket?" I ask.

She probably thought no one would hear her in there, he says. But he got prostate problems. His wife whispers something about Depends. If eyes could slap, she'd get one good across the lips from him. "We're discussing that tramp, not me," he tells her.

"William! Be decent."

He start walking. Cricket's wiggling like a worm. I'm right behind him. My eyes looking back at the window now and then.

He asks about the driver again. "Is he in the bathroom?" He'll hand her over to him if there's no officer of the law around, he tells us. I try to keep up. His wife tries to keep up. But he got long legs, plus he's fired up. Mad.

"April is having a hard time," I say. "Ain't you ever had it bad?"

He in the middle of the room when he stops. "Who hasn't had it hard?! This baby will have it hard too, if someone doesn't intervene."

People stare at us from everywhere. Cricket cries. Screams. Kicks. He look at his wife, starts to hand her over till I snatch her from him. Stepping back, holding her tight as muscle hold on to skin, I tell him if he try to take her from me, I'll scream. "Bad things too."

I turn my back to him and pat her head. "Shhh. Quiet. Your momma's coming soon." I look out the window that faces the trucks. "Them calves," I say. "Where their mothers at?"

"What?"

"The calves on the farms we passed."

He wipe sweat off his forehead with a white napkin he took off a table. "Just give her to me. I'll turn her over to the—"

"You think their mothers may be on one of those trucks out there—on their way to be cut up, turned into steaks and shoes?"

I barely hear him say, "Life's hard."

I hold on to Cricket like I birthed her. Like JuJu held on to me some nights after my parents passed. "I bet them calves wish they had their mothers no matter how bad a mother they had."

His wife looks down at the floor. "I was adopted."

Her husband say not to bring that up again. "It has nothing to do with that trollop who sat her baby on a pissy floor of a Greyhound bus." His hands go in his pants pockets. "I told you, Pat, what I was going to do, and I'm going to do it."

"Leave her be, William."

"No, I—"

"If her mother doesn't return then we will take additional steps. But for now, let's do like the Bible says we should." He hangs his head after she says, "Do unto others as you would have them do unto you."

He talk like he wears the pants in the family, but it's her I see.

"Where's the coffee? I need some coffee—black."

Once he's gone, she give me Cricket's Binky. It should go in the trash since it was on the floor, she says. Pointing to one of the stores, she starts walking. "I will pick up a few things for her. It's the least we can do."

"You mad at your mother for giving you away?"

She stop in her tracks. "Mad? No. I'm thankful. Sincerely and forever grateful. She was fourteen. Never finished high school. Where would I be if she hadn't come to her senses?"

She's gone when I call JuJu.

"Char. I told you—"

"I love you. I'm okay. You don't need to worry about me," I say, right before I hang up.

CHAPTER 20

APRIL WALK ON the bus carrying a shoe in her hand. Wiping lipstick off with tissue, she keep her head down. A woman up front means for everyone to hear her say, "God seen ya nasty."

A fat man who was nice to me ain't the same way with April. He calls her a name that gets the driver mad enough to tell him to apologize. Not that he does. He stares at April even after she pass by—so does everyone else.

It ain't till she close that I notice the shoe she holding is missing a heel. And her right cheek is red. *Did somebody hit you?* I wanna ask. But who can't tell she ain't up for questions?

"I'll take her." She sits down and pinches the fat on the back of Cricket's neck. "Hey, Mommy. Did you miss me?"

Cricket is a baby. She don't know better. She do her best to get to her mom. She throwing a fit, crying. Only she can't go nowhere. I won't let her. I got my arms around her belly tight as rope. "She tired. You can have her after her nap."

"What?"

"Let her sleep! She almost was before you got here!"

April made us late by ten minutes. The driver wouldn't leave without her. He got daughters, he told us for the hundredth time. He paced outside. "It's my last day," we heard him say. "What can they do to me?" He pulled out a cigarette and lit up. I ain't know he smoked.

He was backing up the bus when somebody said, "There she is!"

I try to flip Cricket onto her belly, but she fighting me. Making her legs stiff as sticks, refusing to lie down.

April's hands go under Cricket's arms. Before I know it, she in her momma's lap. "I'm her mother, not you." Her eyes close. Her cheek leans on Cricket's forehead.

"You left her on the floor."

"What did you want me to do? Hire a babysitter?"

I keep my fist where she can't see it balled tight, ready to go off like a gun. Inside I'm counting, trying to do like JuJu said right before I left and not fight the whole daggone blasted world 'cause I'm having a bad day.

"All I'm saying is . . . you ain't have to leave her like that. I like her. Don't mind watching her either. You raised her good, April." It's a sort of apology. Normally, I ain't the type, but sometimes you have to so you get what you want in the end. I want Cricket to be all right. 'Cause I know what it's like to want a mother who ain't there. "You got the right to do with your baby what you want."

How people expect her to eat, she says, or buy diapers or milk? "If I don't— Never mind."

I look out the window. Notice cows beside the road. April lay Cricket across her lap and turn her legs like wheels. "I sold . . . a few pills . . . that's all."

The man behind us laughs.

April raises her voice to make sure people hear her. "I'm starting a new job. With benefits and everything." She looks at me. "I want to be a good mother. But I can't right now." She cuddles Cricket. Puts her nose in her bushy brown hair. "If she stays with me— Never mind."

I ask about her job.

"It's on a ship."

"A boat?"

"A cruise ship."

"You mean the kind people get pushed off sometimes?"

She laughing. "The kind with cabins you live in rent-free. With all the food you can eat. And people from around the world speaking different languages. I'll get the chance to take college courses."

April filled out the application online and sent in money. "Three hundred and fifty dollars," she says.

"For what?"

"The job."

"You gotta pay for a job? I thought they paid you."

"The good ones cost." She still owes 'em money, she says. "I'm supposed to pay the rest when they pick me up."

Truckers drive all night, she say. Sometimes twenty hours straight—not that they supposed to. She reach into her pocketbook, takes out a bottle of pills. There's maybe six left. "I still need to make seventy-five more dollars. Otherwise—"

"They won't give you the job?"

She shakes her head.

The purple-hair girl stands up. "Turn your lights off. Don't you see people sleeping? Driver!"

I never seen so many snitches in my life. I reach for the button. Now the whole bus is dark, except for the moon and car lights shining in.

"April."

"Yeah."

"When you start your job?"

"Tomorrow."

"Tomorrow?"

Her aunt will come and get the baby. Someone from the company is gonna pick her up and drive her to Florida. "I have to be on that ship." April reaches down and pulls out a yellow blanket from her baby bag. She covers Cricket from head to toe. "I'll wear a uniform and everything."

"What kind of job is it again?"

"I'm not sure. They say they got lots of positions. I get to pick, I think."

"Oh."

She closes her eyes. "See. I had to sell those pills. To do whatever I needed to. Otherwise, things for me and Cricket won't ever change."

I think on that some, then go back to my seat. I'm asleep in no time, at home, in my bed dreaming.

CHAPTER 21

THE SUN'S DANG near up when the driver burst out singing. It's a soft song—one I never heard before. I got my fingers on the window ledge, my nose pushed against the glass, listening to him sing people awake. Nobody say for him to shut up. Maybe 'cause his voice is smooth as the Jack Daniel's Black that JuJu serves up when people walk in looking like they got money to burn.

The farmer knows the song, seem like. He hums while the driver is singing; while Mrs. Rodriguez sings under her breath too. Most anybody that's awake or knows the words do the same.

If you think I'm gone
Then you gone crazy, girl, 'cause
Gone ain't nothing but a word someone made up
to keep us apart but, but, but
I'm never leaving you, gonna be gone from you
'cause can't four letters get in between me and you, you, you.

I'm sad again. Partly because of the song, partly because I did have fun on this bus. Now I won't. From here on out, I'm on my own.

"People!" The driver goes through the toll booth and up on the turnpike. "In just a little while we will be at the Greyhound bus terminal."

A few idiots clap.

"It has been my pleasure to be your driver."

More people clap, including me—don't ask me why.

"Thank you for making my final trip a fun, memorable adventure."

Mrs. Rodriguez's children follow her to the back of the bus. The driver give us instructions. People traveling to other cities will find their bus information on their tickets, he tells us. If we got luggage, then wait on the platform until the baggage people open the door to de-board our things, he says. "Folks with a few hours to kill before their buses take off can purchase drinks, food, books, and lottery tickets inside the terminal." He drives onto the highway. Tells everybody to stay put until we get to the station. But people gonna do what they gonna do.

WK grab his bags from underneath his seat. The man behind me asks his wife to let him by so he can get their things from the overhead rack. The driver's nice voice is gone. "Sit down, people. I told you. You can get your things once I'm in the terminal, parked."

Miguel flops down in WK's seat. "Char." He got a hat in his hand, full of ones, fives, and tens. "We're giving the driver money for being nice. You have any?"

I need all I got if I'm gonna be on my own. But I go in my backpack anyhow. Drop a candy bar in that hat.

"Charlese—no!" Mrs. Rodriguez acts like she my mother. "A generous spirit gets generosity. A tight fist—"

"Gets to punch back when people come for you." I ball up my hand.

Her lips get tight. Her arms fold. I don't know why 'cause I'm not giving up my money for the driver or no one else. "Here." It's the farmer. "Ten bucks."

"But you already gave," Mrs. Rodriguez says.

I look up at him staring down at me. "For her." He drops two fives in the hat.

"You don't gotta—"

"You are good with that baby. Better than her own mother."

People don't say that to me much; that I'm good at something. I mess up. I screw up. I'm too loud. I fight too much. But that don't mean I ain't got feelings or don't want what other people want. Who knows, maybe I could be a daycare worker. Or go to school for nursing and be a baby nurse. Or own my own daycare center. I take out a piece of paper, then write down all the things I already know how to do like cook and clean, change babies, make 'em laugh, read to them. Then I make myself a promise. No matter how hard things get, I won't never give up or give in or stop believing I can be somebody my mom and dad would be proud of. I take out my phone and almost call JuJu to tell her that. Only, I know what she would say. "Char, you been in the seventh grade three years straight. Why don't you put your mind to finishing that first?"

CHAPTER 22

IT'S WILD ON this thing. People push and shove, ask for help with their bags—worry they might not make their connections on time. I got nowhere to be. I stay in my seat hoping I get to carry Cricket off.

"Charlese!" I get a big, juicy kiss on the cheek from WK. "I almost forgot." He sits down beside me.

"What?"

"To tell you my real name. Weldon Kingston Kennedy. I got the same first two names as my mother's first boyfriend. Long story. My dad plays the sax. He went on the road when mom was nine months pregnant. Missed my birth and everything. She got him back though. He never left town again when she was ready to give birth."

I laugh. We hug like boyfriend and girlfriend. "Hold up," I say once he stands up. "Did you sneak and kiss Blaine while I was asleep?" I'd ask Blaine, but he already gone. "You owe me ten dollars, if you did."

He gives me air kisses. "Well—maybe a little one. Or three little ones."

I stick my hand out. "Pay up."

He'll donate the money to the National Kidney Foundation in my name, he say. On the steps, when he's almost off the bus, he tells the whole truth this time. "Okay. I kissed him a long, long time. No tongue. Just on the lips."

"I woulda done the same thing!" I yell.

By the time April gets close to my row, I'm standing up with my arms out. She shake her head no. April got two bags on one shoulder, one in her hand, the baby in the carrier in her arms. She in a hurry to get ahold of her aunt, she tells me. "See you inside."

Dag, she know how to use people. Mad for a little while, I sit down.

I'm the last one off. I try to ignore him, but he ain't having it. "Thanks." The driver reach in his jacket pocket. "But I can't use it. I'm a diabetic."

How he know I put the candy in?

"But thank you for thinking of me." He shaking my hand.

"Okay. So, can I go now?"

"In a minute." He unbuttons his uniform jacket and reaches into his shirt pocket. "I wanted you to have this."

I look at the card in his hand. "Why?"

He does private bus trips. He leases minivans and custom buses and takes people wherever they want to go, he say. "This is a business card." He asks if I ever heard of one.

No, why would I? But I lie and say, "Yeah. So?" And I take it 'cause otherwise he won't give me no peace. It has his phone number on it, his name, and the name of his company. My lips twist up tighter than a pretzel. "Company? I thought you worked for Greyhound."

"I have two daughters. They need things—college tuition for starters." He laughs. "One job wasn't gonna hit it."

"Oh." I take my suitcase by the handle and head for the terminal. He like tissue stuck on my shoe. I can't get rid of him no matter what I do. So, I quit walking. Turn and face him. "Why you messing with me? You creep me out."

He backs up so far you could sit a kitchen chair in between us.

"I see girls . . . so many . . . kids . . . like you." His eyes shoot left and right, then find me again. "The big bosses say drive. Keep your eyes on the road. Don't get involved in people's personal lives." He smiles. "I did what they said . . . but, well . . . it's my last ride so . . . I did what I wanted to do, finally."

"Mike." It's another driver. Before I know it, he in between us, slapping Mr. Mike on the back, talking about the cake-and-punch party waiting for him in the locker room. He got mad jokes about Mr. Mike doing nothing all day after he retires. "Come on, man. Get yourself inside." He go open the door.

Mr. Mike grabs my suitcase. "Coming?"

I look at his card, stick it in my back pocket. Inside, I get away from him fast as I can.

LEFT BEHIND

CHAPTER 23

PEOPLE STUFFED IN this terminal like croutons in a box, so it's hard to find April or see if Mrs. Rodriguez is still here.

It's not a big station. Not a small one either. There are ten doors. Which mean they got ten buses coming and going at any one time. I see that man who offered me money. He holding a woman's hand—his wife's I bet. He trying to be a gentleman now. I watch him open the main door, letting her step outside first. The couple who sat behind me is standing in the line for the bus to Charlotte. He's drinking a bottle of water. She sipping grape juice, it look like. They the first in line already. I don't see April nowhere.

I take a few steps and stop. Turn my bag loose and wiggle my fingers. This suitcase is heavier than I thought. But standing in place is a good way to look for April. So, I turn in every direction slow as the minute hand on a clock and try to see where she at. She could be in the bathroom changing Cricket, I guess. Taking my bag, I start walking, not apologizing when it knocks into one lady's knee and rolls over some man's foot. I'm in a hurry. Like they in a hurry. When it happens to me, I keep my mouth closed and keep moving, until my wheels roll over some girl's foot. She got on new sneakers, she say. Just bought 'em yesterday. She step up to me. Put her hands on me. I had to punch her. She got the nerve to hit me back. Which mean she gets hit again—punched harder.

"Hey! You two!"

No matter how clean a dog is, they still stink. So, I smell that shepherd before I see that cop. My feet and knees, private parts and thighs, all get sniffed. So do hers. His paws, big as my whole hand, scratch and scrape the floor. The chain pulling him back is thick and shiny, scary as his wet, slimy teeth. "Evening, girls." The cop jerks hard on the chain, makes the dog stand still beside him. "No trouble here, is there?"

She says it before I do. "No, sir. We just—"

"Talking. She so loud." I swallow. "People think she arguing even when she saying hello."

She nervous like me. The top of my nose is sweating. Her hand opens and closes, opens and closes. "Can I go?" She's not looking at him or this dog. Her eyes stay down, staring at the floor or her feet. "They just said my bus leaves in five minutes."

They said somebody's bus is leaving. I ain't sure it's hers.

He asks to see both our tickets. A few minutes later, he telling us we can go on our way. Him and his partner will be checking people who board the bus, so we can expect to run across him again, he tell us.

I get as far away from him as I can, over to the food counter. I order more than I can eat—nerves, I guess. "Hot chocolate with lots of marshmallows," I tell the cashier. He look me up and down. Says he seen that dog rip a man's kneecap off once. I order more food— two hot dogs with onions and mustard, a pack of glazed donuts, and a whole pickle, plus soda and corn chips. Eighteen dollars it cost. Not that I would think of not paying. I do that here, and I'm dog meat.

CHAPTER 24

I TAKE MY time eating. Like, what else do I got to do? Nothing but try and figure out where I'm going next. But then I also need to exchange my ticket. Not that I know where I want to end up. It won't be Alabama. I know that for sure.

I stop and check out the cities people going to. I know I don't wanna go to some of 'em, based on the people in line. Why would you wear old clothes? Who travel with rollers in their hair—missing teeth? But then again, most of them are with somebody. I'm all by myself.

That dog sees me, looks at me, scares me. So, I turn around, start walking and don't stop until I'm out the main door, on the corner bumming a cigarette. That's when I see her—April—by the curb on the phone with Cricket on her hip. I'm surprised she still here. It's been a while since we got dropped off.

I don't have to ask to hold Cricket. She hand her to me. "I called four times. She never picked up. I came out here to wait for her."

She give the side eye to everybody that pass it seem—a man in a wheelchair with half a leg, a little girl that don't want to hold her mother's hand, some dude who can't take his eyes off April, and the cop with the dog. I watch them get in the police van.

April tries her aunt again. Cricket starts crying. April screams, "Shut up! Be quiet! Let me think."

People around us stare. I wanna give 'em the finger, a piece of my mind, cuss 'em out. But JuJu say I got a way of making things worse, turning a windy day into a hurricane. Anyhow, I see by how upset April is that me wowing out won't help her any. It's my idea for us to go back inside. She on her cell while we walk. "Yo, Snow." Some dude grab her arm. "I got that." He take all her bags. Nobody helps me.

When April and me sit down beside each other, I roll my eyes at the girl sitting across from us. She gossiping about April—I can tell—to a girl next to her. I can't hear what they say, but I notice things. Like her leaning with her phone so her friend can read something on it. If I was in school, I'd get the twins to jump her. Like I got Daphne to beat up Maleeka. But I got to do things different now, or poop gonna keep flying my way. So, I tell April we need to brainstorm and come up with some ideas. Miss Saunders taught our class to do that.

I take out my composition book. Rip one page out for me, one for her. We supposed to make a list of every idea in our heads, I tell April—even the worst ones. Miss Saunders said you should 'cause a bad one might lead to a good one, then to a better one.

> CHAR'S LIST
> Take the baby to April's aunt's house
> Put Cricket in foster care
> Get the baby's daddy to step up
> Leave her with his parents
> Find a job and take care your own baby

Miss Saunders said no idea is a bad one. That's not true. There's some bad ones here, I swear. Foster care? But I keep it on my list. Share it with April. She do the same with me. I point to one line on her list that surprise me. *"Drop her off at a hospital?"*

Hospitals will take your baby, no questions asked, she say. "Fire stations too. I saw one around the corner."

"Wouldn't you worry about her . . . for the rest of your life . . . if you ain't get to be with her no more?"

She heard me. I know she did. But she don't answer the question. She take Cricket from me. "I want a new life." She smiling. "This one is all used up. Beat up. Raggedy. And I don't want her life to turn out like mine."

Cricket's got no better sense than to smile.

"So—you never coming back for her?"

April's staring out a window when Miguel run up to me. Fast as I can, I hand Cricket over, stand up, and spin him around. "I thought y'all left a long time ago."

They had a three-hour layover, Mrs. Rodriguez says. So, they went to a restaurant. They just got back. "We came to say good-bye."

Miguel jumps down. I got my arms open wide. "You're not saying good-bye to me, Gabriella?" She walks up and hugs me hard. So does her mother.

"Char." Mrs. Rodriguez reaches into her bag. "For later."

It's a small bag of pretzels. She offers one to April, but she turn her down.

She ask me to walk them to their gate. Miguel's got his thumb in his mouth when he take my hand. Gabriella holding on to the other one, swinging my arm like rope.

"You are a good girl, Char. Remember that."

"Yeah, right."

She make me promise not to say that no more. I promise, but I ain't sure I mean it. When she hugs me one last time, I hug her right back, extra hard. "Make your mother proud," she say, "your poppa too."

I want to. I do. I'm just not sure how.

CHAPTER 25

WE IN THE bathroom, in the baby-changing stall. Cricket's chewing on her fist, kicking and laughing when I lay her down. I wonder if she know that things about to change for her. That when she wake up tomorrow and her mother's not there, she gonna cry till she run out of tears. Cry worse when April's gone two days—a whole month. When do kids quit expecting their mothers to come home? I wonder. It took me a long time to stop looking out the door—going to the window—wishing my parents would come back. I ain't care what JuJu said. I ain't care that they was buried and I seen 'em in the casket. They was coming home, finding a way to me, I knew it. "But that ain't how it works." I kiss Cricket on her pink lips. "But at least I knew my parents was dead." I unsnap the legs of her pants. "You not ever gonna get over missing her. I feel sorry for you for that."

I'm quick at changing diapers. I'd win if there was a competition on TV for that. Once I'm done, I hold her little fingers under the cold-water faucet and wash 'em clean. She likes poop. Always finds a way to get her hands in it. Some on her mouth too. After I couldn't get it from underneath her nails, I stuck her finger in my mouth and chewed the tips off. "Now you all clean."

Before I can push the door open wide and leave, a woman walks in. "Here. It's free."

I take it before I know what it is. "Whoa. Hold up. I don't need this."

It's a bar of soap with a 800 number on it. If I'm ever in trouble, being held against my will, trafficked, or just need to talk to someone no questions asked, I should call, the lady says. I hand it back. "I can take care of myself."

I push the door open with my hip. People check me and Cricket out. "Yeah, she mine," I want to say. But you can't claim what ain't yours. I done that with Caleb. It ain't work out.

I talked April into calling her aunt again. I told her I would take Cricket while she tried. I walked her all over the building. We ended up outside. April is right. A fireman told me you could leave a baby at the station if you ain't want it. He asked if I was dropping her off. I ran like my hair was on fire. That's how we ended up in the bathroom. Once I calmed down, I noticed that Cricket needed changing. Babies always do, it seem.

"Did she answer? What she say?" I sit down beside April.

"No." She shake her head no when I offer to hand over Cricket. In another hour, the cruise ship people gonna be here expecting their money and to drive off with April. How she gonna go with a baby?

April wipes dribble off Cricket's bottom lip. "Some people's lives never turn out right, huh?"

I pat Cricket's hands together, patty-cake-style. "Maybe I should call her."

"Call who?"

"Your aunt. From a different number, you know."

I don't gotta hand Cricket over to her, she grabbing her out my arms like a present she can't wait to unwrap. I try not to forget the number on my way across the room. I say it out loud, then repeat it. With my fingers crossed, I dial her aunt, hoping she ain't changed her mind.

"Hello. Hello! Oh, good. You answered." Well, somebody did anyhow. "I'm looking for Mrs. Bodine Johnson. April's aunt . . . Huh? But? Wait a minute? Don't hang up! Okay . . . I ain't mean to scream, it's just. She got the baby with her. Your wife said . . . But April's got a job. She paid . . . What? They made her pay for it. Huh? Well . . . I don't know about that. She got the job anyhow. They coming to drive her to Florida. On a cruise ship, yes. Please? Well . . . what she supposed to do with Cricket—? She can't take a baby on a ship. I know it's hers but . . . Hello? Hello? Asshole."

April don't need to ask what happened. It show on my face like a lipstick smudge, I bet. It was her uncle who turned me down. He said his wife work a full-time job and got her own kids to contend with, and she can't shoulder nobody else's burdens. I'm all set to tell her that, but something else he said come out instead. "He said you don't pay for jobs. Employers pay you to work."

She say that plenty of important jobs ask for a down payment before you start. "My uncle doesn't know everything. He only made it to the eighth grade."

"How far did you go? In school I mean."

She flips her hair and screams at me, "What's that have to do with anything! I know more than you and my uncle!"

I jump up. "Here. She yours. Take her." I sit Cricket in her lap. Grab my suitcase and leave. No looking back. 'Cause if I did, I might see Cricket looking sad, needing me. And right now, I need to look out for myself.

CHAPTER 26

I END UP sitting beside him by accident. But I ain't sorry. He cute. I'm tired. Since I got here I ain't had no fun. So, I smile, cross my legs, and say hello. His eyes take a trip all over me. He don't try to hide the places they visit either. What I care anyhow? I don't got nothing better to do.

He smile and the left side of his lip goes up. "I'm Anthony. Are you—?"

"Char."

"Oh." He look at his watch then check out the room like he expecting someone. "I'm in trouble, I think."

JuJu told me to watch out for weirdos and pervs. "Don't tell nobody you traveling alone either," she said. "Sit by yourself. Scream fire if some old man tries something with you."

Anthony ain't some old man. He got hazel eyes, contacts most likely, long arms and legs, ones that look like they used to run up the court, shooting free throws at the gym. His clothes look tight, even down to his shoes. Professional-looking. He even got on a plaid shirt and a tie. What school do I go to? he asks. I lie. "McClenton." He lying too when he say he's in college "working on my PhD." Dudes in college don't wear eight-hundred-dollar sneakers. They too broke to wear four-hundred-dollar jeans too. JuJu taught me how to spot good clothes, the best jewelry—like that Fenix watch he got on. So why he here? Most of us is broke, or we'd be flying.

He look down at his watch again. It's the second or third time he done that. "You got somewhere to be? 'Cause I don't."

He smiling, showing off white teeth straight as a fence. When he ain't checking me out or checking the time, he eyeing the main door in front of us, watching people coming in, going out, walking in front and behind us—just like April.

Anthony ask where I'm going. I tell him my story—the two-minute version. Let him know I don't know where I'm headed, but I'm gonna have fun getting there. A lady on her way by stares him down, then looks at me—disappointed. His hand is on the armrest in between us when he say, "Maybe I should change seats."

"Why? What did you do? Nothing." I look at that woman who can't stop staring at us. "Bet she's a mom. They like that."

"I don't know. A girl like you is trouble," he whisper. "I can tell." He winks at me.

For some reason, I think about my dad. Maybe because he wore a mustache too. My mother hated it. He shaved it now and then to make her happy. "Love does like that," she said once, "sacrifices some things."

I clear my throat and sit up straight. "Maybe you *should* move."

He know I don't mean it. He leaning in closer, whispering in my ear. "Maybe—I want to end up in Pensacola. Not prison." He reach for his wallet and give me a business card. "Look me up. If you want—"

"What?"

"Everything. Pretty dresses. Jewelry. A nice place too—"

A woman walk by with a baby in her arms. I follow her with my eyes till she go into the bathroom. "You don't want a baby," he say. "They ruin your figure." There he go again, eyeing me.

"Why you care?"

For the first time he seem like he telling the truth. I remind him of a girl he grew up with. She died young of leukemia. "You could be her twin."

"Why people got to die?" I get sad for a minute. "That just messes everything up." I think about my house. It used to always smell like cake and cookies, things my mother liked to bake. And cigar smoke from Dad.

He understands, he says after I tell him about them. "You never get over that kind of loss."

I think about Mr. Bobbie. I think about my sister. I hate being sad. So, I'm glad he's here.

Paying attention to Anthony means I'm not paying attention like I should. So, I don't see him walk over to me. "Young lady. You're still here?" It's the driver.

Anthony stands up.

"Ignore him. He not my father. He just a bus driver who likes girls." I cross my arms and turn away from him. The next thing I know he walking out the door. Taking out his card, I stare at it, then rip it up. Stupid man. The number is already stuck in my head.

Anthony keep standing. Says he got business to attend to. But if I change my mind, I should call him. "Anytime, day or night." Maybe he can find me a job or something, he tells me. I mention April—not Cricket though. In one whole sentence, I give him her story. I mix a little of her true life in it, but like sugar in collards—not too much so as not to ruin things.

He smiling. "It's kismet."

"What?"

"Meant to be. Me meeting you." He looking around. "Where is she?"

"I think she's outside. I'll get her."

Sometime God be working things out in your favor. That's something JuJu be saying all the time now. Not that she go to church or the mosque. I think it's Miss Saunders putting ideas in her head.

Out of breath, I catch up to April. She outside with the phone to her ear. "Listen . . . this man . . . he got a job . . ." I hold out my hands and take the baby from her. Bouncing Cricket on my hip, I explain things. She could stay here in this city with her baby, I say. "Me too."

"Oh."

"Don't you want that?"

"What I want, I can't have." She opens the door. "Where is he? What kind of job is it?"

"A good job."

I don't tell her that he the kind of guy that does shady business. You know, hires people under the table, lies to girls and gets away with it if they like Maleeka. But April and me is different. She been on the streets, knows game when she see it. If he ain't careful, he gonna end up buying pills off her.

April take gloss out her bag and redo her lips. Next a bottle of deodorant comes out. Sticking her arm up her shirt, she rolls it under both arms. She blows kisses Cricket's way. "And don't come in looking for me. I mean with her. I'll find you." She look down at her clothes. She changed once she got here. Now she got on a white top that buttons up to her neck, a black pencil skirt down past her knees. Flats. "How do I look?"

"Like somebody's mother." April walks away quick.

Cricket's high in the air when I say, "Don't worry. Your mommy is like me. He can't get over on her." I look through the glass door at April. She look back at us. Her eyes say something I can't read from here. I smile and wave, anyhow.

I kiss Cricket on the lips even if doctors say not to 'cause you can pass diseases on to babies that way. *Your mother loves you. Don't ever forget that,* my teacher told me the day after the funeral, when I was back at school. It's what I tell Cricket. I look her in the eyes and repeat it out loud. She smiling like she know what I'm saying. Hope she do. Your life ain't much if you don't believe somebody got your back out here.

CHAPTER 27

I BEEN SO worried about April and her life, I ain't made plans for my own. So, while Cricket play with her toys, I start another list.

> Go 2 Alabama
> Finish school 1 day
> Find my own place and get a good job
> Find a place where me and April both can live
> Share expenses

I stare at the list, then cross off the first three things. How come I ain't think of it before? If she get the job, we three can live together, help each other out. I'll work nights—at a bar, a restaurant, maybe cleaning at a hotel—and babysit while April is at work. Two jobs gonna mean we'll make enough for us both to live good for a while.

CHAPTER 28

SHE WAS GONE over an hour. So, I came looking for her. She on the corner by herself—but don't seem like herself when I get to her. Seem like she crying. Her back stays to us, so I ain't sure.

"Well—?" I say, holding tight to Cricket.

"He'll pay what I owe if—"

I knew it. Way deep down inside I did. "He a snake, right?"

"Something like that. But—" She walk up to somebody she don't know and asks for a cigarette. It's lit when she get to us. And tears are on her cheeks. I ask what's wrong.

She used to dance, she says. He want her to dance on the ship.

I bring up Cricket. "What you gone do with her?"

"You know I can't take her with me." She start walking. It's hard to keep up, but I do.

April turn the corner. By the time she turn the next one, she done with the cigarette. It's in the street now, still lit. The fire station is across the street when she take Cricket from me. Pushing a red button hoping to make the light change faster, she talk about the Atlantic Ocean. She even knows how deep it is.

"What if he lying to you?"

"So—he lies. Everyone lies." She needs a place to stay, she say, and a job. He can give her both.

We cross the street in a hurry. I tell her about my new list.

Cricket starts up again. "Quit it!" April lifting her high and shaking her.

"Touch her again. Hit her. Shake her and I'll—" My fist just misses her chin.

She is tears and snot and words I can't make out for a while. "I prayed for that job. Prayed that my aunt would take her so we could both have a good life."

This time I tear up. "We can make it. You don't need him."

She walking again. "Maybe somebody nice will adopt her."

"Let's go back to Greyhound. We'll think of something."

She stops. "Like what?"

"Like . . . maybe . . . I don't know . . . maybe my sister will take her."

If JuJu didn't want me, she says, why would she want a baby? She kisses Cricket on the forehead, her cheeks and fingers, leaving red lip gloss everywhere. "They'll find her a good home."

It seem like a long way to the door. "Mommy's sorry, baby." Her hand is on the knob, turning it, when the siren goes off. She and me both back up.

They jump on the truck, putting their hats and jackets on. More come running, yelling. It's kismet—or whatever. There won't be nobody in there to take the baby—April know that, I see it on her face. I turn so she don't see my face, wet.

CHAPTER 29

APRIL TELL ME how she made her money when she was home-less. And it wasn't selling pills. Then she apologize to me and her-self. 'Cause she shoulda known before she paid for the job, she say, that things ain't seem right. "I've been in the game too long to get played."

Sometimes JuJu say I can't see the forest for the trees or my nose right in front of me. "You streetwise, Char, for a girl living on the street in the city we live in. But the world's way bigger than our block. Faster. Got more shit happening in it."

"Someday," she told me, "you gonna end up on the express-way with no way off. Then you'll see—snakes out there just wait-ing for you."

April wanna talk to him. Let him know she changed her mind. He interviewed her in his car up the street, so she on her way there again. She say for me to go inside, and she'll meet me later. I'm at the food counter when she come with good news. She gonna stay here and find a job. He understand why she changed her mind. But she still got to pay the money she owe the company. All she got is those pills. He know the neighborhood, so he'll help her get rid of 'em, he told her. April says they'll be back in a little while.

She got her suitcase by the handle, pulling it. She'll stash it in his car to make it easier for me to get around with the baby.

"Take this." I hand her the carrier. "It's too much to carry with her and everything else." She act like she don't want to do it, but she does. Halfway to the door, she comes right back. "You like her, don't you?"

"I love babies. Anybody's. Any color. Special needs or regular. It don't matter to me."

She hugging me and Cricket at the same time. Soon as she's gone, I think about the kind of curtains we'll get for our apartment. And wonder if there's a Goodwill or thrift shop close by. I got money. We could start early to pick up things for our place. JuJu don't like to shop at those stores. Me either. But you gotta do what you gotta do till you can do better.

I been outside a few times now, watching traffic, walking Cricket, asking people for a cigarette. Once I get back, I call Maleeka.

I have to practically scream for her to hear me over all the people talking and laughing near her, music playing loud. "Maleeka! What y'all doing?!"

"Char! Char! We won—!"

"Oh."

"—first place! Know what that means?! We get to go to California! California, Char! I never been that far away from home in my whole life!"

"Oh. That's nice."

"Stop! Don't y'all see I'm talking?"

Her new friends try to get her to come with them to a restaurant next door. The whole team is going, Maleeka say. She'll meet 'em over there, she tells 'em. "How you like the bus ride, Char?"

"It was okay."

"We rode the bus all the way to New Jersey once. I liked it. Momma didn't."

I say it again. "It was okay." Then I tell her about WK.

She laughing. "What kind of name is that?" Then she bring up the twins, Raina and Raise. "But now that I think about it, they have weird names too."

For like ten whole minutes, Maleeka talks to me, when anybody can see she got better things to do. After she can't stay on the phone no longer, she promise to call me again sometime.

I don't know why, but that make me feel good, like everything ain't always gonna be bad for me.

"Maleeka. Thank you."

"You don't have to thank me, Char. We were friends, girls. Now we'll be different kind of friends, you know."

"I know."

She tells me, like she done the other day, that if I treat her bad, she won't talk to me no more ever.

"Why you keep saying that?" My voice not so nice now.

"So you don't forget, and I don't forget. Otherwise—" Somebody calls her. "I have to go."

"Me too."

Cricket start crying for no reason at all. Before she get too loud, I stick the nipple in her mouth. She sucking in air 'cause we out of milk. I had too much in my hands, dropped the can on the floor, and the Similac went everywhere.

There's a store around the corner, a Greyhound worker says when I ask. I pay six dollars to store our things. I walk to the store. Find out it's four blocks away, not two. Besides the milk, I buy a gallon of pure water. Can't carry that and her, so I buy new bottles. Fill 'em up—all six. I ask the lady to do me a solid and microwave them. Nope, she won't. Can't. That's what she say.

"They don't like this, Cricket," I say, going into Panera. "But you do what you gotta." I buy a cinnamon bun—not that I like wasting my money—and put the bottles in the microwave instead of the bun. After I turn it on, I stand with my back blocking it. And hope nobody catches me.

Using a napkin, I wipe her nose. Holding her tight around the belly, I force her to sit on my lap when all she want to do is fight me, kick and yell. I bounce her on my legs. "It's okay. She coming back." Guess she tired of being here. So am I. "She a little late, is all." I'm lying. She's two hours past the two hours she said she needed to sell them pills. "You'll get another bottle in—" I look at the lady's watch beside me. "Twenty minutes." Cricket is greedy. Every hour she want to drink something. But everything can't be about her.

"Pretty." A woman sits down across from me. "You babysitting till your mom gets back?"

I would answer, but she wouldn't like what I say. Instead of being rude, I keep quiet. I tie Cricket to me with a long, thick scarf I bought after we left Panera. She wiggles and fights me, but finally calms down. I sit her bag and my backpack on top the suitcase and start walking. Dragging it behind me, I walk around looking for another place to sit, mad that I gotta look out for somebody else's baby.

I'm barely in my seat when she start up again. "It's okay." I lay her on her back across my legs. "Want to play patty-cake?" Maybe she's tired of that game. 'Cause she screaming now. "Chill. I know other games." I sing the one about the baby coming down after something breaks. 'Cause I can't remember all the words, I stop. Besides, she don't like that one either. Or maybe she hungry again. I dig deep into her bag and pull up her bottle and give it to her. We both fall asleep while she drinking it.

"You stupid, Char. Stupid, stupid. She not coming back." I smack my forehead, then look around to see who saw me. People staring all right. A woman asks if something is wrong. I tell her I forgot my earbuds. She go back to reading on her iPad. Cricket and me moving again in between people who moving too. When I stop, I'm near a girl lying down on the floor. I find us a spot. Take out Cricket's blankets. And lay 'em on the floor so we can get comfortable. Only, I'm not there long.

"Young lady."

"Huh?" I rub my eyes and sit up.

He don't have a dog, just a smile on his face. But I still don't trust police. One move and I could be shot dead. Only, JuJu ain't raise no fool. I'm smiling when I stand up and put my hand out for him to shake. "Hello, Officer." I try to think up a big word to impress him. "Mighty splendid kind of day, ain't it?"

He says I got a nice firm grip. JuJu said make sure it was when you run across the police. But the last time we did, seem like she was gonna wet herself.

"What a beauty. Yours?"

I look down at Cricket and lie. Then tell him they make pretty babies in my cousin's family. Lifting Cricket, I talk to myself instead of him. "Why she always making us late? Coming to the bus station, forgetting stuff, changing tickets, going back home to get things. Now we won't leave till morning."

He wanna know my age. I tell him I'm eighteen. Got a body that look that old, anyhow. When he mentions my ID and how he wanna see it, my toes go cold. "ID?" He a cop with the city, he say. They come now and then to the station, checking on things. There's been some craziness with people running through grabbing things from the counter, "wreaking havoc," he says. The station don't got a real guard, so they help out now and then. Guess that's why the last cop was here.

I can't get to my wallet holding her. He offers to take her off my hands. A few minutes later, out comes my fake ID. It was my idea, my doing, not JuJu's. I had it made over the summer when I wanted to get in a eighteen-and-over club.

"Okay. Well, if you need anything. I'm here. Have a safe trip." He gives Cricket back. I sit there another hour with him not that far away. That's the only reason I decide to call JuJu. Well, that and the fact that I realize what a blind man can see—April played me.

CHAPTER 30

HOW YOU TELL your sister somebody stuck you with their baby, and you don't know their last name, where they live, or nothing? You don't.

Sitting cross-legged on the floor, I ask how she doing. She already mad because I should be at my grandmother's house by now and I ain't. I keep quiet and listen—then lie. "The bus broke down—twice. We just got here."

"You shoulda called. Greyhound shoulda called. They know you a child."

She ask what time the next bus gets to Alabama, then says never mind, she gonna call and ask herself. I beg her not to. "How can I grow up if you baby me?"

I sound more mature already, she think. For a while, we both quiet, and so is the station. Then Cricket wakes up crying. "That a baby I hear?" I tell JuJu that baby belong to a lady sitting next to me. "Well, tell her to keep her quiet. Who wants to hear all that racket this time of night?" She ask me to hold on while she take care of business.

She got a surprise waiting for me when I get to Alabama, she say once she's back. "I didn't want to tell you but—I got you in a Catholic school. The money from the parties gonna pay your tuition." She swear the one she throwing next weekend will be the last one. But that's what she said about this one.

"It's a new start. A chance for you to make your own life right."

"JuJu. I thank you, but me and school—like water and oil. Hurry . . . get your money back."

She say I'm smarter than she is. That if I only apply myself, I could end up in college . . . with a real good job one day.

"Quit using her words. Thinking you and me is like her or anybody else."

"We can do better. I'm trying. Anything is possible."

Anything is possible? She don't even talk like that. But Miss Saunders do. For spite, I tell JuJu, "I got a baby."

"What?"

I lay Cricket on her blanket on the floor and tell JuJu the whole story.

"Is you nuts? Didn't I raise you better than to fall for something like that?"

"She's coming back."

"Like Tupac coming back."

I'm watching the cop across the room watching me. The place is more filled up than it was before, but empty enough for him to keep an eye on me. "I need to go."

"What station you at? I'll call 'em. Report her. And make sure they put you on a bus."

"What's gonna happen to Cricket?"

"Foster care, Char. Kids end up there all the time."

"Then how will she get her baby back?"

"WHY DO YOU CARE?!"

Cricket looks up at me, smiling. "'Cause . . . 'cause—she don't have nobody like you and me didn't have nobody."

"We had each other."

"But no mother and father."

"I'm trying to give you a better life."

"I ain't ask you for that."

"You won't let nobody help you, Char. I see that now. You a tornado tearing down your own life. Wrecking everything. Miss Saunders said—"

I'm yelling when I say Miss Saunders never did nothing for me. She helped Maleeka, sure, but never me. I was drowning right in front of her, and she was happy to let me go under.

I close my phone and call him. "Answer. Please." I knew he wouldn't.

That cop is on his way over. So, I'm packing as fast as I can. Walking by rows of empty seats and lines with people standing up asleep, I hold her tight, look over my shoulder, almost start running. I got too many things in my hand to open the front door, so a nice old lady does it for me.

I stop at the first car I see in front the bus station. "I need a hotel. A place to stay. Cheap."

He asks my name. Says he's here to pick up someone else. I pull out two twenty-dollar bills. That's his money on top of whatever the ride cost, I say. Inside the car I tell him, "I'm underage. So, it's got to be a hotel ran by somebody that don't care."

THE MOTEL ON
THE CORNER

CHAPTER 31

THE WORLD IS full of crooks and thieves—and half of 'em is grown-ups. That driver wrestled another thirty bucks out of me. He kept the doors locked until I paid it. The guard out front the motel got forty. Said I couldn't step foot in the place unless I paid him first. This neighborhood the same as mine—it ain't kind to strangers at night. Now I'm in the lobby, and this man say they don't rent to minors.

"But the guard—"

"Guard?"

I would explain. But what's the point. I got played—again. Shoulda known better. Seen it coming. "Mister." I look down at Cricket. She slept through everything. "I'm not from here and I got no place to stay."

He's heard that story more times than he can count, he says. "It's that kind of neighborhood. You know."

I know. It's my neighborhood stuck in a different city. It's after two. That driver picked up other people and dropped them off, then done it two more times before he pulled up to the motel. When I got out the car, the club next door was letting out. People was piled on the pavement and curb like parked cars, talking about the next party. Billboards selling lottery tickets and used cars, found me here. Grandmas and girls my age walked up to cars, jumped in some, hoping to get paid. I seen it too many times to feel sorry for 'em.

This man behind the desk says he owns the motel. "Who can I call?" he says after I walk up to him.

I watch him put the last letter in his word puzzle. He smiling down at the word—snobbery. I show him my ID. He look up and repeat the question. "Like I said, who can I call?"

"I got nobody—just me."

He back to his puzzle when he tell me to show myself out.

He the type to call the police. Not to mind if I'm locked up and she in foster care. That's the only reason I'm headed for the door. Only, once I get there, I stop like a red light forced me to. For the first time all day, I don't know what I'm supposed to do.

"You going or what?"

I would if I could.

"Hey. You okay?"

The front desk lifts in the middle to make it easy for workers to get out. It squeaks so I know he on his way. Only, that don't stop the tears or me hiccuping like a five-year-old.

"Jesus." He step in between me and the door. "Here. Here." He stuffs a tissue in my hand. "You kids always crying. Wanna be grown but tear up at the least little thing." He's overweight. Short. In a suit that fit just right but got stains on it, gravy seems like.

He take me by the elbow. Helps me over to a bench that faces a wall with a flat-screen TV on it. "Sit." He go back for my suitcase. "Here." It's beside me when he goes behind the desk again, taking the first cup off a stack sitting on the water cooler. It's full, wetting the floor, when he come running over. "Drink this." He sit down beside me. "Now, that's better." He stands up, leans against the wall, and looks at Cricket lying on her belly across my lap. "You girls . . ." He shakes his head. "I just don't know what to say." He sneezes six times in a row. "Allergies." It's a lie. They let you smoke here anytime you want, anywhere. I can tell. My eyes itch, and I'm sniffing, plus they got cigarette burns in the brown carpet. "This your only one?" he asks.

I nod.

"Keep it that way. Then maybe you'll have a fighting chance in life."

I don't got no words. Nothing to say about nothing. I started on a bus trip to Alabama yesterday, and now I got a baby. That's what I'm thinking. And what if April change her mind, and they put a Amber Alert out for Cricket? "Mister . . . please." I don't beg nobody for nothing usually, but I gotta right now. Nothing good will happen to me or Cricket if I go back out tonight.

His eyes dig into mine the same way mine do when people come to JuJu's parties. I look down at the floor 'cause sometimes your eyes can snitch on you.

I can stay the night, he finally says. But he don't want the police all up in here, so I got to be gone in the morning. I open my purse, pull out half the money I got. "How many days will this get me?"

He staring at it, licking his purple lips. "Well. Now I don't know. The cops—" He walks over to the door and looks out. "Those girls draw attention, the law you know, men from all over town, college boys too." He got his hands behind his back, folded. "They ask to stay sometimes. But I can't have it."

"You won't hear a sound out of me—or her. I promise."

He walk back over to me. Takes the money, counts it twice. "Another fifty gets you three full weeks. After that, you pay on Fridays, weekly starting the fifteenth. Make your own bed. We dust the floors, give you toilet paper, fresh linen and towels—charge extra if your guests relieve themselves where they shouldn't."

"O—kay."

"No male company. Otherwise—"

Who I know? Nobody. April probably long gone by now. I cross my heart, promise "no company—male or female."

"I almost forgot." He's on the opposite side of the room behind the desk before I get a sip down. "I'm giving you my best room."

I look at him.

"Well—maybe not the best. But it's clean."

I blink my eyes; rub the right one a few times and sniff. He know what's up, I guess. And tells me what I know already. "There are no non-smoking rooms. People here free to do like they want as long as they don't burn down the place or bring the cops to my door."

He sound like my sister, JuJu. Seem to like plants as much as she do too. There's a spider plant on the desk, snake plants reaching outta floor pots like fingers beside the front door. They been around a while—years I bet. Some is as tall as me. A few got spiderwebs. "Thank you, sir."

He drop the key in my hand. My room got lots of amenities, he say. I'm glad when he explains what that means. "A stove, refrigerator, plastic dishes—two—cups, ice trays, a desk, bed, dresser, and a TV." He talk about how he been meaning to update the building. "Bad heart. And sons that I paid to go to college that think working in LA is better than working here." He shakes his head, sort of laughs. "Oh, the elevator is out. Take the stairs."

My room is on the second floor, he say. Not far from the elevator that don't work. "Watch yourself on the stairs."

"Can you hold her at least? I can't take her and all this up at one time."

He lifts her out my arms. Says he had open heart surgery and can't carry anything over ten pounds. I pull my suitcase across the room, turn left and take the steps. Dang, no lights.

CHAPTER 32

I STICK THE key in the lock and turn but don't go in. I stand out-side with my hand on the knob and my eyes closed and remember what I told myself before I got to the bus station. "People don't know you, Char. You smarter than they think."

I leave the suitcase in the hall by the door. Flip the switch that work the ceiling light and see it don't work. But the lamps do, so that's something. They sitting on end tables next to the double bed I can't sit on or lay in till I strip it down and wash the bedding. I could catch something from other people if I don't.

I think of all the things I can do here. How much fun Cricket and me gonna have. Then I open the refrigerator and see ants taking a walk in the vegetable bin. I squish 'em with my thumb, wash my hands in cold water. In the bathroom, I start a list in my head of the things I need. Cleanser, ammonia, Pine-Sol, soap powder, bleach— 'cause if that man think I'm leaving, he wrong.

Looking in the medicine cabinet, it hits me. I got my own place. I'm a boss. In charge of my own self for once. The twins, John-John, and Maleeka at home taking orders from their mommas. I'm done with that. Finished with people telling me what to do.

I got a lit cigarette in my hand when I pull back the drapes and lift the blinds in the bedroom. "Wow. A daycare center." I wonder how much it gonna cost to put her in there. Sometimes it's based on income. Taking another hit, I laugh. "Guess I need me a income."

Shapes and letters is painted on the building in crayon colors: Chicken Little Blue, Cherry Tomato Red, Sweet Pea Green, and plain old purple. I'ma use those to teach Cricket her alphabets and colors. *A Child's World* is the name of the place. Two doors up there's a laundromat—good. It's open twenty-four hours. From the laundromat to the corner there's plenty of stores—a Chinese takeout, a pawnshop, the one-dollar store, a liquor store with kids out front, a grocery store, two boarded-up stores, and a junk store lit up like Christmas with old furniture for sale on the sidewalk.

I watch them girls on the corner across the street. Cars pull up. They walk over, jump inside. After a man smoking weed look up at me, I lower the blinds, pull the curtains tight, and stay where I am, smoking till my cigarette is done. I ain't grown, but I feel like it.

By the time I unzip my suitcase, it's three thirty. I take out six pairs of my jeans and lay 'em in the middle dresser drawer I just cleaned. Cricket's thick pink blanket goes in next. Then her.

A baby should be washed before bedtime. But I ain't want to wake her 'cause I might not be able to get her back to sleep. So, I put her to bed in her street clothes, hoping her diaper ain't wet. I'll sleep sitting up in the chair at the desk in the middle of the room. In the morning, I'll see if the one-dollar store got sheet sets, Similac, and other things we need. Standing over her, I watch her sleep on her back with her itty-bitty fists balled. For a minute, I wonder what she dream about. Her mother? Milk? Playing in a crib? I hope she dream about nice things.

I won't go to sleep for a long time. I got money to count. Moves to make. Sitting at my desk, I empty my purse and wallet. All this change make it look like I got a lot of money. When all I got is too many pennies and dimes, not enough dollar, dollar bills. I count everything twice. "Two hundred and . . ." I put down the last bill. ". . . ten dollars." I count once more, just to be sure. Then I walk over to the window and stare out. "Milk costs what?" I look at the sign in the store window again. "And that's a sale?" My eyes find other things the grocery store advertising, like baby food. She don't eat food yet, but maybe she ready. I need her to be ready anyhow. For her belly to stay full longer—for her not to want to drink Similac all the time 'cause it cost too much.

CHAPTER 33

SHE WOKE UP crying. Don't know how long she been at it. I was sleeping so hard I woke up on the floor and ain't know how I got there. All I know is Cricket's face is beet red, and snot bubbles out her nose every time she yell.

I wipe her nose and cheeks with my only washcloth. Which mean I don't have one to use on myself this morning. "That's okay." I lean over her bed and kiss both her cheeks. "We'll get more." Stealing with a baby is easier than taking things when you on your own, I bet. "But don't you grow up and do nothing like that." I tickle her belly. "You wet?" I dig my lighter out my back pocket. Then I get the cigarette butt from last night out the window seal and light up. Gotta save what I have till I can get more. Same with diapers, only you can't reuse those. Well, you could, I think, as long as a baby didn't mess it up too much.

I got my eyes closed when I dig my fingers down her diaper. It's warm, soaked. So is the blanket and two pair of my good jeans. I got the cigarette in the corner on my mouth when I let her know she got five diapers left. "So, chill on this peeing, girl."

She sneezes—coughs so many times in a row I got to pick her up and pat her back. "You getting sick?" My hand is on her forehead. "I can't take you to no doctor. They want papers. Birth certificates, you know. Insurance cards. If you don't got those, they can keep the baby. I think they do anyhow."

I rock her, walk her, trying to calm her down. She in my arms when I switch out the jeans. Now the clean ones is on top the wet ones. I lay Cricket down and explain how our day is gonna go. Her eyes follow me every time I move. I'm on the other side of the room, out of sight when she start crying. In the bathroom, soaking and soaping her blanket in hot water and dish liquid, I sing to her. It's a made-up song—but it quiets her. "JuJu say my voice is pitiful. What she know?"

After I'm done rinsing the blanket out, I hang it over the bathroom door to dry. Next, I make a list in my head of things she'll need: Vaseline, baby wash and wipes, nail clippers, biscuits, clothes. I empty my head out at my desk on the pages of my composition book. There's forty things on it once I'm done. Not that Cricket care. She crying again. Louder by the minute. I don't even think about rushing to her. I need to wash some things out, like my underwear. Wiping sweat off my forehead, I yawn a whole bunch of times. I ain't sure how it happens, but I fall asleep standing on my feet.

CHAPTER 34

IN A NEW neighborhood, it's best to know your surroundings. You might have to run for it. Or report to the police something somebody did to you. "Memorize street names and numbers, landmarks and good alleys to run up," I tell Cricket. She a baby, I know. But a girl got to learn early how to look out for herself.

The motel is on Best Avenue. It ain't too wide or too dirty. Yeah, people drop their trash—pepperoni boxes, iced tea bottles, Tastykake Pie wrappers and stuff—but I seen worse. Done worse.

I'm across the street in front the daycare center when a girl my age pass by, staring. I tell Cricket that every girl ain't gonna be her friend, even if they do her a favor now and again. Her nose wrinkles like a rabbit's. Her fist tightens into balls. "Good. Keep 'em that way. You gonna need to use 'em on somebody someday."

I shift her from my left to my right hip. She bunching up, yawning, holding tight to my collar like she do a lot now. I kiss her fingers. Sniff her baby sweetness. A daycare worker pushing a stroller stops to ask how old Cricket is, if she's my sister. "Three months."

She smiling. I tell her Cricket is mine. Ask if she look like me. "Sure does."

More grown-ups smile at me and stop to ask about Cricket. Only one of 'em says I'm too young to be a mother. Like that's any of her business. Stopping in front the one-dollar store, I see something Cricket could use. A carriage. Expensive. The kind that sit high off the ground and got big wheels and shiny spokes. It's new, I bet. Cost nine hundred dollars or more. I look both ways, then sit her in it. If my phone had a camera, I'd take her picture. Show her that she was balling even when she was a baby. I look around to see who watching me. Not that I would take it. I just want to give her a taste of the good life. It's what I tell the woman when she come running out the store holding a baby. She the kind that people think make neighborhoods like this better. "Okay, all right—dang." I take Cricket out. "It wasn't like I was gonna steal it."

Her blue eyes go up and down the block, like she hoping to find a cop. I speed up. Walk as fast as I can, pushing a cart into the store with Cricket in my arms. On our way up one aisle, down another, I tell Cricket what I'm picking up and why. Babies understand more than we know. Plus, talking and reading to them makes 'em smart— even I know that. "Let's get you a book." I drop two in the cart, including one that pops up. The coloring book and crayons is for me. We stop in front the paper plates last. I like the ones for weddings and baby showers. Six packs go into my cart. Some got baby bottles and blocks on 'em. The rest is covered with silver wedding bells. One day I think I'll be married.

By the time I get to the line, the cart is full, hard to push with one hand. It take forever to get things on the counter. "Sixty dollars," says the cashier.

"What?! For this?!" I look at my things. "I thought y'all only charged a dollar."

Things add up, she say. I can put something back or pay up, she tell me. I sit aside two bags of corn chips, a liter of Mountain Dew, and a deck of playing cards with black people on 'em. Things I bought for myself. Cricket needs Similac. That cost more than a dollar. What I bought is just as good, I hope. Six cans sit in my cart next to Desenex for her bum, ten packs of diapers with five each in it, baby shampoo and conditioner. I put her books in a empty cart near the register, then take one back. I can't make up my mind what else to leave behind. "Y'all hiring?"

The man behind me changes lines. The cashier, around my age, says, "Sometimes."

"Is now the time y'all hiring?" I get rid of more things.

She point to the back of the store. "The manager's that way. You can ask him."

I leave twelve packages of Oodles of Noodles on the counter, plus two candy bars, and wait for her to say what I owe now.

"Forty dollars."

Yeah, I need a job.

I pay up. She pack my things. Cricket and me go see the manager. "Y'all hiring?" I ask as soon as I get in his office.

"Hiring yes. Hiring kids with babies, not today."

"I just asked. I didn't know you had no opening."

"We have an opening." He looks at Cricket. "If you want to make a good impression—next time leave your kid at home."

"So, I should apply another time?"

"No."

CHAPTER 35

SOME PEOPLE TRY to make you feel bad about yourself. Well, I don't. I'ma get a job. Next week. Doing something that pay good.

I push that rude man out my mind and the cart across the street at the same time. You not supposed to take it home, only I do. I can't carry nine bags, a bucket, plus a baby. But when I get to the motel, I still got a problem. I need help taking everything upstairs.

The back door of the Starfleet Motel for the Weary Traveler is on the corner of Best Avenue and Juniper Boulevard. Boulevard traffic runs both ways, with a island in between. Cars shake the ground. Horns beep. People curse. A boy on that island selling water runs up to cars, almost begging people to buy what he selling.

I park my cart in front the motel. Drivers act like they don't see me trying to cross the boulevard. I end up running so me and Cricket don't get hit. He sitting down when I get to him. "I'll give you ten dollars if you help me with them bags." I look at his plastic chair, books, and papers on the ground.

The light turns red. He jumps up, running from car to car, talking fast. Back on his island with them same bottles he left with; he walks over to me. "Fifteen," he say, like I'd ever pay that.

Instead of arguing with him, I lie. "Okay."

We in front the motel when I hand him my key. "Room two thirteen."

He my height. Around my age. Plaid shirt. Black jeans. Fingernails clean. Run-over sneakers. I remember what JuJu said about good shoes. "Hey," I say when he reach for my bags. "I know what I got up there. Take something that ain't yours—" My finger slides across my throat.

I watch too many movies, he say, picking up four bags. He ask me to watch his things. I laugh. "Don't nobody wanna steal water."

"People can be shady."

I wonder if he talking about me.

Three runs and he done. Out of breath too. "Thanks." I hand him a ten.

"Really?"

"Really."

"So, it's like that?"

I have to watch my money. "Yeah, it's like that." I walk the cart over to a tree near the curb and leave it. He still by the door when I get back. *Stupid*, I say to myself. *You forgot to get your keys.* My hand goes out.

"You want something? I want something." His hand goes out.

"My keys. Please."

"Oh, now you got manners?"

I fold my arms. He start walking. Then all of a sudden he stop and turns. "Catch."

The keys sting when they hit my hand.

"They throw things out . . ." He pointing to the daycare center. "Good stuff. They want people to take it. Seem like you gonna need it."

He runs across the street.

I feel bad, sort of, about ripping him off. But that was on him. If he wasn't so soft people couldn't get over on him.

I'm on the first floor of our building when I tell Cricket, "Do not let people take advantage of you. 'Cause they will. Somebody will, anyhow."

CHAPTER 36

THE ONLY REASON I call Maleeka is 'cause it seem like I'ma lose my mind if I don't talk to somebody besides Cricket. Before she start to brag about her own life, I brag about my place. I make it sound better than it is, bigger, cleaner, 'cause I don't want her thinking I'm in some beat-down ratchet motel. "Maybe one day you can come visit me."

She's happy for me, proud. "But what about your grandmother? You ever going to live with her?"

"I changed my mind. Anyhow, my sister said she ain't care where I went."

Maleeka don't say nothing, maybe because for a long time it seemed like JuJu ain't care about me nohow. So, who wouldn't believe that ain't still true?

I walk up to the dresser and pat Cricket's belly. Maleeka just got back from California with her robotics team. They made tenth in the country. Stayed in LA a week. After I heard enough, I tell her, "I got a baby."

"What?"

"I . . . have . . . a . . . baby . . . girl."

"You're lying."

"Her name is Cricket."

"For real? How? Whose?"

I tell her the whole story. She say I must be nuts. "And how can you afford to feed her and buy diapers?" She ask so many questions,

I wanna scream. 'Cause I ain't got all the answers. Don't need all the answers, really. Today she had clean diapers, milk, and a place to live. Who knows about tomorrow?

"What about shots?"

"Huh?"

"Shots, Char. Baby shots. A baby has to have them because if they don't, they can get sick and die."

"Oh. Well, I'll think about that later."

"JuJu know?"

"Yeah, she know." Now that there ain't no lie. "She don't like it. But what can she do? Cricket's mother is coming back, watch and see."

She ask me more questions. I tell her I don't know everything. "But I think I did the right thing . . . taking her with me. Too many kids in foster care anyhow."

I can tell she thinking. So, I'm happy when she finally say, "You're right about that."

I'm smiling.

She's quiet.

I walk over to my desk and pull out a crayon. Before I know it, I'm coloring.

"Why you so quiet? What you doing?"

Now it's me that take a long time to answer. "Nothing."

"Liar. Yes, you are."

I almost don't tell her. But why not? I already told her I got a baby. "Coloring."

"Oh."

"I'm too old for stuff like this, for real. But they was here when I got here, so—"

Last time she colored she was about ten, she say. She would

color at this age too, Maleeka tells me, if that's what she wanted to do. "Raina still plays with dolls."

"No, she don't."

"Remember, her sister told us that one time."

I remember. JuJu keeps a doll in her room that Mom got her one Christmas. She change her clothes with the seasons and holidays. I gave her a haircut once. I was mad at JuJu when I did it.

Picking up a blue crayon, I tell the truth for once. "I'm good at coloring. Better than anybody I bet."

I'm waiting for her to tell me what she good at 'cause she's good at so many things: writing, building robots, math, getting As, making friends. But she don't talk about herself this time. She say, "I'm proud of you, Char."

"Why?"

"'Cause I can see you trying."

Don't nobody else see it, I almost say. "Maleeka, I— Never mind."

"What, Char?"

"Nothing," I say at first. Then more words come out me, fast as water out a fireplug, and not 'cause she making me. "I apologize— for always calling you names, picking on you, getting Daphne to beat you up while the twins and me talked about you like you was dirt when you always was smarter than us, gooder too." I breathe in deep, let it out slow. "You ain't deserve none of that."

"I know. But why are you just seeing it now, Char? Never mind."

"My parents died. And I got so mad. God ain't leave me nobody but JuJu."

She start crying too. "I'm sorry . . . about your mom . . . and father. I wish they never died. My father either."

"I was real nice before then. People don't remember that, but I was."

"I remember. We was in elementary school and—"

"I didn't like you then either." I laugh.

"But you wasn't mean to me back then."

"No, and I was still cute." I wipe my eyes with the heel of my hand. "Wasn't nobody prettier than me. Wasn't nobody dressed better than me. My mother kept me like that."

"Sure did. Your mother was something else."

"She was, wasn't she?"

"Remember that time she made Valentine cookies for your class and my classroom next door?"

I tell her that I cook as good as my mom. "So does JuJu."

"See, Char. You still got something to hold on to." She talk about the mirror her dad left her, the poems.

I think about my mother's cast-iron pans under the sink. Dad's bat. "Yeah, I still got something," I say, walking over and taking his baseball out my backpack. Holding it tight, I tell Maleeka I need to go. "The baby—"

"I know. You gotta change her. I'll call you sometime, Char. Promise."

"Okay."

I didn't want to stop talking to Maleeka. But most likely she woulda hung up on me first. That mighta made me mad. And I don't want her to think I'm the same old Char.

CHAPTER 37

"SHHH."

"Ba . . . ba . . . ba."

"Quiet. He'll hear you," I whisper in her ear. Then I cover her mouth with my hand. Not tight so she can't breathe. Just enough so that baby talk she talking don't give us away.

He knock on the door again. "I'm getting complaints about that kid. If you can't keep her—"

"It wasn't us. We just got back from a long walk. Maybe it was somebody else's baby."

Cricket is the only one in the building, he say. Then he tell me the lady next door asked to change rooms. Since we got back from our walk, Cricket's been fussy. I fed her, changed her, rocked her, played a counting game with her—and she still whining about something.

I shove a chair under the knob to make sure he stay out. He brings up the rent. Says it's overdue. "Everybody has to pay—no exceptions."

"All right."

"And if I get one more complaint. You and that baby are out!"

"Okay, all right." I crack open the door. See him walking up the hall, stopping the elevator. It's fixed for now, he told me the other day.

I tell Cricket she got to learn to be quiet. Only, she don't listen so well. I end up holding and rocking her two whole hours. After she go to sleep. I go to work.

At home, I'd be doing what I'm about to do now—scrub the place clean. Plus, I had other duties—sit out ashtrays and shot glasses, count liquor bottles, make sure we had enough small bills for change and my tips. Otherwise, JuJu would need to make a bank run. I hated when she did that. 'Cause there was always somebody who'd come earlier than we'd want. And it would be me there by myself with some grown-ass man trying to get me to let him in. I'd stand with the door cracked. "We not open yet." He'd try to force it open wider with his foot. "I thought y'all was always open."

"Well—we still getting things ready." That was my favorite line. It ain't always keep folks out. The bat my daddy played ball with in high school helped. JuJu kept it by the door. All I had to do was reach over, pick it up.

"How many strikes?" one guy asked, like that was funny.

"I knocked a man out once," I said. It wasn't true. "Wanna see." I swung. My father taught me how to pitch, hit, box, and throw. Guess he wanted a boy. People said I act like one sometime.

"Ahhh! Ahhh!"

I kick the door shut so I don't hear her.

"Ahhh, ahhh."

I lift glass shelves out the bathroom cabinet and sit 'em in bleach and hot water in the tub.

"AHHHHH!"

How she hungry again? Wet again? Crying again? Wanting to be held again?

I get on my knees by the tub. "And how you expect me to clean and wash the place, if you won't be good and shut up?"

"Ahhhh!"

Ignoring her, I wash the shelves, dry 'em, put 'em back, then light a cigarette. She still yelling when the lady next door bangs on the wall. I snatch the door open. Throw a scrub brush Cricket's way. It misses her, hits the window hard, but don't crack it. That only make her cry harder.

I get to her so fast seem like I got wings. "I can't do everything!" Grabbing her up, I carry her into the kitchen holding her away from me like a stinky diaper. "You gotta sleep longer, let me get things done." I look at the list on the kitchen counter. *Find a food bank*, that's there on the list, number three. *Go to a church*, see if they got free diapers. That's number five. Number six is call JuJu. Ask her to send money. I ain't get to nothing on the list yet. And I can't because of her. She *still* crying. "All I do is babysit you. Do for you. Can't you just—" I scream.

She get stiff as a deer in the road hoping not to get run down.

I take her to my bed. Make sure she got a bottle when I leave. Outside in the hallway, I sit on the floor with my back against the wall. 'Cause I don't want to do nothing bad to a baby.

CHAPTER 38

IT'S NOT LIKE I planned it. It just happened, me walking down to the first floor and leaving the building altogether with her in the room by herself. I got the right to have some time for me, I think. I been a good mother, better than her real one. Plus, she asleep, washed and changed. If I stayed with her one more minute, she and me would both be sorry.

The line to the club next door is bananas—down the block wrapped around the corner. Weed and cigarette smoke call my name. Men in fast cars call me out my name, hang out the windows with their tongues dancing, ask if I need a ride, got someplace to go, wanna hook up. I give one the finger, ignore the rest, smile inside 'cause some girls don't get no love.

Cars pull up to the curb across the street—junkers, SUVs, Lincolns. A Subaru full of white dudes, parked. Two women walk up to the car. The lady in the room up the hall from mine waves on her way out the building. "Watch yourself out here, sugar." Gemini stops traffic on her way across the street. Her heels, tall as light poles it seem, don't slow her down none. Her silver pleated skirt and see-through top mean she in a car before she get to the other side. She independent, on her on, got no master, she told me once. "And I don't bring my work home."

There's plenty of ways to make money, JuJu would tell me. And ways not to make money. "I taught you the best I could. Make good choices." I don't judge. Folks got to eat. Now that I got a baby, I see how you end up doing things you never planned.

It's nice out, breezy, warm. The moon ain't full, but it's bright like a searchlight shining on us. I got on my bunny rabbit slippers and pajama bottoms. I ain't out here long when a little kid stops me. He begging for loosies. I laugh when he get to me. Grabbing my smokes out my back pocket, I ask if his kindergarten teacher know he out here. He crack me up when he say she the one that sent him. I give him the cigarette, light it up. He see somebody he know and walk off without saying thanks.

He long gone when I start to count every person in line outside the club. They got to pay to get in, so all I'm looking at is money, dollar bills. For an hour, I stay there thinking of ways to get some of what they got. I put in an application at the one-dollar store yesterday while Cricket was napping. Went in the club too, asking if they needed someone to wash dishes, sweep up. I'm too young they say, so did the pawnshop owner. How people expect me to eat, pay rent, and buy diapers if I can't get paid?

When I head for the boulevard, it's 'cause I got nothing better to do. He's there, like usual, selling water. On his island, not far from him, I smile. He can't help but check me out. I'm cute. He sweaty, making good money tonight. That's what I want. What I need: money, lots and lots of it—like yesterday.

When he get a break, he sit in that chair, puts a book up to his face, ignores me. "You want those?" His eyes follow my finger pointing at the ground to a page full of Wendy's coupons.

"I'll sell 'em to you."

"They free, ain't they?"

"Not for you." He laughing.

"Oh, so you got jokes." I tell him my name, I ain't sure why.

He says his name is Solomon. I ask his age. He's seventeen since last month. He wanna know what school I go to. I tell him I ain't from around here. He look over his shoulder at the Starfleet, then at me. He live with his grandmother, he says. She on Medicare. All her money goes to medicine and the mortgage. He pat his pocket. "I buy the groceries."

Wanna buy me some? I feel like asking. But I ain't that desperate—yet.

He asks about Cricket. I tell him I'm leaving to check on her right now. It ain't true. I just don't like people all up in my business. Walking away, I look over my shoulder, notice him checking me out again. Jiggling, I cross the street and almost go back inside. Only, I can't. She might start up again, and I ain't in the mood.

Leaning against the motel, I watch six girls walk by in red, tall heels with crisscrossed straps covered in yellow glitter. They dressed in skirts that almost ain't. The tallest got two thick long plaits down to her belly, with silver ribbons running through 'em. The first two went to the hairdresser. Their weaves is tight. I'm wearing a baseball cap. The braids I left home with is in the trash. "Hey. What's there to do around here at night?" I ask.

One girl pointing to the line in front the club. Another girl rolls her eyes. The last one say they going to a house party. She give the address, like I'd go dressed like this. When they far enough away, I start walking too. I'm four blocks away, across the street from a nice hotel when I finally stop. I didn't know it was here, never seen it before. They got a doorman. A restaurant inside. People coming and going. I look at my slippers. Wonder if they'd hold it against me if I put in a application with 'em on. Then I remember the one-dollar-store man and take myself home.

CHAPTER 39

Pay up by tomorrow or leave!

I pull the note off my door and go inside. I ain't mad that he put it there. I'm three weeks past due with the rent. Gemini from up the hall told me that the only reason I'm still here is 'cause his bark is worse than his bite. "Sugar, his wife left with his daughter years ago. His sons never come home. I think he'd be hard pressed to throw you out. But don't push your luck." She lifted my hand and put a twenty in it. "Don't you have a home to go to, sweetie? A momma?"

I told her the truth. "No."

"Oh, that's not good" was all she said. Then she went to work.

CHAPTER 40

"WHAT IN THE world?" one lady says. Her eyes bounce from me to the flyer I try to hand her. She tells the man she's with to let me know that what I'm doing ain't safe.

He holding her hand when he say, "Stay out of people's business, Gail. She know what she gotta do."

The line outside the club is stupid long like it always is. I'm near the middle. Three dudes standing one behind the other smile at me. One of 'em follows my legs with his eyes till he staring at my face. His friend's elbow hits him in the ribs. "She a kid, man. Quit it."

"I'm just looking."

"To get us locked up?" They move with the line.

Bet there's two hundred people still trying to get in. Only ten so far took my flyers. Six more stopped on their way past to ask for one. "I'm having a party," I told them. "In that motel. Next Saturday after the club lets out." They all ask the same thing. Which floor? I didn't say. I ain't no fool. The night of the party I'll leave the back door open. Tell people to go up to the second floor. Nobody need to know where the party is till then. I'll buy food, pick up shot glasses and soda at the one-dollar store, pay someone to buy wine and liquor—the cheap kind. Bet I'll make five hundred for the night.

"Who touched me?" I spin around. "Bet I cut you if you do it again." For the first time in a while, I think about WK.

"If you didn't want to be touched, why are you wearing those?"

It's the woman with the man who told her to leave me alone. She step out of line and point at my shorts. They red and match my lips. I sewed on the rhinestone decal. *Priceless* it say when you see me from behind.

I look at her. She Miss Saunders's age. Should be at home, anyhow, not out here. "Okay, boomer," I say, shaking my butt on my way by. "You just jealous, is all."

He take her by the hand. Gets out the line and walks up front. The bouncer lets 'em jump the line and go inside. Maybe they knew him. Paid him off.

I wave flyers at two boys walking up the sidewalk. They my age. They take and read 'em. I get so close to one, I smell toothpaste on his breath. "You coming? Come," I say. Then I give them extras for their friends. Guess I shoulda hit up the the basketball courts and sneaker stores. But I'm more used to grown-ups being around me when it's party time.

"No soliciting." It's the bouncer. He look down at the ground where people dropped my flyers. "Pick those up." He a mountain, tall and wide, hard to look around.

"I ain't drop 'em." I hand the next person in line a flyer, then the next.

He take me by the arm, pulling me into the street. His fat fingers go in his pocket and a badge comes out. He not a real police officer, just a pretend one, a guard. I do like he say anyhow, especially after he talk about calling the police.

My shoes is in my hand when I sit down in front the post office, smoking my last cigarette. "Plan B—you need one."

I try to think of other ways to make money—some legal, some not. Selling weed from my room could bring the cops to my door, get me kicked out the Starfleet, my things piled outside the motel on the street. Homeless don't look good on nobody. So, I stand up, drop my flyers in the mailbox. Put my high heels back on. Cross the street and walk into the lobby of The Fount Hotel. There's a chandelier hanging from the ceiling, a water fountain shooting blue water up high in front the building and another one inside, pictures of angels painted on the ceiling, real plants everywhere. The Fount remind me of a grandma that used to be young and pretty. It needs painted now, wax striped off the floor, curtains that ain't so thick and dark. But I like it. The people working in here dress like they got money, look important. I'm gonna be important one day.

I stand in the line for guests, ignore people staring. "I want to put in a application," I say once it's my turn. "I can work anytime day or night."

The lady at the front desk smiles. "You have to be eighteen or older." I think that's a lie. But she nice, so I don't get mad. I lower my voice. Tell her I'll work under the table. That's against the law, she say.

"I know. But—" I lean in close, try to explain how things is for me.

She reach underneath the counter. Grabs a brown bag and fills it up with water, a small bottle, a snack bar, an apple, and a bag of chips. She folds the bag over, winks, and sits it on the counter. "Next," she say to the man in line behind me.

On my way out, I make myself a promise. "I'ma live in a place like this one day."

If I was paying attention, I woulda seen him. Not bumped into him. Maybe he wanted it that way, 'cause he don't move after I back up and say, "Sorry." I keep my eyes on the mailbox across the street. You look some men in the eyes, and they think that mean yes to whatever question they got rolling around in their head. I look down, keep walking. I already left Cricket alone too long anyway.

"Oh, it's like that?" He follows me to the curb.

If I talk to him, he'll think I'm interested. Tonight, I don't want him to think nothing about me—I ain't in the mood.

We cross the street at the same time. He think he cool wearing shades when it's dark out, a black trench coat even though it's warm, leather gloves like he expecting snow. "Where's your daddy?" he ask.

I look at him. "You wanna be my daddy?" I almost say. But that would be an invitation. A way in for him, when I got the door locked and don't plan to open it—not tonight anyhow. But when he start talking again, I turn and look him over. I got to, 'cause I know him—his voice from somewhere. The motel, maybe? The one-dollar store? I think a minute about where else I been. He look up the street at men in cars and girls near cars wearing shorts shorter than mine. My eyes stay on him. "Hey? You're him."

He lifts his shades. Smiles and nods.

"Your mustache. You shaved it. That's how come I ain't recognize you." I step up to him with my hand up to my eyes like a visor. "Where's April? I got something for her."

He drove her to Florida. He tells me the name of the highway they took and everything.

"For real? Seriously? You lying." He take out his wallet, shows me a picture of the ship she on. "She dancing? She didn't want that kind of job no more."

He found her something else, he say. Something better. "Good work. Good wages." He points to his head. "Using her brains too."

I think on it some. "Well, I hope she like it."

I let down my guard when I spoke to him. He know that. Does something about it when he hold on to my wrist tight as a handcuff. A car at the end of the block start up the street slow, close to the curb, then stops in front of us. It's black with black windows, probably got black seats inside. "That your ride?" I smile. Look up at him. "Nice." I correct my posture. "You got a chauffeur? You seem the type. I want one." I ask about the car at the bus station. He got more than one, he say, a van too. "You will one day too. I can tell."

He facing the hotel when he tell me about April's uniform and job. It's white like they wear on TV ships, he say. She supervises people already and plans activities for kids. I ask for her address. He'll get it to me another time. I ain't say I wanted to see him again.

"Hungry?"

I look at the bag in my hand. "What?"

"Are you hungry? There's a place that's open all night. Close by. I can take you home afterward."

I look at his car. Imagine myself inside. "Ahhh, nope. I'm expected home."

He take a toothpick out, sticks it between his lips. ". . . Expected home. Where is home?"

My sister ain't raise no fool. "Wherever I say it is." I start walking away, jiggling on purpose. When I stop, I got that bag tight in my hand. "I need a job, Anthony. You know anybody hiring?"

"How much do you need?" He slide his hand in his jacket pocket.

"I clean, and I don't mind hard work." It's not easy, but I turn away from the money and look across the street back at the hotel. "They hiring? You stay there, right? They wouldn't let me put in a application."

He'll ask the manager if he's got any work for me, he says. "If I had your number—"

"I got your card." I look at The Fount. "It always that busy?" If he answers, I don't hear. I'm watching more cars pull into their driveway. Counting the floors, I try to guess how many rooms a maid would clean a day, how much she'd make. Plenty, I bet. Ignoring him, I take myself home.

CHAPTER 41

I PUT THE key in the lock, tiptoe my way up the steps, hope the owner ain't waiting for me with the cops.

Cricket asleep in my bed. She quiet as a mouse, still blocked in by pillows when I get in. Good. She don't make a sound when I kick my shoes into a corner, hurry and change out my clothes in the dark. I think about changing her diaper, then decide not to. She did me a solid, slept the night away, ain't get me in trouble—so I ain't gonna trouble her neither. I lie down on the floor to go to sleep. I don't mean to cry, but I do. I'm tired, I guess. Tired of playing grown, tired of changing diapers, being broke, tired of everybody getting what they want except me. Lying on my back, I think about Maleeka. What would she do? Go home, probably. But I can't do that.

Sad, I crawl into bed beside her. Put my arm around her. That's when I notice that she burning up. I touch her forehead, her legs and hands. They on fire too. So is the part of the bed she lying on. I run and turn on the lights. See her eyes crusted over, glued shut with green pus in the corners.

It's a bug maybe. Could be something worse. What I'm gonna do if she need to go to the hospital?

In the bathroom, I pull down her pants and diaper, lay her belly down across my lap. "This gonna hurt. But we need to know." I pat her back for a while. Tell her everything will be okay. Slide the thermometer in and close one eye. She too sick to cry or fight me. "A hundred and three," I say, holding the thermometer up to the light.

Once on TV, I saw them put a baby in ice water to get her fever down. I plug up the tub. Turn the cold-water faucet on high. Shivering, with water up past my stomach, I hold her tight. She limp as lettuce, whining like a kitten I found almost frozen in the snow one time. It died the next day.

CHAPTER 42

"HEY, YOU! STOP!"

Running past the rice, breadcrumbs, and cereal boxes, I ignore the guard like he ain't talking to me. He catch up to me anyhow.

"Hey!" He grabs the back of my arm. "Don't make it hard on yourself." He in front of me when he say, "I saw what you did."

I'm loud when I say I was only looking. Then I ask why people can't leave kids like me alone. If I didn't have a baby with me, he would call the police, he says.

"For a dollar bottle of Tylenol? It ain't even Tylenol. It's pretend Tylenol." I pull it out the front pocket of Cricket's carrier. "Take it." I start walking, then come back. "Here." It's a dollar for the medicine. I can't afford it, but I need it. I ran out of what I had. This the third day she been sick. Yesterday, the landlord caught me walking her up and down the hall. I had to pay him something, he said. I gave him thirty-seven dollars and kept ten for myself. And I still owe him. Don't know how I'm gonna buy her diapers and food with what I got left.

The girl rings me up. The guard walks me out. If I step foot in this store again, he'll have me locked up, he says. I got no choice. I take her home. Strip her down to her underwear, give her the medicine, and hold her until she asleep. I put on my high heels when I go out the next time, a skirt that ain't too short, and the kind of shirt Maleeka would wear: not tight or see-through or nothing.

CHAPTER 43

"YOU SURE YOU don't need no help?" I'm at the front desk. Cricket's upstairs in her bed sleeping. "I could use the money."

He working on another puzzle, got his head down, his pencil filling in blanks. "Rent's due. Overdue."

"I know. That's why—" I point to his puzzle. "Reality. That's the word."

He write down the last two letters and say, "So, you want me to pay you so you can pay me the rent you owe me that's already late?"

My head goes up and down, only he can't see 'cause his eyes don't leave the page.

"I'll be a little late getting the rest to you."

"No kidding."

"Like I said, I could work off some of what I owe." I could scrub, I tell him, dust down here, wash towels, paint. JuJu taught me how to do some of everything.

"Spanish." He look up. Sits the pencil on the desk. "Good word." He tell me that he ain't hiring. That the maid only works three days a week now, instead of seven, 'cause his money's not what it used to be. "If you need extra toilet paper, soap, and such, get yourself some. It's in the hall." He grab the pencil again. "But rent ain't negotiable. You stay, you pay like all the rest."

"But—"

"Haven't I already given you one break after the other?"

"Yeah, but—"

"Go home, child." He fills in another block. "Ain't nothing good out here for you." He must be smart 'cause he write down a twelve-letter word, plus two more before he says anything else. "Y'all kids don't listen. My daughter didn't either." His eyes water.

He drops the pencil. Stands up and comes from behind the desk. I follow him over to the door.

"Look, people left fingerprints on the glass." I stand beside him. "I could fix that for you."

He don't answer. He waves to Gemini on her way in carrying grocery bags. She waves, winks, keeps on moving. He and me keep doing what we doing. "Thank you," I say.

"I was wondering when it was coming. A simple thank-you go a long way. But I still want my money."

I think about his sons and wonder how a man can end up with no family. "What happened to your wife and kids?"

"You don't pay, I'll put you out. Won't be my fault if you—" His eyes is on me when he say, "Take your baby and go home, little girl. Wherever it is. These streets is mean. And you can't beat 'em."

CHAPTER 44

THE KETCHUP IS almost empty when I sit it on the counter. Then turn on the stove, fill a pot with water, and heat it to boiling. Using a washcloth for a pot holder, I pour scalding water in the bowl. Once it's full, I flip the ketchup top open and squeeze. Garlic, salt, and pepper go in next. By the time I'm standing at the window, I'm spooning it in my mouth.

It's Sunday, quiet out. Slow. After me and Cricket both done eating, we go visit him.

A trash can chained to the streetlight on our corner is running over. I kick the paper, look at the ground for loose change. Do the same thing while I'm crossing the street. I found ten pennies outside the laundromat yesterday. A quarter on the sidewalk by the daycare center. Two nickels stuck in the hot tar in the street last week. Wish people threw dollar bills away.

I guess you could say he a gentleman. We step on his island, and he give us his seat. Offers me water. Sees me staring at his chips, giant size, picks up the bag and offers me some. I take a handful, then ask for more. After he make a few sales, he come back and sits on the ground facing our way.

He staring at me. Making me uncomfortable. I don't know why. Maybe it's because of my hair. I washed it. Braided it too. You can tell I done it myself. The girls I saw that night on the street would laugh.

He got his arms out when he ask to hold her. Who's done that since I been here? Nobody. So, I turn her over right away. She smiling, sitting in his lap, happy. I'm happy too. People don't know what it's like to have a baby and no help. "Hey, you got customers." I lean down, get myself more chips.

He's up, running, carrying her and three bottles. Soon as he get over there, another car stops, then another one and two behind that one. I sit up, watching. Then run bottles of water over to him when he ask. That car pulls off, but more stop. It's 'cause of her. Don't nobody stop and give me nothing when she with me.

We here two hours sweating in the sun. And the cars keep coming. I take her for a minute so he can drag the cooler to the cars. Next, I go inside for her hat and suntan lotion and soak her good. Them cars don't let up. Most people buy more than one bottle. They don't pay me no mind or see me, I guess. That's okay. I ain't mad. He better share, though.

"What you tell 'em? That she yours?" I ask when things slow down.

"Just that I'm babysitting." He hand her over, gets back to sitting on the ground. Knees up, elbows on his knees, he say he never knew a baby could be a money machine.

I stick out my hand. "So, where's my cut?"

He deduct the five dollars he thinks I still owe him. After he hand me twenty bucks, I look at him like he out his mind. I see all the dollars he got. But he's good at math. Tells me how much he paid for the water, the taxes, everything including gas his friend gets paid to bring him here. He gotta take care of all them expenses, he says, before he makes a dime.

I stand up to leave.

"Where you going?"

"Wendy's." I rub my belly.

"If you ever need a babysitter—"

I laugh. "You wanna pimp my baby?"

"You need money. I need money. You need a break. Her too, probably." He gets up to open a case of water, sticks some of 'em in a cooler full of ice. "I know I'd be sick of you if I had to be around you all the time."

He sound like John-John. That's why I'm smiling. Plus, I got money, not a lot, but more than I started with this morning. "Anytime you want her you can have her," I tell him. But that ain't come out right. "Sorry, Cricket." I kiss her forehead. "We need money, is all."

He try to get in my business, asking where my family is, her father too. "She don't look like you."

We was having a good time, and he had to go there. Which is why I leave without saying good-bye or thank you. He don't know, I got questions about him too. Like what happened to his parents? What kind of grandma let a kid work in this neighborhood all times of night? I wouldn't ask though.

Everybody's got something that they want to keep private or all to themselves.

CHAPTER 45

IT'S BEEN RAINING all week, seven days straight. I'm watching
it run down the windows, make puddles in the streets. He got
on a see-through poncho. Not that it do any good. His clothes
still getting soaked. His sneakers drown in water every time his
feet take a step. That hat he wearing dripping water in his face.
And the cars don't stop. They fly up the boulevard faster than ever,
like that'll keep 'em drier. Sometimes seem like they splash him
on purpose.

Once the rain slow down, I walk out the door. Leave the building. Cross the street. On the way, I check for loose change. Soon as
I get in the store, here he come. "I'm not stealing nothing. I got an
interview," I tell the guard. He ask me to leave anyhow.

I done my hair up real nice. It got wet on the way here. I put on
my best pants, a shirt I don't like 'cause it's old lady like, but the
kind the cashier girl wears. "Here." I pull out the paper that says the
time of my interview and who it's with. I printed it out at the motel.
The owner let me, 'cause he say I better get something quick. "See.
That's me. Charlese Jones. This is the store, right?" I point to the
name and address and hope he don't hold that Tylenol thing against
me. Nobody else will hire me.

We still near the front door. Close to the aisle with the seasonal
stuff. Skeletons and scarecrows face us. Spiderwebs and candy corn
sitting on shelves behind my back. He talking loud. Says before I do

the interview, he got to "inform the manager about my prior activities in the store."

"What that mean?" I say, like I don't know.

He explain. My eyes go from his face to his feet. "Mister," I say. "Please." I clear my throat. "I need this job. I got a child." I don't want to. But I gotta look in his face to see if I stand a chance of getting what I want.

He move out my way. Says he can do it now or do it later. But he's gonna do it. And once it's done, my application will end up in the trash. "So, you'll only be wasting your time, and his."

He smiling like he done me a favor.

I turn around and go back to where I came from. Soon as I'm back inside almost about to cry, she call me. "How you doing, Char?"

I look at all the pictures I colored since I been here. One whole wall is full, top to bottom. "I'm all right. You?"

"I don't know. That's why I called you."

That make me feel better, her needing something from me. "Awright, talk?"

"Don't get mad."

"You been talking about me or something? I knew I shoulda—"

"I wouldn't do nothing like that, Char. It's about—Caleb."

"Oh." I walk over to Cricket.

"I didn't want to tell you because—"

"What? He gay? I knew it."

"Char."

"Okay, so he ain't gay. Wish he was. Then he'd have a good reason for not liking me. So, what he do? Feel you up, try to kiss you."

"You know he's not like that."

I don't want to hear about Caleb. Not about him being with her. I liked him a lot. He ain't notice me at all, unless I was being mean to him. I might as well have been invisible, air. But if I hada kissed him—man—he would never ever forget me. He'd be hurting for me hard, chasing me like the cops. "Well—what he do?" I walk up to the window and watch him, wondering if water boy is a good kisser.

"Nothing. That's the problem."

"Oooh, Maleeka ready to—"

"I'm in high school, Char, and I never been kissed."

I shut up and listen. She the only one out of seven of her girls who ain't been kissed ever, she tells me. Some ain't even virgins anymore, she say. "So, I gotta get kissed—quick. And by Caleb."

"Why him? Why now?"

"'Cause I lied and told them—"

"Maleeka Madison done something bad for once." I crack up. "And I didn't make her."

"Char—I'm serious."

I tell her you can't kiss a boy 'cause you lied and told somebody you already done it. Caleb likes Maleeka. A lot. Who don't know that? If he ain't kissed her, he's got reasons. "And you shouldn't do nothing stupid just because of them girls."

He packs up. Looks up. Waves at me. I keep a red shirt in the window now so he know which room is mine.

Caleb never tried nothing, Maleeka say, and she's glad because she wasn't ready to do nothing, not even kiss.

"Then why you gonna do it now?"

"We're going to a party. They said I should invite him. They all got boyfriends. They'll be kissing and . . . well, you know."

I think about the time we played spin the bottle at a party in sixth grade. Somebody took their top off. I got kissed by a boy I ain't like and punched him. He came to school with his lips swelled up. High school parties are worse. I went to one the first time I was in seventh grade. Maleeka ain't ready for that.

Cricket's on her knees trying not to fall over. In her mind, she think she ready to crawl. Like Maleeka think she ready for more than she is. "Ain't I taught you nothing, girl? You still following people, doing whatever they want?"

"But, Char—"

I scream at her on purpose. "Quit kissing everybody's ass!"

"Don't holler at me! Don't you holler at me never no more or—"

"Yeah. Do that. Go off on people. Otherwise, they won't respect you." I swallow. "I didn't—before anyhow."

She don't say nothing, but I bet she shaking her head yes. She laughing when she say maybe I should give lessons on how to quit getting bullied and learn to speak up for yourself.

I smile. She ask how things is going for me. For the first time, I tell her the truth. "It's hard. I be hungry a lot. Last week, I bought some material and safety pins and made diapers." I look at 'em piled in a corner by the door, washed, ready for folding.

"Come home, Char."

I talk about the women who work on the corner. Tell her 'bout my rent situation. "I worry he gonna put me out. But he ain't done it yet, so—"

If I give her my address, she'll send me some money, she tells me. She gets an allowance now. Has her own bank account. "You would do that for me," she say.

"No, I wouldn't. Not back then."

"You helped me, Char . . . lent me them clothes. Without those—"

"Maleeka? You crying?"

146

"Everybody wants to look nice and feel pretty." She asks for the address again.

I change the subject back to where it started. "So, how come y'all ain't kissed?"

"I guess it's because I'm scared. He could be too."

"Scared of kissing? That's like being scared of breathing, walking, laughing." I tell her I was born kissing. That don't sound good, so I say I'm the best kisser in the world and, if she want lessons, I will give them to her once I get back. That don't come out like I want either, but she get what I mean.

Seem like we talk all afternoon. Neither one of us want the call to end, but her cell is running out of juice. Plus, Cricket needs a bath and bottle and clean pajamas on before she go to bed. "Hey, Char?"

"Yeah."

"I like us this way."

"That's because you corny, lame, a nerd," I say. But inside I don't feel like that at all. I'm watching her, learning, like she a book or something.

"Bye."

"Hey—tell them girls your friend will bust 'em in the head if they don't leave you alone."

"I will, Char! And thanks."

I lift Cricket up so fast, I take her breath away. We dance around the room to a song I'm singing. Before I know it, she ready for bed, asleep. Once she's down for the night, I sit at my desk, facing the window, coloring. I color most things on this page black. Some people don't like that color. But stars can't show through without it, and a date ain't as much fun either. In my mind, I color my old neighborhood. Turn cars on the corner Razzle Dazzle Red, and the clothes girls wear around our way Sonic Silver, Unmellow Yellow, Mango Tango, and maroon. I color the sidewalks cinnamon, and sprinkle sparkles everywhere.

In bed beside Cricket, I close my eyes and see myself at home in my own room, in my own neighborhood, happy.

CHAPTER 46

IT'S MALEEKA'S FAULT. We talked three days in a row, even this morning before the sun was up. She start school tomorrow. The building is brand-new. The kids get new laptops and free bus passes. No more than twelve kids gonna be in a room. I think she lying when she say they got a chef.

Maleeka make me want to go to school and back home. "Call your sister," she told me, "maybe she'll let you come back and bring Cricket too." It took me six days to get up the nerve. But I think she's right. What choice I got? I'm down to no money at all, and the milk's gone.

"JuJu? It's me. Char."

"Oh, like I don't know that?"

"I—"

Do I know how worried she's been? she says. How could I be so selfish? My being gone made her have to lie to our grandparents about why I never made it there because she did not want to give them a heart attack worrying over me.

I hold the phone far from my ear and stare at it. "I'm sorry."

"You still got that baby?"

"Yes."

"She better be gone when I get there, Char. I'm not raising somebody else's child."

"Well, that's what I was calling about. Can I—"

She tells me to hold on. She has to get a pen, paper. I hear her talking to somebody, complaining about me. When she back on the phone, it just comes out. "You don't need to come, JuJu, I'm fine."

"How you fine? You sixteen, a dropout, homeless, with a baby that's not yours." Seem like she brings up every bad thing I done since my parents passed. "Your teacher called, checking—"

"Miss Saunders ain't my teacher no more."

"I told her everything. Call her, Char—maybe she can talk some sense into you."

Sometimes firecrackers go off inside of me. Bombs. I'm surprised that the walls don't crack when I scream at her. "Don't! Tell people my business!"

I scared Cricket. She crying, screaming. I walk past her anyhow. "So, I screwed up. I'm not the only one in the world that's done bad things!" I step on the blanket and squat. "Shut up, Cricket!"

"See, I told you. You can't—"

I walk back and forth across the room. "I'm trying, JuJu! You should be here, then you would see how really, really hard I'm trying."

Seem like she ain't heard a word I said. "I know what city you in. Just give me the address, Char. I'm coming—"

"I got a job—cleaning. You know I'm good at that. It's at a hotel. They gave me a room for free. The baby gets to go to work with me."

"Her mother is taking advantage of you. Somebody else probably is too. You not as tough as you think." She's quiet for a long time, same as me. "What's the use? You gonna do what you want anyhow. What you doing for money? I can wire you some."

"I'm cool." I smile when I want to cry. "They pay good. I'll get a raise soon 'cause I clean better than anybody here." I sit at my desk. Pull out my coloring book. Try to calm myself.

"Char—"

"Bye, JuJu." I hang up. And call him.

It's his voice mail I get, not him. I call three more times before he gets back to me. He out of town. Meet his driver at The Fount, he tell me. I get dressed and out the door, fast as I can.

DADDY'S GIRL

CHAPTER 47

SOON AS I get to the car, the window roll down. He don't smile or even say hi. He leans over, opens the glove compartment, and takes out money. A thick yellow rubber band holds it all together. "Three hundred enough?"

"You can do that?"

"You want it or not?"

I look at the hotel, then at him. "Did he tell you—"

"He said that you're a nice girl. That if you show up, I should use my discretion. Help you out."

"I—can't—pay him back yet."

"He doesn't need your money. Here." He peels off three one-hundred-dollar bills, then sits 'em in my hand.

I stand up straight, look up at the hotel. "Why he wanna give me money anyhow?"

"Some girls he just likes. Treats 'em like daughters. Don't worry."

"I ain't worried. I can take care of myself." I back up before he change his mind.

"No worries." He starts the engine. "He helps kids like you all the time."

I think about April. Ask if Anthony got children. He puts on the blinker. "You're lucky. He don't take to everyone." Up goes the window.

I slide the money in my back pocket, waving while he driving off.

CHAPTER 48

I TAKE THE plant out the blue bag and sit it on the window ledge. "What should we name it?" I ask Cricket. "Hickory?" I laugh 'cause that was my great-grandfather's name. "Dude? That's a good one. What's up, Dude?" I carry Cricket over to the kitchen and fill a cup with warm water. "You the man of the house," I tell Dude. "Anybody come in here—do what you gotta."

Dude is a cactus. The kind with spikes that hurt. I bought it to celebrate us having money again. I pour water in the dry, hard dirt, walk over to the desk, and read over my list. Pay your rent was first on the list. I ain't all the way caught up, but he smiled when I gave him the money. Take the bus to the store in the white neighborhood was number two on the list. I did that already. I bought six bags of popcorn, a hundred dollars' worth of Similac, fifteen jars of baby food, a case of Oodles of Noodles for myself, soda, new crayons, and three coloring books—a pack of cigarettes too. I even bought a seventh-grade math book. Miss Saunders would laugh. So would JuJu. I never read my work or did it for that matter. Spending so much time by myself—being bored—got me doing things I wouldn't normally. Plus, Maleeka said if I did it, she would help.

Sitting down on the floor with Cricket, I empty out another bag. "These are books. Yours. They like medicine. They good for you. Only, most kids don't like how they taste.

"Be still. I'm reading." Falling over, she start to cry, then stops when she see it won't get her nowhere with me. *"Goodnight Moon."* I start with that one. I read it slow with different voices, like my mother used to. Stopping, I apologize to Cricket for things being how they been the last few months. When I promise it won't happen no more, I'm not exactly telling the truth. But now that Anthony got my back, maybe things won't be as hard as they been.

CHAPTER 49

I SEE HIM on that island selling water, so I go to him. For the first time in a long time I ain't worried about nothing. I just came back from the nail salon. My toenails is barely dry. His forehead is sweaty. His underarms stink. Sweat dripping off his chin almost get on me. He don't hardly notice. It's Cricket he like the most anyway. Taking her from me, he gets back to work.

I look at his books—*Law for Dummies, How to Hire a Good Lawyer*—and laugh. "Somebody in trouble," I say, then sit down in his lawn chair. Take a bottle out the water cooler and open it. I got money now, so I don't mind paying. When Solomon come up to me, I got a dollar in my hand. I came to ask him a favor, I said. Would he help me move some furniture? They gonna clear out a apartment building around the corner. In a few days, my landlord heard, they gonna be throwing out furniture. Good stuff.

This time he makes me pay in advance. Twenty dollars. He said it could be more, depending on how hard he had to work. I feel like a baller, shot caller. So, I give him what he asked for—plus five dollars extra. After we move the new furniture in—a couch, mirror, floor lamp, microwave with a dent on the side, he reminds me about something he told me before. The daycare center across the street be giving lots of things away too. I bought Cricket five new one-dollar-store outfits, shoes, and more books. But she could use more.

"Stay asleep," I tell her before I leave our place. "If you cry, they will figure me out. If they figure me out, they will find you. Take you from me. Put you in foster care or something." I'm at the door when I make her a promise. "This the last time for real for real that I will leave you alone 'cause I know it's the wrong thing to do."

It's five thirty in the morning. Black out. They getting off work. Kicking off shoes, snatching off wigs on their way up the street two by two, a few all by themselves. Some are my age. A couple of boys is mixed in there too. A car drives up to one. He gets in. Ride off. 'Cause I guess there's always work to do.

Gemini and me meet in the middle of the street. She don't ask where I'm going. Just says for me to be careful. I see in her red tired eyes she got no time for me. But then she say, "I'll be out of town maybe a week or two, could be three." She got food she don't want to rot. She'll give it to me, she say, hugging me hard. "But you gotta come get it."

Walking away backward, happy, I tell her I got all I need.

The daycare center got bars at every window, but no fence to keep people off their property. The floodlights make it seem like daylight over here. For a little while, I play hopscotch by myself—one game anyhow. After that, I sit on a swing in back, stare up at the stars—coloring everything I see.

A half hour is gone when I hop off, walk to go find the bin. FREE STUFF is written on the outside in a bright yellow marker. "People stupid." I pick up a pink rattle. "They throw away good stuff and go buy more stuff they gonna throw away." I find a talking toy. "B," it says when I touch that letter. "F," it yells when I hit the red button with that shape. I sit it on the ground and start my pile.

Most of the toys are dirty. But that's better than being broken or worn to pieces. Digging deep, I find a set of plastic baby keys in good condition. She'll chew on it. Hit me in the head with 'em. Have fun shaking 'em. I dance when I see a box of diapers—Cricket's size. Four inside. Soon, the ground is filling up with what I don't want and what I do.

I don't hear them come up behind me. But when somebody says, "Hey!" I jump up with a plastic phone in my hand, ready to knock somebody upside the head.

It's three women. Two got on uniforms. "Y'all almost got hit with this." I drop the phone in the bin.

They work at the nursing home a mile from here, they say. The other lady run a program for teen mothers. "At the alternative school ten blocks away." She walk up to me smiling, with her hand out for me to shake. "This bin allows us to stretch our program dollars."

I rub my hand down the side of my pants, then shake all three of their hands. "You can call me Char. I got a baby girl. Somebody told me about this place."

The janitor sets things in the bin after his shift ends, they tell me. This time of morning is when you get the best of what they have. My hands are full when they ask how old my baby is. I tell 'em Cricket is five months. The teacher ask about her shots.

"Shots? You mean needles?"

"Yes. Are they up to date?"

"Yeah. I'm a good mother."

She say they got a nurse at her facility. "No charge for shots. But you'll have to be part of the program. Think about it." I can get back in school and everything, she tells me.

How she know I don't go?

She digging through the bin. "Here you go, sweetie." She handing me clothes she say Cricket might be able to wear. "Why pay hard-earned money for something you don't have to pay for?" She warns me to be careful out here.

I smile and tell her I'm used to taking care of myself. Crossing the street with my hands full, I wonder what JuJu would think. I'm being responsible. Just like she said I should be. Wish she was here to see.

CHAPTER 50

HE CALLED ME from Mexico to check on me. Good thing, 'cause the money is gone.

CHAPTER 51

"YOU OKAY? EATING enough? Getting to bed on time?"

I turn onto my belly, smiling. "Yes, Anthony."

"Good. I wouldn't want anything to happen to you—"

"It won't. I promise."

"I know. Because I won't let it. You understand?"

"I understand."

"So, tell me the truth. You're broke again, right?"

I tell him the truth.

"Never lie to me. You cannot trust a liar or turn your back on them. You understand?"

"I understand."

"Good. Now, get back to sleep. Sweet dreams."

"Yes, Anthony."

He only got one rule, he told me yesterday. He wants me to say "Yes, Anthony" or "No, Anthony," not yeah or okay or uh-huh. That's low-life, he told me, disrespectful. It's a little thing to give him what he wants. He been so good to me, I don't mind.

As soon as I wake up, I put my clothes on and go get my money. Cricket gets to hang out with Solomon for a while. When he ask where I'm off to, I lie. I lie to Maleeka too when she wanna know how come I ain't been answering my phone. "I accidentally left it in a store. I finally figured out which one yesterday. And picked it up this morning." The truth is that I can't concentrate on math when

I'm worried about food, money, and everything else. And when I got money, I feel better, smart.

She on her way to gym class. Her school got exercise bikes, little trampolines, and everything. She think she may join the gymnastics team, but the basketball coach is trying to recruit her hard.

I turn another corner, see the hotel fountain splashing water. Rub my arms 'cause it's a little chilly today. "I never hear you talk about Sweets." I stop at the light on the corner. Pushing the button to make the streetlight turn faster, I listen to her tell me that she and Sweets don't talk no more.

"Everything in high school is so different, Char. The teachers. The kids. The cliques." We both say it at the same time. "I sure do miss McClenton Middle."

I laugh. Then she laugh. "Well, I have to get to work."

"You found a job?"

"Sure did."

I cross the street, look both ways. Roll my eyes when some old man asks my name. "Maleeka."

"Yeah."

"Tell me what you see. The colors and everything."

I head for his car.

If clean was a color, she says, it would look like Cottingham High. "White walls, baby-blue lockers, brand-new light brown shiny wooden floors all over the building. Trees—you believe that, Char—right in the building, live ones on every floor. And it smell like lemons everywhere."

Seem like the schools you see in the movies. Nothing like McClenton with doors off the bathroom stalls, gum stuck on the ceiling.

"You sure is lucky."

"Hey. Don't forget to do your homework."

He had the car washed and waxed. Water beads still hang on the fender and hood. "Gotta go." I put my phone away. Smile real nice. Jiggle some. And try not to forget what Maleeka said about commas. She got it in her head that I need to be doing other kinds of schoolwork. "Write five sentences using two commas three different ways," she told me. I ain't know what she meant till she explained. I still can't remember everything she said about conjunctions and how to use *and, or, but.* When I'm at his window, a sentence pops in my mind. *Anthony is good to me, and his driver is always nice.* I'm proud of how I use the conjunction, even if I can't tell her about it.

I need to pay him back. I can't keep taking and taking. I could go by his place, scrub the floors on my knees, wash the windows by hand, do his dishes, anything he want. But he won't accept no help from me. He don't want his money paid back either. "Accept it, baby girl. I like to do for you. No strings."

"Is that what you say to April?"

He tell me that I'm different. Smart. Only him and Maleeka ever said that about me. His words feel like honey on my skin, a warm sun in the sky. I laugh because some words that come in my head now don't sound like me at all. Coloring is changing me inside and out. How something that little do that? I don't know. But I like it. Like talking to Maleeka all the time now too.

"You got a baby, right?"

I ain't sure exactly what to say. Only, I don't want April to get in trouble. So, I lie. Tell him that Cricket is mine. Then I make up a whole story about us. Might as well. Once you start lying, why stop along the way?

"Well—there you go. I help you, and you help me."

"Yes, Anthony. Anything you want."

Usually our conversations end quick—faster than a mouse running 'cross the kitchen. Seems like he got all the time in the world today. I'm at my desk, one leg tucked, coloring. Cricket's on her back on the floor pulling on a one-dollar-store mobile, trying to lift herself up.

"Anthony."

"Yes."

"Did you go to college? You talk real nice, sound smart."

He went to community college, he say. And took a few courses at the university downtown. He quit once his mother got sick. "We had a family business. She died. I had to take over." He sound disappointed, like he sorry he did that. I ask what business she was in. Only, he don't say.

CHAPTER 52

"WANNA SAY HI to Cricket?" I hold the phone up to Cricket's ear. She know Maleeka's voice, sometimes anyhow. Today is one of them times. Whatever Maleeka says makes Cricket laugh and giggle, kick and smile. I take the phone back. "How's Caleb?"

Seem like she don't want to talk to me about him sometime. I used to bully her in front of him on purpose so he would quit liking her and wanna be with me. "I don't like him no more, Maleeka. And I don't care if you do," I say. And I mean it.

He taking her to the movies this weekend. He bought her flowers, daisies, for no reason at all the other day. She found 'em in a vase of water on her porch when she got home. "I wish we went to the same school," she says.

Cottingham High is a charter school in the next county. Black kids from the top of their class come from all over the city, she say. You gotta take a test to get in. Caleb don't go there, not that he couldn't. He at the neighborhood school, HR High. Maleeka say he's running for class president. I ain't surprised. I used to be smart, got skipped in third grade. I been stuck in seventh grade so long that last year they just said forget it and put me in eighth grade. I punched somebody the first day and got myself outta there. If I couldn't pass seventh grade, what made them think eighth grade was gonna be any easier for me?

I rush Maleeka off the phone 'cause he calling me. While I'm clicking over my heart beats hard, my hands sweat. "Anthony?"

"How's my baby girl?"

"Thank you for the Pampers and Similac." He left 'em at the back door. I ran down quick as I could after his driver called. "Am I gonna see you?"

He hangs up.

Should I call him? What if he mad? Maybe I said something wrong. Did something wrong. "Stupid," I say to myself. "You ain't thank him the right way." Sitting on my desk hugging my knees, I try not to cry.

CHAPTER 53

HE LEFT TOWN for two weeks. Bet I called him a hundred times. He never picked up. "I missed you," I say. "Can't you . . . take us next time?" I look at Cricket. "She won't be no bother." Maybe he didn't hear me. 'Cause he act like he didn't. He says he knows I need my hair done, my nails. "I have a woman friend at another shop."

I write down the address. Think about Maleeka. She got no time for fun at her school. She had to study all last week, and take a bunch of tests, so we ain't talked much. She gave me homework before she disappeared. I never did it. Haven't even colored. Mostly, I been thinking about Anthony and what I done wrong. I always screw up, JuJu say. I wanna do better. Gotta.

His voice is smooth as sixty-dollar Scotch. "When you get there ask for Lilly. Tell her to put it on my tab." And he's a gentleman. He ask my permission to discuss the way I dress. He don't mean to be offensive, he say, "But you could use some new clothes. Outfits that show off your figure and how mature and sophisticated you are." Before I open my mouth, he says, "I'm speaking like your father, your daddy."

"Thank you, Anthony." He so good to me, I got no words.

He know a Asian woman at another shop not far from the nail salon. He'll pay for me to get my hair done too. "If I don't look out for you, Char, who will?"

"Nobody, Anthony. Only you."

I think about Maleeka coming and going whenever she want. About my sister still mad at me, Miss Saunders who never cared. Cradling Cricket in my arms, I whisper in her ear, "I can't do everything. I need somebody grown to help me. Anthony's willing. There's worse people in the world."

CHAPTER 54

HE GOT ON a navy-blue blazer, black slacks, and a tie when we hook up. Standing outside my building next to his car he say, "Here." Then he reach into the breast pocket of his jacket. "Ask for George." He gives me a white envelope.

I rip it open. "The Fount! You got me a job at The Fount!" I hug him. "You don't know how bad I need this."

"Daddy always knows."

He opens the back door, buckles me in. He in the front seat of the car when he tells me his brother is the night manager there. "He likes to hire people from the neighborhood. To keep the money flowing in the community. There's a big party next weekend. They need extra help." He looking back at me, winking. "I told him you would be perfect."

I ask why he didn't tell me about his brother before. He don't answer. Maybe he's like JuJu. "Don't be so quick to tell people everything you know," she'd say.

"You want breakfast?"

"Yes, Anthony."

"Jerome, you know where to go."

I feel like Cinderella. My dress is pink sherbet with sparkles. My hair bounces with the car, stops past my shoulders. Black lipstick and lots of makeup make me look grown up, amazing. Even the driver say how pretty I am. Not Anthony though, so I ain't sure he like it. Maybe I'll ask his opinion before I get something done next time.

I never ate in a restaurant with a real tablecloth. Before I sit down, Anthony pull my seat out. Then he sits across from me, not next to me. He snaps the white napkin like a magician, spreads it over my lap. At first, I think it's meant to hide my short dress. Then Anthony said what he just done is good etiquette. Bet Maleeka know how to spell that word. He explaining what it means. "How you know so much?" I ask.

He always wanted the best out of life, he says. "Good wine. A great place to eat. Plenty of money in the bank. A house in the sub-urbs. You know, a easy, comfortable life. Remember this, Char—if you don't work hard and watch your money, you'll die broke."

I smile really big and tell him I'll remember.

"Good." He pats my hand.

I read over the menu. Scrambled eggs and bacon; French toast with powdered sugar; blueberry pancakes, home fries, and sparkling water—I order it all. Anthony said I could.

I got eggs in my mouth when he asks my father's name. I swallow and say it for the first time in years. "Nate. Nathanial Hunter Jones."

"Nate raised you well." He pointing to his cup. A waiter fills it with black coffee. "He would want someone looking out for you. Protecting you."

"I miss him. Nobody knows how much I miss my father."

"I do."

I put another forkful of eggs in my mouth but don't feel much like eating. He pushes a curl behind my ear. "What was his nick-name for you?"

"How you know he had one?"

He slides his warm cup my way. Says he bets I'd like coffee if I gave it a real try. I do it for him. It's bitter. I don't like it. Guess the expression on my face tells him that. Anthony mixes plenty of sugar and cream in the cup. I sip till it's gone. He wipes drops of coffee off my bottom lip, licks the spoon. "So, what was his nickname for you?"

"Charlie. He was the only one who called me that."

"Charlie. Maybe I could call you that."

"If you call me that I'll think about my dad. I used to think about him all the time. Till it got too hard."

"Okay, then I will not call you Charlie. Not unless you want me to."

"Thanks." I cut my pancakes and pour warm syrup on 'em, lift my fork and eat.

"You could call me Daddy, if you wanted."

"No, I only got one daddy."

His hand covers mine again. Pressing down hard, he say, "No thank you, Anthony."

"That's what I meant to say. Ouch! No—thank you, Anthony."

He smile at me, then snap his fingers. The waiter bring the check. "Sixty-five dollars for that?" I say.

He don't answer. Doesn't let me finish my food either. He stands up. Pulling my chair out. Walking out the door ahead of me. On the ride back, he don't talk to me at all, even though I'm trying to talk to him.

Soon as I get in the building, I call him to apologize. He don't answer. All night long, I worry and think about what I did wrong. Five in the morning, I leave another message. "Daddy, I promise never to do nothing to make you mad at me again."

This time he takes my call. "You my baby girl, Char?"

"Yes, Daddy. Thank you, Daddy." While I'm at it, I tell him it's okay for him to call me Charlie.

CHAPTER 55

"MALEEKA."

"Yeah, Char."

"If I told you something weird would you laugh at me?"

"No."

I tell her about Anthony. How he wants me to call him Daddy. "Creep," she says.

"He's not like that!"

"Yes, he is. And you know it."

I try to help her understand. "He just somebody who looks out for me. Lends me money when I need it. Makes sure my bills get paid." It sounds wrong when I say it out loud. So, no wonder she say she don't want to hear no more. That she got to go. Gymnastics tryouts are early tomorrow morning.

"Good luck."

"You too," she says. Then she's gone. Only, not for long. Ten minutes later she calling me back.

It's daylight and dark almost at the same time. I need to leave soon, do Anthony that favor I promised him. I see now I can't tell Maleeka everything, even about me working for Anthony's brother tonight. She'd say something negative about that too, 'cause she one of *those* girls now. The kind with a scholarship to a good school, a cute boyfriend that don't believe in feeling her up, and a mother at home who loves her. All I got is me.

Stepping into my heels, I tell her I'll need to go soon. Her voice turns soft, sweet. "Listen, Char. If he does something to you that you don't want done, call me—call somebody." Her mom don't drive, but she think she'd come get me anyhow, she says.

That's the nicest thing a girl ever said to me.

"You my big sister now, huh?" I ask.

She bring up them boys who followed her from my house one day. They put their hands on her, tried to kiss her, seem like they wanted to do more. Every once in a while, they turn up in her dreams, she say. "I always get away. Some girls ain't so lucky."

I walk up to the window. "You miss your father, Maleeka?"

"Every day."

"Me too. And—" I almost tell her that Anthony remind me of my dad. And I need a father out here. Somebody to look out for me. What Anthony asked me to do is a little thing. So, I'm gonna do it. He won't let nothing bad happen to me.

"It's late. Time for you to go to bed." Maleeka sound like my mom and JuJu.

We both laugh. "Okay, big sis."

"Yeah, Char. Listen to your big sister. I'm the most responsible and mature." It's supposed to be a joke. Not funny, I wanna tell her. But I got other things to do. Like go to work.

I pull up the window and stick my head out, yelling for Solomon to bring my baby home. I wanna kiss her before I leave. He gonna babysit tonight. We made a deal. She can hang out with him, and he gets to keep anything extra she helps him make.

Never enter through the front door, Anthony told me. "Employees working under the table use the one in the rear."

No one ever called me an employee before.

When I pass by the fountain at The Fount, the wind blows the water and my hair. Old men whistle. Tongues jump out. Anthony picked out my outfit—bloodred short shorts with super-high heels to match and a top with no sleeves or back. The temperature dropped, so I'm chilly, freezing. But I walk like its summertime, warm, with me crossing the sand on the beach, my shoes in my hand. The whole time, I'm thinking about a girl I seen earlier. She laughed at me, then took my picture. Girls like her want to be girls like me. They too scared, is all.

I'm late. In a hurry. Which is why I took my shoes off. Walking through the parking lot, I run by green bushes with red berries growing in between 'em, and a row of faded white flowers that make the air smell like candy. Men in their twenties or thirties, standing around drinking beer, eye me on my way by. One dude asks how much. By the time the floodlights come on, I'm at the back of the hotel, knocking on a dingy gray metal door, looking back.

He told me to ask for Carolina. "I don't ask for your brother?" I said. "Give me his name anyway in case she make me mad or something."

If I did that, it would be disrespectful, he said, and ruin his reputation. He rubbed the back of his hand against my cheek. "You wouldn't want to do that to Daddy, would you?"

"No . . . Anthony. I mean, Daddy."

He kissed my forehead. Said he know my father is up in heaven happy that another man is looking out for me. I been wanting a father for a long time. Only, you can't tell nobody that. Your dad or mom dies, and people forget about them quick. I know Anthony ain't perfect. But he's here—making sure me and Cricket's stomach is full. That we ain't living in no alley or on the street. Ain't that what fathers do?

While I'm waiting, I go in my purse—redo my lip gloss and chew on a mint. My finger gets poked by the Phillips screwdriver I brought with me just in case. Men at the party can look, even say more than I want 'cause I'm being paid. But if they touch me, I don't care what Anthony think, I will stab somebody.

Someone buzzes me in. I need both hands to pull open the door. It's dark inside. I stand in front the door, giving my eyes time to adjust. Walking slow, I see trash dumpsters lined up against one side of the hall. Boxes up to the ceiling on the other side. The stink make me hold my nose. "Miss Carolina. Miss Carolina. It's me. Char . . . I mean Charlie." Looking in front of me and behind, I call her again, then start walking up another hall like I know where I'm going.

She come out of nowhere—like a bat. Sneaking up behind me, mad, she says, "What the fuck are you yelling about?"

CHAPTER 56

CAROLINA'S GOT ON a tight red skirt and red-bottom shoes. Her hair is red as fire, tight in a bun at the back of her neck, straight and shiny. She didn't polish her nails. But they neat and clean, low cut. She ain't got on much jewelry. Just a gold chain, white posts in her ear. She look important, out of place in this part of The Fount just like the stains on the basement rugs and the walls that they never bothered to paint.

She walk by the freight elevator, past the steps, past a double-decker washer and dryer and a vending machine that sell pink and purple condoms. She writing on a sheet of paper. Checking things off when she say I don't got to worry about buying condoms 'cause they provide me with 'em.

I quit walking. "Huh? Hold up, what?"

It's a requirement, she say. People are pigs, nasty—them her words, not mine. "You get an infection, we don't make money."

I walk until I'm ahead of her. Standing in front of her, facing her, I tell her she musta made a mistake. Got me confused with somebody else. "I'm Char." I got my hand on my hips, my back straight. "Charlese. I'm supposed to work the bar, make the drinks. Not—" I look at the machine. "I don't do that."

"Do I need to call Anthony?" She walking again.

I try to keep up again, explain again. "No . . . no, ma'am. But Anthony told me—I'm doing him a favor. Some girl ain't show up, he said. I'm supposed to serve drinks. That's all he asked me to do. I don't know nothing about doing nothing else. That ain't me."

We turn up another hall that only got two light bulbs, no covers. There's about forty rooms on this floor. And it smells . . . foul. I hear noises coming from behind them doors, men who sound like bears.

A dungeon—that's what this remind me of. The kind that castles sit on top of. Mr. Bobbie gave me a whole coloring book full of 'em once. I drew in snakes and crocodiles, colored the water so black it looked like the devil lived in it. JuJu said that wasn't my best work.

I turn around and start running. Maybe she ran track, the 400 like JuJu. 'Cause when she catch up to me, she still in her heels, not even out of breath. Before I know it, she turn into one of them guards at county. So, I do what she wants. She got the pistol, not me.

JuJu always said I never knew when to be quiet. This time I keep my mouth closed and my eyes open. I try to remember every room number I pass, every person that go by. Some of 'em work here. Wear uniforms. Empty trash. They listen to music, walk, push carts. Act like they don't see me.

She stick the key in the lock, chains the door once we inside. Room 387 got double beds, a brown pullout couch, a flat screen, and orange rugs that went out of style a long time ago. My back's against the door when she put her things away, tells me to sit.

"I . . . I can make . . . rum and Coke, gin with vermouth . . . uh . . . uh . . ." I can't think up nothing else I'm good at making.

This room is for her, Anthony, and the driver, I hear her say. If I feel unsafe in the room next door, knock twice on the wall. She put her hand out. "And give me your purse and phone."

"No . . . I got a baby. If she get sick—"

"I tell him all the time. No kids with kids. But he— Never mind." She mumbling something about family.

She rolling her eyes. Taking my purse. Going through my phone. Asking where I hang out online. I don't know why she need to know. But I tell anyhow. Then she tells me that whatever the customer wants is what I'm supposed to do. I think about noises in the hall, men in the parking lot. Before I know it, I'm in the bathroom throwing up in the toilet—twice.

She good at showing up without you hearing her coming. "Do that again and"—she whispers in my ear like somebody else might hear her—"I'll tell him. You want me to tell him? He likes you . . . says you are the smartest, prettiest girl he knows."

Sour spit dribbles down my chin when I stand up. "Don't. Please." I turn on the faucet, splash water on my face, in my mouth.

She open the bathroom cabinet. Takes out toothpaste and squirts it on the brush. "Here. And quit crying. Girls like us—"

"Like us?"

"I worked my way up. Started at thirteen. Now I got a Benz. A kid in Catholic school. Don't you want nice things?"

I do.

Her face get so close to mine, I see glue on her lashes. "You should be glad you ain't gotta give it away for free no more."

"I'm a virgin."

She smiles. Says at least Anthony done one thing right.

Carolina watches me brush. Once I'm done, I follow her into the bedroom. She takes a seat at a computer on the desk next to the wall across the room. My eyes go from the chain on the door, to the window, to the balcony, then back to her. "Anthony said I'm like his daughter."

"Anthony is a businessman. All he cares about is making money."

"But—"

She coming my way again. Standing over me, she seem taller . . . a giraffe looking down on grass. "He lent you money?"

"No. He gave me that money."

"That means you owe him money."

"But he said—"

"You owe him money, yes or no?"

"Yes . . . I guess."

She got a smirk on her face, her arms crossed when she say, "Then pay up. Two thousand dollars plus interest. You pay now, you can leave now."

I don't got it, I tell her. Plus, it wasn't no two thousand, not even a thousand, I don't think. "And he didn't say nothing about interest or paying it back."

She sitting next to me when she run her finger down that yellow paper on her clipboard. She stop when she finds my name. There it is, Carolina tells me. In black and white. What I owe circled in red.

My name seem wrong there, misspelled when it ain't. But what choice do I got but to give her what she want—my full name, plus the middle one, my social security number, address, and where I went to middle school. They need to know everything about me, she say, 'cause if I run, they coming for me.

CHAPTER 57

I KNOCK TWICE. "Anybody in there?"

Carolina standing outside the room next door. "Go on. Open it."

It take a minute for my eyes to adjust to the dark after I walk in. Then I see him. Running like I'm thirsty and he the only water around, I wrap my arms and legs around him, cry on his shoulder.

He let me get it all out: the tears, everything Carolina said and done to me, how much I want to go home. It don't take him long to say he's disappointed in me. I seemed so mature, he tells me. So responsible. "Did I make a mistake choosing you, Charlie?"

"No, Daddy. It's just that—"

It's a little thing he's asking me to do, he say. "The first time is the hardest." He holding on to both my hands. "After that it's a piece of cake."

Breathing in and out, fast and hard, I tell him I think I might faint. He rub my back till I calm down. My throat dries up like I swallowed dirt, so I ask for a drink of water.

"Charlie, you want to make me happy, right?"

I nod.

"I can't hear you."

"Yes, Daddy. I want to make you happy, Daddy."

"Then do what you're told."

All of a sudden, I start shaking all over. Like I'm in a cold shower. He hold me close, tells me everything is gonna be all right. I believe him. He believes I can do it. That I'll earn a lot of money for him and me. I'm still shaking after he leave.

CHAPTER 58

HOW MANY ARE there? I don't know. I'm in the bathroom with the door locked, standing on the toilet holding a hanger like a bat. Somebody knocks again. He drunk, I think. Cussing when he tell me he about to go get Anthony.

I say the first thing that come to my mind. "I'll be out soon as I pee."

That's funny to them. They say they want refunds if I come out stinking. I jump down. Throw the hanger in the tub. Unlock the door. It's hardly open when they come for me, black-haired lions, cows, and snakes.

They black and white, friends here for a bachelor party. The one getting married is already wasted, so they walk him over to the bed while he unzips.

In kindergarten, kids fought to be first in line. Nobody wanted to be last. It's the same here. They stand around the room and argue 'bout who gonna follow the one who's getting married. Somebody drags me to him. "I'm in seventh grade." I close my eyes when his hand goes up my skirt. "Somebody call my sister. Tell her I want to go home."

There's five of 'em. One is on the balcony sitting on a lounge chair, smoking a cigar. Two got their backs against the wall, sipping something brown on ice, watching me. The other one asks the groom-to-be if he need some help. When the door opens, everybody look surprised.

"Shit." He closes the door quick. "I told you, no underage girls." His feet and legs move fast as wheels. They all agreed, he says, to each pay their share. "But, man . . . look at her. She's a kid."

The man on the bed tries to stand up. "She wants to be here. Tell him." Grabbing for my hand, he fall down on the bed.

"Mister, I wanna go home."

Sam is his name. He pull out his wallet, drops bills on the floor like he at the club. "Do whatever you want with her. But leave me out of it." The man on the balcony shaking his head. Another man's face is red.

The door squeaks when it opens this time. Everything happens fast after that. The one who's gonna get married stands up and falls again. But this time he end up on the floor. I kick him. He grabs hisself and yells. His friends back up like I got a straight razor or gun in my hand. Running for the door, I scream. They got good jobs, didn't ask for no drama, I hear some of 'em say following me out.

I hear Anthony yelling my name. See doors up the hall open, Carolina coming for me. I scream some more. "Don't stop. Keep going," I can hear JuJu say.

Skipping steps. Falling. I run and run. In the lobby, I remember what my sister taught me: "If somebody's after you, don't be quiet. Let the whole world know." So, I scream all the way home.

CHAPTER 59

I CALL MY sister and leave another message. Her voice mail say she ain't there. That she's on a retreat, the kind where you leave your phone locked in a drawer in a room all weekend. "Call me," I say again. "I want to come home."

I got money to take a bus. There's one that leaves five in the morning, while it's still dark. "You want these, Solomon?" I'm holding Cricket, standing in the kitchen with all the cabinets open. I don't have much left but who don't like noodles and fruit drinks, eggs, white bread, and cheddar cheese?

He nods his head and says his grandmother might let me stay. "You know, until you can reach your sister." He try to take her from me.

I hold her tighter, turn my back on him. "That's okay." Using one hand, I start packing his things in a brown shopping bag.

He ask why I'm so stubborn. I'm used to doing things for myself. Not asking for nobody else's permission or help. 'Cause you can't trust people, really. "Cricket," I whisper in her ear. "I told you. People are janky. Especially men. Don't trust none of 'em."

He takes it personally, what I said. For a minute, me and him argue. I got a ketchup bottle in my hand, ready to throw it at him right before he brings up his dad. "He's in jail for being a stand-up guy."

"Bet Anthony say that every time he end up in jail."

He come in closer. Tickles her chin. Makes it so I got no choice but to look him in his big brown eyes. His father was an accountant, so he say. At a small company. Right after they hired him, he seen that something was wrong with the books. He told his boss. His boss said he'd look into it. Six months later, he called the police on his dad. "He doing five to seven right now."

I don't like it when boys cry. It don't seem right. So soon as his tears start, I hand her over. And keep on packing. "Guess everybody's got problems," I say.

"He needs things—money for cigarettes, phone cards, a new lawyer."

"That why you read those law books?"

He lifts her up. Sits her on his shoulders. Cricket drools on his head, pats it like a drum. "Yeah. He's not a gangster, a crook. But they're treating him like one anyhow." He keep talking. I'm half listening, half thinking about what to do next. Maybe I'll catch the bus home anyhow. Maybe when JuJu see Cricket, she'll love her as much as I do.

Before I know it, he FaceTiming his grandmother. Holding the phone my way, he force me to wave at her. She's gray, but got no wrinkles, brags about being "a young seventy-eight." Solomon lies for me. Tells her I was in a group home that kicked me out because the state quit paying for me to be there. Right away, she offering me her basement to stay in awhile. She don't care if I got a baby. "We'll be good company for each other." She smiles.

I'm nice when I turn her down. He don't say that what I did was a bonehead move, but it show in his eyes. Anthony is probably at the bus station already, he says. I never thought about that. I do think about my sister, though, my grandmother. If I had gone to Alabama like they wanted me to, none of this woulda happened.

At the window, watching out for him, I remind Solomon about the first day we met and how mean I was to him. "But you always been nice to me. Why?"

Him and his grandmother ain't doing me no favors, he say, walking up to me. "She got eight cats. They live in the basement."

We laugh, get real quiet, then listen to music from the club next door. Luther, I think. My mother's favorite. We get the same idea at the same time, it seem. Leaning in close, our lips almost touch. Then he stop, lifts Cricket off his shoulders careful as a Christmas bulb from a tree. She on the floor with her toys when I say, "I always mess up, Solomon. Watch. Something else bad will happen. Keep yourself and your grandmother away from me."

He remind me of Maleeka. They both the kind of people who see the best in you until it's too late. If he wasn't sad about his father, he wouldn't even want to kiss nobody like me. And if I wasn't scared and sad, I wouldn't want to kiss him neither. He so corny, I could boil and butter him.

I use his phone to dial my grandparents' number. They don't answer either. It's late. They got church in the morning. Plus, they wouldn't recognize this number. I try again anyhow. The third time I dial, somebody knocks on my door. Solomon gets the broom. I take a butcher knife out the drawer.

"Char. It's me, April. Open up."

"April?"

"He's outside. I swear."

"Don't lie to me, girl."

"I'm not. I promise. Let me see my baby. She okay?"

Solomon runs to the window, opens it wide, sticks his head out. There's a black Cadillac, a '97, parked on the sidewalk, he tells me. "And a man, six five maybe, two fifty, looking up here."

"That's his driver." I turn the bottom lock real slow. Take off the chain. Twist the key in the dead-bolt lock. Sticking my head out the door, I look up and down the hall. "Get in here—quick!"

April look way older now—like thirty. Her toes and fingers is polished, hot pink, shiny, chipped in spots. Her hair is white blond. Long. Matted at the ends. Her lipstick match her dress and JuJu's favorite red wine, merlot. She look cheap as a one-dollar-store dress on clearance.

She got Cricket in her arms by the time the chains and locks go back on. "No!" I take her from her. "You can't walk up in here and—" Holding on to Cricket, I tell her we'll be okay. But it's like that time on the bus, she want her mother no matter what. So, she kicking, crying, fighting me, like it wasn't just her and me all this time.

April follow me and Cricket from the door to the window back past the bed to the kitchen and back to the window again. The woman next door bangs on the wall. Asks if she need to send the owner up here to make us shut up. I apologize. April whispers, "If you don't come—" She pulls the curtains closed. "He'll sell her."

I point my finger at April like a gun and tell her she the worst mother in the world. But she say it ain't true. "I left her with you, didn't I?"

I roll my eyes.

"She's clean, no cuts or bruises, happy. I did the right thing for once."

She goes to the door and unlocks it. Puts her arms out, so I hand her over, finally. Then I get my backpack and put it on. It's packed, full, ready. While April kisses her and talks to her, I let Solomon know I may not be back no time soon. "Since your grandmother don't mind me and Cricket coming, maybe she won't mind just Cricket there till you reach my sister."

"But, Char—"

"Take her home soon as his car leaves. Keep calling my sister till she answer. Don't tell her what happened to me. She not the same person she used to be. She may call the police. And I don't want to make him madder than he already is."

I hand Solomon her baby bag. It's filled with bottles of milk, toys, her Binky, books, blanket, and snacks. Kissing her, I tell him what nobody told me. "She likes getting her hair washed. Hates soap in her eyes. She think she ready for the sippy cup. But she ain't. Keep trying though. She a fast learner."

CHAPTER 60

ON THE FIRST floor by the door that lead to the street, I ask April what she think Anthony gonna do to me. She say I gotta learn my lesson—the sooner the better. It'll hurt, she tells me. Worse than anything I ever felt before. "But you earned it. Anyhow, you'll get used to it."

I got used to a lot: failing seventh grade, cutting class, bullying people who was scared of me. But I ain't never gonna get used to the things that happen at The Fount, I tell her.

"That's what I said."

I push the door open. "What's Cricket supposed to get used to? A different mother every two months? Men who—"

"Shut up! You talk too much."

She step out the building like she leaving one of JuJu's parties, swinging her hair and everything else. Stopping at the car she say, "Here she is, Daddy," even though his window is shut tight.

I get in first. Sliding across the back seat, I sit behind the driver. "I'm sorry, Daddy."

Anthony don't look my way or say a word. He on the phone taking care of business. The car start moving, backing up before April's door is closed. The driver tell us to buckle up—like it matters.

April leans her head against the window, like she's tired, then closes her eyes. When I pat the seat in between us, she ignore me. Next, I tap my foot on hers. It's like I ain't here. So, I take out a pen, writing on my hand what I got to say. *What if he sells her anyhow?*

Her purse is on the floor between her legs when she unzips it and takes out pills. She got two in the middle of her hand when she say, "Take them. You'll feel what he's doing. But you won't care as much."

My palms is sweating. I wipe 'em on my shorts. Wipe sweat off my nose and cheeks too. But I don't take the pills. I pray under my breath. Not for myself but for Cricket. She only a baby. Too young to run out of good luck or for God to forget about her.

He covers the phone with his hand. Yells for me to shut my big, fat, stinking mouth before he does it for me.

She swallows the pills without water, even though there's a bottle in the pocket behind Daddy's seat. When she start crying, his hand reaches back. He grabs her by the hair and bangs her head on his headrest. She don't make a sound, not a peep. Me neither.

The car turns corners fast. Flies by a restaurant, The Fount, and a park I never seen before. By the time it's on the highway, we doing eighty.

I see Walmart in a strip mall in the next town over, Barnes & Noble and TJ Maxx two exits past that. I try to memorize that, plus other things about him. He's tall, maybe six four, I remind myself. He shaved his head last week, so he bald. Always wears a watch on his right hand—Apple today. I lock that picture in my brain. The license plate number too. And hope Solomon do like I said and get JuJu to come for the baby soon as she can.

April picks at a knot at the end of her hair. I try the lock again, the window too. He tells the driver to go back for Cricket once they're done.

For the first time she look scared. "Daddy, you said it wasn't true. That it was just something for me to tell Char to get her to come. Please—don't sell my baby."

He tell her to shut up. That he's a full-grown man, and he'll do what he wants.

We both get quiet. Soon I see April lifting her purse off the floor. Sitting it in her lap. Her fingers move slow as slugs when they go inside it. My eyes get big as the moon after I see it—pink as Pepto-Bismol. Loaded, I hope.

CHAPTER 61

RAILROAD TRACKS AND raggedy streets that need fixing make the wheels on the car bounce, and us too. The car slows down, turns left, goes under a bridge. The driver cuts the lights off, but the car keep moving, rolling over bumps, smashing bottles.

Once it stops, the locks pop up. April tells me to pretend I'm somebody else, somewhere else. He say for me to leave my coat and backpack here. We right by the water. So, it's really cold. Even my long sleeves won't keep me warm. But I do like I'm told.

The moon give enough light that we see each other easy as we see broken bottles and rocks stuck in the dirt we standing on.

"Here." I got my fingers in my back pockets. "Sixty dollars. It's all I got. Please let me go home."

He take out a lighter, then two cigarettes, and lights 'em both up. "Cigarette?"

I take a long drag. "I'm sorry, Daddy."

"Of course. No harm, no foul." He put one foot on the fender of the car. Makes rings with the smoke. "I rarely set a finger on my girls. It's bad protocol." April can vouch for him, he says.

She come out the car like he called for her. Standing under a tree, she watches. My hand shakes. So does the cigarette. "I wanna do right by you, Daddy, but I don't think—"

He grab my arm and twists it behind my back. "Don't ever—"

His other hand hits my cheek hard as a baseball bat. So, I scream. He punch me in the face and my head.

She don't say a thing. After he push me down on the ground, he bang his knee into my chin. My teeth bite my tongue. I spit blood. He say I better not lift my hands and wipe it. Or get it on his new shoes.

"Yes . . . Dad . . . dy." My voice melts like sugar in water. I look up at April. She look away.

"And don't move."

My knees and hands hurt. They shake after a while. When I ask permission to stand up, he grab me by the hair and pulls me like a dog on a leash. Crawling, I beg him to turn me loose. "I'll . . . behave. I promise. I promise. Please, Daddy." Glass and rocks dig into my knees and hands. "Whatever you want. I'll do it. I'll do it. I'll do it."

He drag me past the car parked in front of his, past the next one and the next over to a sixteen-wheeler parked with its cab facing us. You can't see over it so whatever gets done behind it, only us and God gonna know.

"Look up at me!"

He spits in my face. "And don't wipe it off."

It slides down my nose. Runs over my lips. Drips on my hand like tears.

"You're ugly."

"Yes, Daddy."

"And you too fat, bitch."

"I know, Daddy. I'll lose weight for you, Daddy. Don't hurt me no more."

Out the corner of my eyes I see her getting closer.

"Did I say you could talk?"

I put my head down so I don't get smacked. He tell me to moo.

"What?" I look up.

"Moo, bitch—like a cow. You're a fat-ass cow, aren't you?" He lifts his foot, stands on my hand, smashes it like a cigarette butt.

Glass bites into my palm, cuts places already cut. I moo anyhow—like them cows I seen off the turnpike. He laughs, takes his foot off my hand, and laughs again after he hear me say, "Moo! Moo! Moo!" I shake, wiggle, and jiggle. "Look, Daddy. I'm a cow."

He turn my hair loose. Tells her to come closer because this is what she can expect next.

"Charlie. Daddy loves you. Say it." He unbuckles his pants.

"Daddy loves me."

Her eyes stay on mine.

"And he's going to take care of you."

I swallow. "And you'll take good care of me."

"But first you have to learn your lesson. Don't you?"

"Yes, Daddy." I back up.

His pants drop.

He don't see her hand go in her purse. Or seem to care that she getting closer, walking up behind him. The gun is pushed up to his ribs when she say, "Take care of my baby, Char. And tell her I always loved her."

He laughs.

She put the gun up to his head.

He reach down and pulls up his pants.

She backs up. "Why are you still here, Char? Go!"

I stand up. Trip. Fall down and get up again. Looking over my shoulder, I see the driver coming. And Anthony with that gun pointed at his chest. On the ramp to the bridge, I hear it go off a whole bunch of times. But I don't stop. I can't.

THE LIFE I'M IN

CHAPTER 62

SHE'S GONE. DEAD in the river. He never told me if she was alive before she went in. I was barefooted, sitting on the side of the road when the driver found me. Anthony was still under the bridge with April, I guess. Running in and out of traffic, I cried and screamed, but ain't nobody care. They kept driving, beeping, giving me the finger 'cause I was in their way. You can smell the river up there, or maybe it's the bodies that people dump in it, or gas fumes and tailpipes that needed fixing. Everything on me hurt, so I couldn't fight back. On the way to the car, I thought about April. She helped me and Cricket both at the same time. I ain't never gonna forget that.

CHAPTER 63

HE KEEP THE drapes closed, the room dark, me under the sheets without no clothes on. I don't know how long I been here. It was Friday night when I came, I know that. I think I heard a preacher on the radio a little while ago.

Cuts and purple bruises—different shades of crayons in the box—showed up every place he punched me, bit me, forced me. I hurt inside and out.

He on break now, across the room at the computer, taking care of business. Now I'm his business too. Lying on my back, crying, I tell him I need a shower. That I need to go home. I ball up when I hear his feet, curl up tight as the knots in my hair, then put my head under the blankets trying to disappear. Did he tell me I could cover up, sit up, breathe? he asks. No. Did he say I could move? No. No. No. The answer to everything that got to do with me is no till he say it ain't, he tells me.

"Okay, Daddy." I think it's okay to say that.

He pulls the blanket off. Crayons pour on my head like rain. Purple, silver, green, black, gray, and everything in between spill out over me, lay on the blankets and in between the folds of the sheets, fall off the mattress and roll across the floor like they want to get away from him too.

He hits me upside the head with the box, slips on a crayon, and stomps it. I don't care. I'm too old for crayons now, anyhow.

I get to clean up the mess he just made. So, I run over to the wooden trash can by his desk and drop the crayons in. Then run back to bed. He wants a shower. I run to his bathroom and start the water. Then run back to bed. He showers twice a day, rain or shine. Wants jazz music playing while he in there. I run to his desk and turn the radio up loud. Sitting on the bed, I fold my hands.

It don't take long for him to look brand-new. His suit and tie cost more than some people make in three months, Daddy tells me, sitting on the edge of the bed. I put on his cuff links. Off comes one of his rings, then three more. I lotion his hands, in between his fingers. He whistles while he smiling at what he see in the mirror beside the couch across the room. I sit in the same spot looking at all he's got: a bedroom big as our living room, a chandelier and two couches, a bookcase with a whole row of dictionaries, plus a globe—black—that spins on his desk when he get to thinking. He work all day in A-hole motels and hotels, he told me last night, so when he come home, he wanna live the way people do on the internet and TV, and in them condominiums by the river downtown.

I walk like a mummy, shuffle, feel broken as my crayons. She don't care. "Hurry up. You think you special? Every bitch here been through what you been through or worse."

Two girls run past us, into one of the bedrooms, laughing. I gag and throw up.

"On my clean floor! Kianna."

One of them laughing girls runs up to us. She look down, rolls her eyes at me, then gets downstairs and back ASAP with the bucket of warm water Carolina asked for.

"Clean it up."

They got wooden floors, light brown, shiny, and pretty. It's hard getting down on my knees, but I do it with a quickness. Once I'm done wiping, she make me go wash my face and hands. The bathroom at the end of the hall is for us girls only. The tub and sink so white they hurt your eyes. I take care of my business and get back to Carolina and her tour.

Anthony's room is on the second floor, she say like I don't know. "When he want you to come, you come. No matter what time of day or night, if you sick or not." She says I'll get used to it.

"When do I get to go home?" I close my eyes and wait for what I earned.

Pinching my chin, she whisper in my ear, "He had to break you, so you know he owns you, like he own this house and everything in it. One day you'll thank him."

My eyes open slow and stab her.

"I woulda killed you. Can't trust a bitch who did what you done. And knows what you know. But college boys—think they're smarter than everyone else. She shoulda left the business to me."

She point to doors in the hallway. This closet is for linens, she say, opening it. Different color towels and washrags fill up the shelves, sweet-smelling body wash, soap too. The next closet got T-shirts in it, shorts, ironed and folded, plus blouses. Shoes in different sizes, some with plastic heels with fake fish floating in 'em, wait on a rack on the floor.

We don't own nothing in here, not even ourselves, she telling me. "Anthony does." We fight over any of this shit, she'll whip us good, then take it out our pay.

I look up at her. "We get paid?"

"You work. You get paid."

Carolina opens the double doors to the closet at the end of the hall. It got baskets of hair in it, packs of weave, Styrofoam heads with hair on 'em: short and brown, long, curly and black, platinum blond. "Everything you need. But ain't nothing free."

I rub my eyes with the heel of my hand. Walk behind her past windows painted black so we can't see out and they can't see in, she say. In the bathroom cabinet, she show me toothpaste and brushes, condoms, sanitary napkins, boxes of Tylenol 3's. We pay for them too, plus security and food.

She take me down one floor, past Anthony's room to one with a padlock on it. Us girls can't go in this room, she say, but we'll see her and him in there a lot. His business partners too. It smell like weed, but he don't partake. She showing me the room so I don't go snooping, she say. "And end up like your friend." She laughs, then unlocks the door.

Laptops and desktops is on all three desks. Cell phones is piled on the bed. Money is tied together with thick rubber bands. He hides most of his money, she says. Buys gift cards a lot too. So cops can't trace his profits. Vanilla gift cards is how he pay us mostly. So, if we steal, we steal from the family and ourselves. For the first time, she touches me. Hugs me a good long time. "You're family too now, Charlie. Never forget that." Her arms is soft and warm, like my mother's, when she say what Anthony said—all of this was my fault. That some girls is harder to break than others. Then she asks if I learned my lesson.

I shake my head yes. "He won't have to do that to me no more."

She walk me over to a camera on a stand in the corner. "You don't advertise in this business, you don't make no money." Then Carolina tell me how things are done here. They post our pictures wherever perverts be.

Clients contact Anthony online, by phone, or text, and place orders for the kind of girl they want like we pizza or fried chicken dinners. She gonna take pictures of me after the bruises heal. Till then, I still got to work, she say.

I start tonight.

CHAPTER 64

THEY IN THE family room, most of 'em in their underwear. Carolina is in the kitchen. She said it was up to me to introduce myself.

I stay where I am in the living room, staring in. The two I seen upstairs wave at me at the same time. "Hi, I'm Rosalie." The other one don't have to say that her name is Kianna. But I'm glad when she smile. A girl lying on the floor, belly down, playing Fortnite, tell me to call her Earle. Her lipstick is dark purple, maybe blue. She got yellow cat eyes. Contacts. Kate, the white girl on the rocker, walks up to me. "It gets better," she say, helping me in. Katrina nods her head.

Rosalie is sitting on the floor between Kianna's legs getting her hair braided. "I only charge fifteen dollars." She stop to crack her back. "I'll do yours anytime you want."

I stop in the middle of the room. "I'm Char—I mean Charlie."

A girl at a card table by the window say it's okay if I use my real name around them. "But not around the customers. Always keep something for yourself." She lays down four cards—spades. "He makes me call myself Roxanna. My real name is Roxanne." Roxanne got a face full of freckles, tiny brown flat bubbles sitting in the middle of her face. She say she's fourteen, but she look more like twelve. She stick her hand out, gets paid in cigarettes from the girl next to her. I walk up to their table, limping. They act like they don't see. She pat the seat on the other side of hers and says, "You won't always be sad. Right, Gem?"

Gem is thick all over, short, maybe five two. She got cute dimples and wears braces. When she smile, her face shines. "I was never sad." She pick up the four of spades and sits down a club. "Daddy took me off the street." Her nails seem long as chopsticks. She talk about girls on the stroll. The ones she know anyhow. "They got nobody to take care of them or to handle the crazies." Some girls get beat by their daddies on the regular, she says. "Not us. Not if we good." Her eyes stay on me. "He say you don't listen so well."

"Did y'all know April?"

Seem like they deaf or I didn't say nothing at all. 'Cause everybody ignores me, look any place else in the room but right here where I am.

"She was my friend and—" I think about Carolina. Her telling me Daddy had to break me 'cause I don't listen so good, and he would do it again if I didn't learn the first time. "Never mind." I sniff. "She wasn't nobody." I try not to think about her in the river, or Cricket crying for me.

"Daddy got all kinds of businesses, different girls," Gem says. "We're his favorites. He keeps us close." She tells me that I'm lucky. "This is a nice house, warm. There's a Jacuzzi in our bathroom."

"A pretty-ass prison." Earle look back at me. "And don't pay attention to Gem. She like to drink the Kool-Aid."

"Leave, then." A pack of new cards fly over Earle's head. "But you won't." Gem smiles at me. "She did twice and—"

Kianna asks me to go to the kitchen and get them some snacks. I don't want to go, but I do. A bag of honey mustard pretzels and bowl of dip is waiting for me when I get there. Carolina is flouring chicken to fry for dinner. She say not to believe everything them girls say. Earle is gone when I get back.

I take the chips and dip from one girl to the next. Some dig in the bag with their hands. Roxanne uses napkins to get hers, then asks if I ever done this before. I never liked games all that much, I tell her. They think that's funny. She stick two pretzels in the dip, eats 'em at the same time. It's the worst job you ever gonna have, she say, licking her fingers. "A lot of times you gonna wish you was dead."

"I wish I was dead now."

Gem hunches her shoulders, changes the subject. "I do nails." She move her fingers like she typing on a laptop. "Plus, if you need your makeup done right—I'm your girl—not Earle." Gem wants to be a cosmetologist. To work in Hollywood with movie stars. "Go to Roxanne for—"

"I'm not good at anything." Roxanne lift up the chain on her neck and make the cross swing. She asks how I met Anthony but don't wait to hear the answer. She was at work, pumping gas, when she first ran into him. "Hungrier than I ever been." She got a chip in her mouth when she say that Anthony came in the store and offered to buy her lunch. At first, she ain't go. But he came three days in a row. "He probably heard my stomach growling."

"Where we at?" I say. "What part of town, what's the address?"

They don't know. He don't say. There ain't no address outside the house neither. We all get quiet, sit still for a long time. "God knows," Roxanne says.

"Daddy's God to me." Gem was on her own, getting beat up almost every day till Daddy found her and brung her here to live.

I ask who been here the longest. Rosalie raise her hand. She met Daddy online. Thought he was sixteen. Left with him anyway after he showed up at school one day. Gem's hand goes up next. She been here two years, three months, fifteen days. She fourteen. Her mom got her the braces, she say, before she gave her back to the state. She clicks her teeth. "One day they'll come off, I guess." For the first time, she seem sad.

"When your birthday comes," Roxanne says, "Carolina will make you a cake. Then we'll make you one that taste good."

I laugh. Them too.

"Rum cake!" It's Katrina. "That's what I want for my birthday next month. With plenty of sprinkles."

Gem always buy the candles and gift wrap. Roxanne offers to get me a gift. Katrina wants a pack of cigarettes from every one of us. "And no loosies. Plus, I want my hair did. Flat-ironed."

They got rules about birthdays. If you in this house one minute or ten years, you give something to the birthday girl. "You can make it," Roxanne says. "What you good at?"

"Nothing."

Her eyes roll.

"Well, I used to be good at coloring."

"Good. Do that."

I think about my crayons, smashed, broken. And remind myself to throw my coloring books in the trash. They get back to doing whatever they was doing before I walked in. I don't know what I'm supposed to be doing, so I sit at the card table, listen, watch, and try to remember.

CHAPTER 65

IT SMELL LIKE Christmas out here because of the trees. Carolina says they're pine. The needles crunch under our feet like cereal. The ones still on the trees pull at the fur on my coat. I stop and stick my tongue out, catch me some snowflakes.

Every day we use the back door to leave the house. Sometime it's dark. Sometimes not. Guess it don't matter. People don't see us nohow. It's like our house is invisible. Buried in trees. Seems like we live in a park or forest, but we don't. Earle say we got neighbors 'bout ten, fifteen blocks away. Maybe they'll see us one day, find us or call the police, I said the other day. Gem told me to shut up and be quiet.

Air blows on my cheeks, scrubs my chin till it hurts. I'm freezing in fishnet stockings and a short skirt that was too short 'fore it shrunk in the last wash. Roxanne's in front of me. The other girls is ahead of her. I say for them to step it up, but it's hard walking on sticks in heels. Sometimes, I count the trees. I got up to seventy last time I tried. I drop stuff too. A red fingernail, a yellow pencil, bread, broken glass. Daddy figured it out. Asked who done it. Roxanne took the beating for me. So, I owe her like I owe April. Roxanne say God don't keep score.

It's the first snow to fall since I been here. It melts on my tongue and lips. Gem swiped the lipstick for me when she was out by herself with Daddy. So, I guess I owe her too. It's called Ripe Red

Raspberries. It don't come off no matter how much kissing gets done. Plus, it's expensive.

"Here." I brush snow off Roxanne's bangs with my hand and wipe her wet cheeks. "You look pretty tonight." Kate done her hair. It's down her back, strawberry blond, a million curls. My wig is black, stops at my chin. I'm happy my bruises is all gone.

"Make a wish," Roxanne say once she walking again.

I say it to myself. *I wish I was home.* I look up at the moon instead of where we going. It's a half-moon with half of that half stuck behind a cloud. I look down at my shoes and icicle toes. And ask Roxanne what she wishing for.

"A Christmas tree." She been here a whole year and a half and they ain't never had one.

I watch the moon while she telling me what all she'll put on it. "I hope you get your wish." She hope the same for me.

The van don't got no seats, or rugs on the floor, just benches and a window so Carolina and the driver can look back and keep their eyes on us. We get in, slide across the seat far as we can, then sit facing each other. They padlock us in. There ain't no windows, so we don't know where we going until we get there. He uses The Fount, motels, and other places. He's got other girls too. Says he wants to be a billionaire. Me too.

I rub my hands, blow on my cold fingers, pull out a cigarette and light up. Roxanne hums. Kate talks 'bout her daughters. Twins. They live with her grandmother somewhere in California. The state took 'em from her. Put Kate in a group home. Left her father free. She ran two months after that. That's something we all got in common. We run, but trouble always catch up to us.

"I had my first pimp at thirteen." Kate pops a pill in her mouth. She snuck on a train going from DC to Virginia, hitched a ride to

New York. Found another pimp there. Anthony is number three. Kate sneezes, digs up her nose, checking her nose ring for snot. She Irish with a bunch of freckles and red hair that look like it never stops. She got a Irish accent when she want one. Says it gets her bigger tips. Daddy take most of those too, but he still let us keep some. Shaking her legs to warm 'em, she bang on the wall. "Heat! We need heat, Miss Carolina. Those men don't come to buy Popsicles."

I ain't like the rest of them. They don't belong to nobody. I bet nobody is looking for 'em, wishing they was home either. I got JuJu, Mr. Bobbie, and Maleeka. Maybe even Miss Saunders. At work, I think about 'em, in my head I talk to 'em, 'cause if I didn't, maybe I would be like Gem and think I was supposed to be here, stay here, like it here. I don't. I never will.

CHAPTER 66

"HEY, SUGAR." I walk across the room jiggling. "What you want, sugar?" I stick gum in my mouth so he don't smell my sour breath. He on the bed in the middle of the room—undressing. Says he wants to watch me undress too. I already done worked four hours. Got ten more to go. I smile really big 'cause I gotta. I taught myself to ignore some things: faded wallpaper, dirty sheets, holes in the rugs, screams up the hall. Sometimes, I think about Cricket—and smile. Soon as we start, I close my eyes and see me and Maleeka back at school—cutting in the halls. She laughing. I'm laughing. We both happy for once.

CHAPTER 67

WHAT CITY IS this? I can't remember. Yesterday was Philadelphia. The day before was Erie. Last week we drove to Baltimore, New York, Chicago. It's the holiday season. Big games and parties everywhere. We busy as Santa Claus.

When we out of town and ain't working, we sleep in the van. Change clothes in the van. He give us a little extra when we traveling. The other day I bought a sweater with my extras, a turtleneck shirt too. They only good for wearing in the house though.

The next trick steps in the room, slams the door. No need to move, I'll end up here anyway. "It ain't snowing in here?" he say. "I thought it was snowing. Damn." He step on my clothes on his way over to me.

I smile, and he think it's for him. He wrong . . . about everything. "You like snow, baby?" I get on my knees. "You like 'em white as rice, light as rum?" I wonder what he tell his girlfriend, wife, or daughters. "You in DC, Chocolate City, sugar." I jump on the floor and twirl like I'm a ballerina, when inside I feel like a dragon ready to set fire to this room, burn the whole building down. The snow outside is doing a dance too, pretending that it's something it ain't—flurries instead of a snowstorm.

CHAPTER 68

My eyes is April's eyes now, always watching,
looking, seeing—
cops who pretend they ain't
chickens everywhere
competition trying to move in on Daddy
men who beat girls like me 'cause they hate,
love, can't stay away
from girls like me—
My eyes is pinballs bouncing left right, side to
side, up and down
'cause in this job you gotta be ready
for anything
anybody
anywhere
anytime
sometimes I wish I was dead.

In my sleep, I sit straight up, look around, watching, checking in front me, behind me, inside the closet too, 'cause you never know. Anything can happen to you out here in the streets, in hotels, motels, parking lots, and Daddy's house too. People see girls like me and don't see us at the same time. When I'm gone, it'll be like I was never here.

CHAPTER 69

WE LAUGHING SO hard we slobber and spit on ourselves. We all in our underwear sitting in the family room, like usual. Rosalie just told us about the time her father came to school and whipped her for cheating on a test. He work at a pickle factory. Came in smelling like pickle juice when she was in third grade. For the rest of the year, kids called her peewee pickle head.

Kianna goes next, telling us 'bout the time she spent the night at a white friend's house and got her hair washed. Kianna liked how straight that girl's hair got when it was wet. So, she asked her friend's mom to wash her hair next. A hour later, that girl's momma was calling Kianna's mom telling her to come over quick. Kianna say she cried two whole hours while her mother detangled her hair and brought back her curls. "So, Earle, now you know why I don't just let anybody do my hair."

We check on Earle to see if she smiling yet. She is a little. We joking around mostly to cheer her up, especially after what Carolina done to her. The makeup hide the bruises, but she still hurting.

"You cool over there, Earle?" I ask.

She in the rocking chair, not moving. I'm 'cross the room at the card table with Roxanne. She doing my nails. I'll do hers next. Earle start talking 'bout that night like we wasn't there. Everything went wrong it seem. She was tired. We always tired. And she ain't wanna leave the house. Carolina dragged her down the steps by one leg.

Daddy was at the bottom of the steps finishing his corned beef sandwich. Burping, he asked Carolina why she couldn't control us.

Sometime Earle just be asking for it. At the motel, she argued with Carolina in front of customers. Later on, them two brung that mess back home. That's how I found out Anthony and Carolina is related, sister and brother. I shoulda known by the things Carolina say sometime. Plus, they do got the same nose and skin color—ears with tips that curl under. We was all piled in one room lying across the floor like sardines in a can, when Earle spilled the tea.

"They grew up in a house like this," she said. "Had a younger sister with leukemia and everything."

My head almost explode when she say that.

"Anthony was in college, till his mother got sick. He left school to run the business 'cause she made him. Then she died, and he sold the house. Carolina's been mad ever since, because their mother promised the house and the business to her."

"How you know all this?" I asked.

"We from the same hood." So, it was easy for Anthony to get her to come work for him, Earle say. "Kids 'round my way know about his big cars, expensive clothes, and trips."

I asked if they knew about us. "They knew about his momma, and they know about him. Now they know about me too." Anthony made sure they did, after Earle ran off the last time. He posted pictures everywhere. "That why they wanna know," she said, "where you be at online. My grandmother seen them pictures. I can't go home no more."

Daddy would never do that to me.

We tell Earle more stories, make some jokes. Kianna and Gem fall asleep on the floor. After a while, me and Roxanne follow Earle upstairs 'cause she asks. We in front of Carolina's room when Earle stops. Normally, Carolina padlocks her door whenever she not there.

A hour ago she flew out the house, cussing all the way to her car. She still out there arguing with her husband, Earle says. She walk into Carolina's room. Not us, we too scared. She opening and closing drawers. "There's gotta be a cell phone here."

I walk in after I hear that. Roxanne does what I do. Quiet, we hold our breath. Moving fast. We find stuff we don't care about— cards and notes from her kids, pictures, good underwear, not the cheap kind they buy us. "Hey. Look."

We run over to Roxanne. She found it under a box in the closet. It's different from the one we see her writing in all the time. Earle swears she's seen it before. We're all here, even some girls that been gone for years. "Carolina told him," Earle said, "that this should only be on his laptop or phone. But he old-school." She turns some pages. "I'ma pay him back one day for what he done to me."

We find our names.

Roxanne Roxanna Early 14 Medium brown 5'3 Church girl $428,400 x4 yrs. sale

"What's that mean?" she say. "Sale?" She look at me. "Am I leaving the house?" She looks at the door. "Carolina!"

I cover her mouth with my hand. "Shut up, stupid. We for sale every day—twelve, fifteen hours a day every day of the month. So, what's it matter what she wrote there?"

My fingers slide over my name. I read everything twice.

Charlese Charlie Jones 16 Medium brown 5'5 Virgin. Runaway. Orphan. Baggage: Sister and a kid $680,000 x3 yrs.

I'm older, Earle told me. Anthony probably don't see me around long as he does Roxanne. Guess I don't get sold. Maybe I get put on the street, thrown in the river.

"You're a diamond, Charlie. It's hard to break you. JuJu did a good job raising you. It's up to me to undo some of what she's done."

Every time he say my sister's name, I wanna throw up. 'Cause if I go home, he's coming for her and me, he told me. "And that baby too. What's her name? Cricket." He stomps the ground whenever he say that, like she a bug under his feet.

Kate yells upstairs, "She's on her way."

We run to our room. Lying across the bed, I tell 'em about the time Miss Saunders brung something to school I don't never wanna forgot. "She's not like regular people," I tell 'em. "She go to museums, buys old postcards people already wrote on, newspapers, and other stuff most people don't want."

Earle lay on the floor with her feet on the bed. "Miss Saunders brought in a ledger one day."

"A what?" Roxanne asks.

"A book where a farmer wrote down stuff like how many pigs and cows, chickens and mules they had. I can't remember everything. But I remember he had people on that list too. Slaves."

I remember some of the names. Maleeka ain't the only one with a good memory.

"James Beard, Negro, thirty-seven years old, married, two hundred dollars," I say. "Nellie Beard, Negro, twenty-six years old, wife of James, five hundred dollars."

Roxanne picking at the edges of her hair. "They the same as us—"

"Property," she and me both say.

CHAPTER 70

I'VE BEEN A good girl. So, he let me go to the store with him today. It's the first time he done that.

It's freezing out. I'm in shorts like always. Plus, a new white fur. He say it's real. I know it ain't. It stops at my waist. Keeps me warm up top. Lets me show off what customers like on the bottom. Him and me together get stared at a lot. "Ignore 'em, Charlie," he say.

"Yes, Daddy."

But he don't ignore that girl at the register putting on lip gloss. She not pretty, not ugly. For sure she too immature to see he out here hunting. "Come on, Daddy." I put my arms through his.

Him and me walk up one aisle, down the next. We watch everything and everybody. I check her out again. If she lucky, he'll leave her alone.

We in Detroit. Only for three days. There's a basketball game going on. I'm one of his most requested now. That give you privileges, he say. "Daddy, can you buy this for me, please?"

He wrap his arm around my waist. Whispers in my ear, "Daddy says yes you may have it today."

I jump up and down. Wrap my arms around his neck. Kiss him real good. People in the aisle stare. "I'm gonna work extra hard for you, Daddy. You watch."

It ain't for me, really. It's for Cricket. A bracelet wrapped up in plastic so he can't tell the size or see the initial C. When I get back home, if I get back—it'll be my present to her.

I follow him up the next aisle. Licorice and Tootsie Pops, a caramel candy apple, and chocolate doughnut holes go into our basket next. He eyeing me but don't say I should stop. I remember how much Roxanne likes Kool-Aid straws and throw a handful of them in too. He on the phone, way up the aisle, when I steal liquor off the shelf. A pint just for me. I stick it inside my coat pocket before I catch up to him.

Daddy wanna have a word with me. Earle is gone. After work the other night, she disappeared. He don't say what happened to her. We don't ask. Now Daddy asking me what I think about having another little sister. I check out the cashier again, and shake my head no. "She stuck up. And skinny."

His lips touch my ear while he talking. "This is what I do, Charlie: recruit, market, make money, invest money, to give y'all a better life." One day he gonna need a top girl to replace Carolina, he say, for the hundredth time "You wanna be that girl?"

I wanna go home. If I say that I'll be picking myself off the floor. So, I lie. I'm really good at that now. "Yes, please let me be that girl, Daddy." I don't tell him what Earle told me, that Daddy and Carolina promise all the girls the same thing.

Daddy work all the time. He takes her picture, and she don't even know. Right there by the peas, he send it someplace, who knows where. The man stacking mangoes in aisle two been staring at me since I came in. When Daddy takes a call, that man asks me how much. His nails are dirty, split. His dark blue pants seem like they got pork fat hanging from 'em. I smile and give him the finger.

At the register, Daddy asks if she'd like to meet us for pizza. He complimenting her long, pretty hair, asking if she want free tickets to the game. His eyes stay on her a long time. His cell goes off. He goes up aisle six to talk.

Under my breath, I tell her what he want, how things be for girls like me. She put that lip gloss down. "Whatever."

"You been told."

Soon as he's back, he gets rid of me. "I got work to do, Charlie. Go outside and wait. If you're gone when I get out there—" He smacks my behind.

When I leave, she scratching her head.

Stamping my feet to keep warm, I see him. "Hey!" He got a cell in his hand. "Could you help me, mister?" I can't follow him, walk over to him, or chase after him, 'cause Daddy may see me. "Mister, please. I got a sister. You can call her for me. Tell her—" He stops. Don't hardly look up from his phone. "I don't wanna be out here. He making me. Can you—"

He texting and ignoring me. I do what I shouldn't, start walking, running some too. Over my shoulder, I see the door open, Daddy step out. That man and his phone get away.

Me and him both get to the car at the same time. "I had to potty, Daddy," I say out of breath. Then I point to a SUV with nobody in it. "Over there." He goes to slap me. I duck. He misses. "You think I don't know what you did? You thought she wouldn't tell your Daddy the truth?" She standing at the window watching. "Every girl in this city want what you got."

"Yes, Daddy. I know, Daddy."

I follow him to the car and get what's coming to me. I earned it, he says.

CHAPTER 71

IT'S A CHARLIE Brown Christmas tree. But we ain't complaining—we decorating. Gem got a sewing needle in her hand. She threads it, knots the ends together. Then sticks the needle through pieces of popcorn till she got a whole row, maybe forty pieces, strung together. She call it popcorn garland. It's my job to hang it on the tree. I already done two rows. Only one more to go.

I'm at the tree when Rosalie bumps my hips with hers, laughs, and hangs more bulbs. They small as quarters, red, green, and silver. Them our colors this year. At least that's what Gem say. We got silver tinsel on the tree; silver garland taped on the wood around the front door. Branches full of pine needles is on the mantel with fake candles in between. Roxanne gave all us girls the same exact reindeer socks—Rudolph with a little bell on his nose.

Katrina the only one in here not working. She in the middle of the room on her belly facing the television. She look up at the tree and smiles, then gets back to her show. This the fourth time today she watched *Home Alone*. The first two times the family watched it together. Not Daddy. He out of town on business. We work every day, weekends plus holidays. Today is Christmas and we off for once.

Kate's under the card table on her knees plugging in Christmas tree lights. They blink and play music—"Jingle Bells." Roxanne walk in singing. Nobody joins in. She a whole choir by herself, singing sweet and soft, making me miss home. I go stand at the front door so they don't see me crying.

Daddy don't allow it, but we got Carolina to let us leave the front door open. I wipe steam off the storm door with my sleeve. See the snow piled on the ground and trees, making outside look like a Christmas card. All day long, the sky's been dropping snow. When the wind blow, seem like we stuck in a snow globe.

Folding my arms, I think about Cricket. If she's with my sister, she got so many toys she won't know which ones to play with first. Is you walking now? I ask her in my head. Crawling? Teething? I sniff. Clear my throat. Hope the other girls don't hear. But Roxanne got cat ears, I say all the time. Here she come standing beside me. Putting her arm around me. Next thing I know, Gem is on the other side doing the same thing. It don't take long before there's two rows of us, side by side, staring out, quiet as snow. "What you miss?" I ask.

"I miss my mom and dad," Rosalie whispers. "We baked gingerbread cookies the night before Christmas every year till— Never mind."

"The church across the street from us brung us Christmas presents every year." They gave her a talking doll once, Roxanne says. "She upstairs under my bed." For the first time since I been here, she look sad enough to cry.

Kianna's brother burned their house down, but not on purpose. Her mother and two sisters was in there. Her and her dad went to a homeless shelter. One day she woke up, and he was gone. She never found out what happened to her brother. Daddy found her near the shelter the next day, crying.

I close my eyes and see myself in my own bed under my own blankets with Mom, Dad, and JuJu downstairs wrapping presents.

"What that girl say in that movie with the bear and lion in it?" I ask. "Ain't no place like home," Kate, me, and Rosalie say together.

"This is home." Gem stabs the popcorn with the needle. "My present at Christmas at my house was a stepmother who beat me and a mother on meth. I ran, left. And I'm never going back. So, quit talking about how nice things was before because if it was—y'all wouldn't be here."

Carolina's heels always let us know when she coming. By the time she in the family room, we back to decorating right along with Gem—at least pretending to. She dressed in all red down to her shoes, wearing an apron that used to be her mother's. "I need help with the pies."

She point to me and Roxanne, so we right behind her when she get to the kitchen. Pans and flour, brown eggs, sugar, fruit, lard, butter, and spices, fill up the whole table. Carolina gonna bake sweet potato pies, apple pies, and one blueberry pie even though she don't like blueberry and none of us either. Her mother made it every year, now so do she. She cooked the collards early this morning. Gem and Kate helped her stuff the turkey that's in one of the ovens. Rosalie made the cranberry punch too sweet. Kianna and me made three-cheese macaroni and cheese yesterday before work. Katrina ain't do nothing at all.

I dig my hand in the flour and spray Roxanne's face. She pays me back. Carolina yells that we got no time to be playing around, acting like kids. But before we know it, Gem, Kate, and everyone else come in here. We make the biggest mess. Flour in our hair, on the floor—everywhere. It's Christmas, so maybe that's why Carolina hands us brooms and mops, but don't get mad or cuss.

At dinner, she asks me to say grace. The table is full. Everything is hot and smells good. The only thing missing is Daddy. He in LA, stuck at the airport now, trying to get home to us. I pray for him first. Ask God to bring him home safe to us. Maleeka would say I'm nuts. But he ain't beat me lately. Him and Carolina feed us and give us clothes—so they not all the way bad. I pray for the girls here next. We like sisters. Better than sisters 'cause they would cut or kill somebody for me. Gem is right, I guess. There are worse houses to be in, worse daddies to have. I know that for sure now. So, I close my eyes and thank God I got it as good as I do.

Licking sweet potato pie from between her fingers, Kate opens the gift Rosalie gave her. Wrapped up or not, we can tell it's a cup. Jumping up and down, Kate act like it's filled with money. She give Rosalie a big, long hug. "Just what I wanted." It got her real name on it—Katie. Only her real family ever calls her that, she say.

"Merry Christmas." Roxanne hands me my present.

"Oh," I say once I open it.

She cleans Daddy's room sometimes. Says she saw the coloring book and crayons in the trash. "I knew they were yours so—"

"I . . . used . . . to color but I don't no more . . . so thanks . . . anyhow. But I don't want nothing from back then."

CHAPTER 72

HE ONE OF my regulars. I got six here in town. They ask for Charlie not Char. Good 'cause Char ain't here no more.

I'm sitting on the floor with my back to the door, smoking. I finish the bottle of rum next. Harrison is nice to me. He bring me things. Nothing big or expensive. Anthony would beat me if he knew—or take it. He got a wife, kids. A daughter in college who want to be a doctor like him.

I watch him. Wait for him to move. But he still dead to the world, snoring when I stand up and tiptoe past him. The whole time I'm looking over my shoulder. Sometime, I swear Anthony can see through walls, hear what you think. So, I try to be good. I try to be quiet. I wouldn't call nobody I know, ever—till now. Because of Christmas and New Year's, I been thinking about my sister a lot. So, I had to take a chance.

Shaking, I lift his cell out his pocket with two fingers. Then walk on my toes to the other side of the room.

"JuJu," I whisper.

"Char—"

"I'm fine. He treats me good." My neck stretches when Harrison turns onto his belly. "I don't want to leave; I like it here."

I don't tell her all he said about me being his property, that nowhere on earth is safe from him, how he will cut Cricket up like sausage if I left, feed her to the bears at the zoo. He talked about doing worse to my sister, my friends.

She crying. "Char, who's doing this to you?"

"Nobody." I wipe under my eye with the back of my hand. "You know . . . I always liked money. I'm making my own now, plenty, so I'm good."

She gonna have the call traced, she say, get the FBI involved.

"I have to hang up." I look at the time. Then at him—naked—no covers to hide him. He pays for an hour. Only last half that time. Falls asleep every week like an old man.

"I'm taking good care of her."

His arm reaches for me on the other side on the bed. My heart jumps—beats fast as eggs boiling in hot water. "Can I talk to her?" I thought by now JuJu woulda put her in foster care.

Solomon done what I asked and called her, she say. She took a plane. Got Cricket from his grandmother's place. "We home waiting for you."

He yawns. Smiles in his sleep.

"Ma . . . ma . . . ma."

"Cricket. It's me. Momma." Too many tears roll in my mouth for me to say anything else.

My sister gets back on the phone. "I knew you would want me to take care of her."

I tiptoe past him. "I just called to say Merry Christmas and thanks. You did a good job raising me. It's all my fault. I shoulda listened."

"Mr. Bobbie asked about you. He told me everything."

"I'm sorry."

"I'm glad. He kept you off the street, and you wasn't with some boy. He was out of town when you left them messages," she say. "But he's back now. Him, Miss Saunders, Maleeka, other kids at your old school—they put up posters back home. I put signs up in your neighborhood before I left the motel."

Anthony won't like that.

"Char—I was wrong. You smart . . . going places in this world." She cries some more.

I tell her I ain't the same Char she knew. I done so many things, seen so much—I don't know myself no more.

"We know you, Char. Me, the people at your old school—Mom and Dad."

I tell her they're dead. She say they up in heaven talking to God about me.

I snort when I laugh. "God—Where he at?"

He's inside of me, she says, all around me, everywhere.

I cover myself. "I don't want him in here, JuJu . . . seeing me."

"He's seen worse, Char." She asks to pray for me. Does it before I say yes or no.

"Merry Christmas. Happy New Year," I whisper.

This the best present she had in her whole life, she say.

I end the call, put his phone back in his pants pocket, then sit on the edge of the bed and drink my rum. It's gone in no time. Harrison too. He don't even notice that I'm drunk. But Anthony do.

"Bitch!" His fist is a rock slamming into the back of my head. "Throwing up on customers." He kick my legs out from under me. "You cost me money, Charlie, three weeks in a row."

He dragging me up the hall by my hair. Smacking me until I almost pass out. I try to tell him, but he won't hear it, I was nervous 'cause he got rid of Earle, and I was scared I'd be next. It's a lie. All we do in this business is lie, so what's it matter? He think I'm blaming him for all this and everything else. That give him more reason to hit me again.

The men lined up ignore me. The manager downstairs pick his teeth with the end of a straw, watches me get drug out the door. Out on the sidewalk, people pay for the movies and get a free show too.

I quit begging in the car. I'm up front next to him, 'cause the driver is on vacation in Aruba. I don't know where that is.

Daddy puts the car in reverse, backs into the street, speeds us away from there in no time 'cause he got no time to waste no more on me, he say.

Mostly rats and mangy cats they say live in Daddy's other house next door to us. The last girl who ended up here got sold, they say, sent overseas. She was part Japanese, five three, my age. She ran away from Daddy five times, Earle told me. Came back every time on her own 'cause we love him and hate him, need him and don't, all at the same time. When I step in between the trees, I wonder if my shoes sitting on the dirt, her shoes kicked up, walked over. And which of them I'll see soon—her or April?

He's beside me, holding on to my arms like he the police. If Daddy bring you to this house, shut your mouth and take what you got coming, Carolina told me that first day. So, I let him walk me up the crooked steps without opening my mouth. Watch him unlock the back door, turn on the lights, push spiderwebs out his face.

"You made me do this."

Should I talk or be quiet?

"The problem is you're hardheaded, Charlie. You don't learn."

Maybe I should beg.

"Damn girls with babies. Y'all the worse kind."

This a old house. Cold as ice cubes. You breathe and see your breath. We in the basement when I think about the dungeons I colored. In movies, ain't nothing good happens in a place like this.

"Get in."

I do what I'm told.

"Daddy."

"You are not her. I have to keep telling myself that."

I look in his dark, tired eyes.

"She had that baby. Got leukemia. Died at your age. And she's not coming back."

I look away so I don't get hit for seeing what I'm seeing—him crying—tears dripping on his seven-hundred-dollar jacket. On my way in, I tell him he can beat me, cut me, do what he want to me. "Just don't leave me."

The door is almost closed when he say I better be alive when he come back.

CHAPTER 73

HOW LONG I been here? Six hours? Ten? It's the next day, I know that. I talk to myself a lot. But I don't cry. I walk. Back and forth, up and down, in circles to keep warm. And I count. I made it up to five hundred with no mistakes. I wet myself some too, 'cause I ain't wanna do like dogs do and go in the corner. But I did anyhow. He think we dogs. He think we animals. That's how come he can do us the way he do. Even my bones are cold. If I die, how would JuJu know?

CHAPTER 74

I LICK MY lips like they a fountain that I can drink from. They cracked and dry, hard. Hurting me bad. My stomach hurts worse. It's empty, burning, bubbling, sending air up to my mouth like I can eat burps. Can you die from not eating two days in a row? Would he let me? I bet he would. I still ain't cried yet. I got no tears anyhow. I got a coat with a hood, so that's something. I'm still freezing, though. Can people freeze like Popsicles? Would he send my body to my sister if I did? I wanna be buried next to my parents. I lie down on the cold hard ground and close my eyes. Then I'm up again, talking out loud to myself. Maybe I'm going crazy. I start dancing to keep warm. But you can't stay warm in here no matter what you do. So, I lie down again. Close my eyes again. Then open 'em wide again. "Don't you go to sleep, Char. Don't you cry either." Sitting up. Using my finger for a stick, I write in the dirt.

Charlie is here.

I cross out Charlie.

Char is here.

I cross out Char.

God is here.

I erase his name.

CHAPTER 75

SHE COMES HUMMING. Otherwise, I wouldn't know it was her out there. "Roxanne?"

"Yeah—it's me, Char."

I cry. She don't tell me everything is gonna be okay, just that she'll stay here with me as long as she can. The door is too short on the bottom for the space it's in. Her fingers slide under it and wiggle. I sit down as close as I can and hold on. My words come out in a whisper. "Where's everybody else?"

"Sleeping. Bone tired."

"Where's Daddy? You think Carolina would talk to him for me?"

"He had to leave. Carolina is asleep, I think, in her room with the door closed."

"Roxanne?"

"Yeah."

"Get the key. Let me out. Then me and you could run."

"You know I can't do that, Char."

I know.

"But here." They come rolling in like they on skates. Straws filled with water, chewing gum stuck in both ends. A pack of Mentos— the pretty color ones—comes next. Then there's pretzel rods— dragging dust on the way in. I drink first, empty all ten straws, save the used gum. I'm starving, eating while food is still coming. A pack of peanut butter crackers slides under last. I keep quiet and eat.

Choking on the crackers, I pat my chest. Once I'm full, I hold on to her fingers again.

She tell me that he never keep a girl here more than a day or two. Some get sent off for good after that. Some he lets Carolina take care of. I bring up April. He don't do that too often, she say. "It's bad for business and don't make him no money."

"Roxanne?"

"Yeah?"

"Why would God let this happen to us?"

She thinks on it some. "I don't know."

My forehead is leaning against the door when she ask if I want to pray. "Why? Is God gonna bring me a key and get me out of here?"

I hear her yawn, so I tell her it's okay for her to go back in the house. She'll leave when she hears Daddy's tires outside, she tell me. Then out of nowhere she ask if I knew she was born in a orphanage for teenage mothers.

"They still got those?"

It wasn't called an orphanage, she say, but that's what it was. "The church across the street ran it."

"That's why you talk 'bout God so much?"

"He the only father I ever knew besides Pastor and Daddy."

I ask if something happened to her there like we hear about on the news with priests.

"No."

"So, why you leave?"

They paddled one of the girls. She called child welfare to report them, she says. "Then they came for the rest of us. Some kids went into foster care. Some to group homes. Some got sent back to their real families. I ran away."

"We can run now too."

"Where would I go? Anyhow, if I left, he would get another girl to take my place. And I don't want that."

"But—"

She say for me to hush. Then I hear it too. Car wheels spitting gravel.

She don't leave when I say go. Next thing we know, the door opens. His feet stomp around upstairs while he talking on the phone. I don't hear all her words, but I do hear her say father, God help us.

His feet is on the steps, on their way down, when I close my eyes and pray for her. Roxanne is everybody's friend. I don't want nothing bad to happen to her 'cause of me.

"Char," she says. "I think he brought somebody with him."

I put my head to the door and listen, then I tell Roxanne to run fast as she can. "And don't stop for nothing, or nobody, even me. You hear me?"

"But—"

"You stupid, girl? Go!"

I'm crying by the time the door opens. But don't nobody care.

CHAPTER 76

Cows.
Mooing.
Like the kind I seen at the truck stop.
Walk in with Daddy.
And find me.
Stomp me.
Break me.
I scream. "Daddy! Please!"
I made him do this, he say, leaving me behind.

He walk out the kitchen, through the living room telling Carolina to shut up. She right behind him, louder than him sometimes. "Momma knew! Yeah, I said it. She knew I would be better at this than you." Carolina runs past him in silver heels, stopping him at the front door.

I don't say nothing. I'm just glad to be inside. Alive. It was Roxanne who told Carolina that she should come get me. She found a way out of the basement. Stayed gone until the next afternoon. I was still crying when Carolina and her came for me. It wasn't that Carolina cared all that much about me. But I'm money on the table, a sure bet. At least I used to be. And she don't like losing money, she told me on my way out of there. I kept thanking her like I was a freed slave. She sounded like Anthony when she told me, "To us, you're the same as that flat-screen TV, the curtains, that grandfather clock. They stop being useful, we throw them in the trash."

"I'm useful," I whispered. Then I closed my eyes and waited to get hit. She got Roxanne instead. 'Cause she had no business being over there in the first place, Carolina told her. Plus, she lied. She told Carolina she saw blood sneaking out from under the door like a snake. That was last week. I only started walking like my normal self yesterday.

Anthony walking out the door in the cold without a coat, with her behind him. I stare at the sidewalk and the trees that follow the road. Carolina's words blow in the wind. "Just before she died, Momma said she made a mistake picking you. She knew you would ruin this business. The new girl will probably be trouble too."

Anthony brought her here this morning. The sun wasn't even up. A little while ago, I saw her putting gloss on her lips, walking upstairs behind Gem. Did she come on her own? Get knocked out, drug here? Last time I seen her she was working the register at the grocery store.

Carolina and me alike. We don't know until it's too late that people done had enough of us. So, I see his knife before she do. It's up to her throat by the time she shut up. "I run this!" I close my eyes so I don't see blood. "Just because you're my sister—"

She bring up his mother and their sister who died. I keep my eyes closed and listen. Anna, that's what they call her, was the baby of the family. She had herself a baby right when their mother took sick. Then she got sick too. "Girls with babies. Girls on pills. You can't make things up to Anna by taking them in." I open my eyes. She poke his chest. Then stares at me. "And dead girls, plus the ones you give away for free, won't make us no money."

"I was supposed to finish college." He puts the knife back in his pocket. "Earn my degree. Go to work on Wall Street." He punches the door. "I wasn't her husband! I wasn't Anna's father. It wasn't right to make me responsible for them."

This the first time I see her hug him or act like she care about anybody. He don't say nothing. Her fingers squeeze his chin. "You were the man of the house."

"I was eighteen. In my second year of college. On scholarship."

"I was in high school. But I woulda done it. I told her that. But she wanted you." She goes to stand in the doorway, watching him. "Momma was in this business twenty-five years and didn't learn a thing about men."

"What's that supposed to mean?"

"They always get the credit when it's the women who do all the work."

"You think you can run this?! Then run it." He's stomping down the porch steps when he say, "I got business out of town anyhow. I'll be back in three weeks. But if you mess up—"

"I won't. I promise. I swear." She runs and hug him till he got to peel her arms off him. For the first time, I notice dark clouds over their heads.

Closing the door, she rub her hands together like she won the lottery. Laughing, she says maybe she ought to thank me. She been trying to get through to him for years. "This time I think I did."

She walking out the room. I'm staring at the dead-bolt lock she left open. When she come back, I figure it's 'cause she remembered. But it's her cell she wants. Grabbing it off the end table, she start talking, bragging. "I wanted you gone the first day you showed up. The money's in younger girls. We need some nine-year-olds in here. I told him that. But does he listen?" Her voice is a siren going off at the other girls. "Get up! Listen up! There's going to be some new rules around here! Meet me in the kitchen in ten."

Feet start running up and down the hall. I watch the door, then the steps Carolina walked up, then the door again. The new girl comes up from the basement, stops, and stares at me. She roll her eyes like I did something to her, then goes upstairs. Carolina screams at somebody.

I'm slow standing up. Slow getting to the door. Holding my breath the whole time, I stop like Carolina's down here ordering me to. What if he still out there? I run back to the couch. But what if Carolina gets rid of me, sells me, while he's gone? I think about the basement next door. The van, johns, police. I run this time. My hands is on the knob, shaking, when I hear her say my name.

"Charlese."

It's Roxanne.

"Don't forget about us."

I got one arm reaching back when I walk out the door. Outside in the cold, I say, "Roxanne, come with me."

She shaking her head no when the rain starts.

"We got room at our place for you." She's at the door when I say he don't own you.

"I don't want him to get no other girls."

"But he will. Whether we here or not."

She backs up.

I got no more words. Just bare feet on a cold wet sidewalk. Rain pouring down on me. Slipping, I run as fast as I can.

HOME AGAIN

CHAPTER 77

WHEN HE GETS to my house, they all there. Miss Saunders, Maleeka, JuJu, Cricket, and Mr. Bobbie, who sitting on the porch with a shotgun in his hand.

I almost hug the bus driver, but I can't. I repeat myself. "Thank you." Then my eyes find the sign over the porch again.

WELCOME HOME, CHAR!
WE LOVE YOU

The bus driver drove all night. His wife slept most of the way. I stayed awake the entire time, eyeballing every car, truck, motorcycle, and bike I saw. "Don't let him get me." I said that to the bus driver so many times I can't count. He said he wouldn't. And he didn't, just like he promised.

A woman twelve blocks from Daddy's house took me in. I ain't tell her the whole truth about what happened. I was too scared. "My boyfriend did this to me," I said. Then I asked her not to call the police. And to let me call my father.

"Help me," I said to him on the phone. He was at her house in twenty minutes. I showered and got dressed at their place. Put on their daughter's clothes. Two hours later we was leaving.

Bus drivers know all the back roads, little towns and places where there's lots of state troopers and police watching out. I begged him again not to call the cops. But I ain't tell him the whole truth either. I lied. Told him an old man with hair in his ears was stalking me, threatening to kill me, and all I wanted was to go home.

Walking up to the porch steps, I break down crying. JuJu run over and hands Cricket to me. They all circle around me, rub my back, pat my arm—even the driver and his wife.

Bet they think I'm the same Char they used to know. I'm not. She gone. And she ain't never coming back.

CHAPTER 78

IT'S FOR ME, this party. So, I smile sometimes, clap when JuJu and Mr. Bobbie do the electric slide in the middle of the room with everybody watching. Miss Saunders don't dance. She got two left feet, she told me a long while ago. From across the room, she smiles at me. It's a little smile, quiet, not like JuJu's at all. My sister been grinning since I got home. And all her answers to me is yes, yes, and yes. "Char's home, y'all. Praise God," she say with both hands up high pushing the air. That's funny, 'cause she never talked all that much about God before. Now it seem like she praying and thanking Him all the time.

The doorbell ring and another neighbor walk in, so do another one of JuJu's customers. I go back in my mind to where I came from, sitting in the family room in my underwear. We at the card table, me and Roxanne laughing at something silly Gem said. I do that a lot, think about the way things was—even the bad stuff seem less bad.

Maleeka wiping food off her hands with a napkin when she sit down next to me. "Hey, Char."

"Hey."

We at the window seat, on thick, soft cushions. I smile, then stare at the empty paper plate in my hand. It was full of food. I ate it, I know I did. But I can't hardly remember doing it. "You get enough to eat? JuJu cooked all of it. You know she can throw down."

She rub her belly, burps, and balls up the napkin. "Sure did."
She been here a whole hour, mostly with Miss Saunders. I think
that's because I couldn't talk to her much. People kept coming up to
me. Asking how I was, if I was okay. I ain't sure how much my sister
told 'em, not that she can say much. 'Cause she don't know nothing
herself. Since I been home, I tell her all the time that I'm fine, okay,
that it wasn't no big deal. She look at me like she don't believe me.
Next thing I know she hugging me, whispering in my ear that
she love me, that everything's gonna be all right. It won't.

I picked this seat so I could see outside. Look up and down the
street. Plus, keep a eye on who comes through our front door. He know
this address, my sister's name, that she work at a bank. One day
he gonna show up, I know it. "Be sure to lock the door in between
people coming and going," I say to JuJu on her way by. She tell me
that Mr. Bobbie is on the porch, like Anthony care about a old man
with a gun.

The grown-ups dance, talk smack, drink too much Hennessy,
rum and Coke. Eat too many spicy hot garlic chicken wings. "Nice
party," Maleeka say, just to have something to say, I think.

I smile. Wish the music wasn't so loud and I was in my bedroom under the covers asleep.

Me and her stare and watch the people in the room, but don't
talk to each other. I catch her once in a while, side-eyeing me.
Wondering, I guess. She not the only one. The rest of the people
here doing the same thing. One day they'll see them pictures—I
know it. I'll cut my wrists if they do. Hang myself, I swear. 'Cause
once something like that is out there, what's the use of living?

It's slow, her hand coming my way. But I don't stop it from sliding into mine, holding on. I hold on tight and squeeze Maleeka's
hand right back, hoping not to cry. Her voice is so little right now, I

don't know how it climbs over the music to get to me. But I hear her anyhow. "You got this, Char."

She been calling every day since I came home. I ain't been answering or returning calls. It don't matter to her. She leave me a message anyhow. "Welcome home, Char. It's gonna get better," or "Glad you back, Char. Call me if you wanna walk or talk, get a pretzel at Cookies and Beans." I listened to 'em, every one. But I been too sad inside to call.

I fake a smile. "Your hair looking nice. You done it yourself?"

She pats her fro. It's big as the moon, with white cowrie shells in some places. One of her friends did it for her, she says. I check out the hoops, wooden, so big they touch her shoulders. She rocking in her school uniform. It's Thursday, early so she came in it. It's Boy Scout beige color. The skirt got pleats. The tie she wearing stops at the waist. It's olive green. Them her school colors, she says. Since I been home, JuJu bring up my education a lot. But I got my education, all I need, plus a PhD. Bet she don't wanna know nothing about that.

I stand up, letting Maleeka know she can follow me if she want. Walking straight through the middle of the room, I keep my eye on them and the door. My shoulders get squeezed from behind. My arm gets patted. I flinch when they do that, and speed up. I wish they wouldn't touch me at all, but I can't say that.

Me and Maleeka are rocks in a river, tadpoles in a jar of loud laughing grown-ups who think everything will be all right with me now that I'm back home. Miss Saunders's eyes follow me like high beams. Sometimes I think my life woulda turned out different, if I never set fire to her room.

She kick off her flats in the hall. Walk in barefooted, every toenail painted a different color blue. I lock the door after we get in.

Then check to make sure it's locked. At the window, I check to see if he here, anywhere near, coming for me. She sitting on my desk, swinging her legs. "Char. You okay?"

I tell her I'm cool, everything is fine.

My mind be racing a lot, so I move a lot. Leaving the window, I sit on my bed, lie on my bed, put the covers over me. Then push back the covers, jump up, and sit on the edge of the desk looking at her. I do that breathing thing my old therapist taught me. It don't work as good as she said it would.

There goes her hand again, in mine again. "Breathe," she say. So I do. At least I try to.

I go check the lock. Both our eyes look around the room, then find each other. It take a while before her eyes notice the trash can beside my desk filled with crayons and coloring books, the last doll Mom gave me, and a crown I won in a second-grade pageant that I never wanted to be in. "I thought you liked to color."

"Used to."

"So, you throwing all that away?"

"Yeah."

Can she have my coloring book and crayons? she asks. "Maybe somebody can use 'em."

Soon as I say yes, she bags it up, leaves the bald-headed doll and paper crown. I bite my bottom lip to stop it from trembling. "Maleeka."

"Yeah, Char." She ties the plastic bag in a knot.

"Ain't that the worst party ever."

We laugh. She sitting beside me again. I ask what she think about Cricket. My sister's friend took her for the night to give me a break. I ain't want no break. But I did what JuJu said because I think Cricket knows I'm depressed and that's not good for her.

"I can't believe you have a baby, Char."

Cracking my knuckles, I get up and walk over to the window. Her too. She standing next to me when she asks if I like being a mother. "Sure do."

"Is it hard? I mean changing diapers all day, waking up at night . . . I think I would hate that part."

I tell her Cricket is different, a good baby. I leave out April and how she got killed. Then my mind goes back to my first day home. Cricket's little fingers held on tight to my shirt, wouldn't let go. That's what she do all the time now. She cries a lot too. JuJu say that's because I be crying while I'm holding her. "Let me put you back in therapy." JuJu must say that every day. "You should talk about what you been through." I talk to Cricket about it.

"Maleeka."

"Yeah, Char."

"Nothing."

"If you ever want to talk about anything, Char. You can call me—day or night. I swear."

"Maleeka. What's the worst thing you ever done?"

She says it with a quickness. "Set fire to Miss Saunders's room."

That crack me up. Gets her to laughing too. We holding our stomachs, can't stop laughing. When she start hiccuping, I laugh harder. Then just like that, I stop. "Maybe I deserved it."

"Deserved what?"

"Everything that happened. Payback, for all the bad I done."

It's only a tear, one, so I guess that's why it's taking its time rolling down my face, off my chin. She wipes it away, not me.

"You think I deserved what you done to me? Being bullied every day, teased for no reason."

I shake my head no.

"Char, I wasn't no angel. And you for sure wasn't. But that don't give people the right to—" Now she crying. "What did he do, Char? Something bad I know. Tell somebody or—"

"He—he—" I shake my head. "Never mind. It wasn't nothing. I had fun living on my own. See." I point to my face, my lips, grinning.

She use the side of her hand like a napkin to wipe my tears this time. Then up she jumps, walking over to my closet, shaking the junk in her trunk. She wanna know what I got new since she last seen me. "Lots," I tell her. I'm beside her before I know it. Sliding open the doors, picking through sweaters and pants. "JuJu specials," I say. She laughing 'cause she know what that mean.

It's easy, seem like, for us to go from one thing to another. For the music to go from fast to faster, to slow, rap to line dance. The DJ seem like he's on break when I tell Maleeka that JuJu told me she asked Miss Saunders to tutor me on Saturdays here at the house. JuJu wants to call it the Charlese Jones Academy of Excellence. It's supposed to help me catch up, maybe even get me on track to take a test to get me into my real grade. I don't wanna do it. JuJu wants me, needs me, to be my old self again quick as I can, so she making me do this. I ain't mad. It's been hard on her, like it's been hard on me. But that's a lot of school and studying. Too much of Miss Saunders too.

I ask if she'll do it with me. Otherwise, it'll be weird. She such a nerd. She say she loves school. Wishes we went seven days a week. "So, yeah. I'll do it with you."

At the window, we watch the moon, full, shining on everything, even us. I hold my breath after she say to me one more time, "Char, don't worry. You got this."

CHAPTER 79

SHE SMELLS. I smell. We smell—rotten. I ain't bathed myself or her in over a week. Bending low, I sniff her scalp and frown. I smell my underarms, get a whiff of my stank breath, shake my head.

"It's time for her bottle. Feed her." That's what I do now, remind myself to do things. Sometimes it works—sometimes not.

"One bottle," I tell myself. "That's all she need." I'd move if I could. I can't.

"Cricket."

They coming again—the tears.

"I'm—" I apologize to her every day, all day it seem. "I'm trying."

Since I came home, my sister put a microwave and small fridge in my room to make things easier. She having second thoughts now 'cause I'm melting in front of her eyes, she say. Too scared to go downstairs or outside, I stay in my room locked up.

JuJu can't stay home and babysit me. She got to go to work. Make that money. But when she home, she's knocking on my door. Leaving supper and lunch. Begging me. She's caught in between a rock and a hard place, she say. If she call the authorities, they may commit me. Keep me for good. Charge me for some of the things I done, even though she don't know all the things I done. But she been on the streets, so she knows what's up.

My hands shake when I lift Cricket—so does she. If we was standing on ice in the middle of winter, dressed for summer, we couldn't be shaking more. My sister's voice pops in my head. "Charlese Jones. We have to go to the police and tell them."

"If you do, he'll kill me."

I just need time, I keep telling her, to forget about everything. Only, I can't forget, and I can't tell. So it stay in my head like a bad dream.

I lay Cricket in the middle of my bed. Stare at the dresser I keep in front the door whenever my sister is at work. Sitting on the floor with my back against the bed, I cry. She cries. We cry all the time now.

CHAPTER 80

MY CELL KEEPS ringing, so I gotta answer. "Char."

"What, Maleeka?"

"You up?"

"Duh. I'm talking to you, ain't I?"

"I'm outside."

"What?"

"Open the front door."

"I can't—I'm in bed."

JuJu gave her a key to our house, she says. She put it in Maleeka's hand when she seen her at the pizza shop the other day. "So, I'm on my way in."

My sister told Maleeka she might need her to check on me sometime while she at work or school. JuJu leave by eight and gets in by nine at night, calls me in between, but I don't pick up most times.

I hang up. 'Cause I need sleep. Need my brain to shut up, to stop making me sad. Next thing I know she outside my bedroom door knocking.

"Go away, Maleeka—"

"I'm just gonna sit out here, Char, till you open up."

I turn and face the wall, close my eyes, wake up a whole hour later and ask, "You still there?"

"JuJu's thinking about calling the city social workers or somebody like that. She doesn't want to, Char, because maybe they'll put you in a psychiatric hospital or take you from her." She mentions Cricket. JuJu told her what happened, I see. She with JuJu's friend again, Miss Eleonora. She fosters children. I ain't want her to leave. But I see the truth JuJu was trying to show me when the diaper rash wouldn't go away and she rolled off the bed right in front of me. "Cricket need a full-time mother, Char. Not a girl so sad that tears done turned into her middle name," my sister said.

I step over last night's dishes. Walk by a pizza box with dried-up slices in it. Take a tray of glasses into the bathroom. See the rest sitting in the tub. Then I move the dresser and unlock the door.

She walk by me like she ain't here to see me. I'm still near the door when she pull my desk chair over to the bed, sits down and takes a book out her backpack.

In bed with the covers up to my chin, I watch fingers pinch her nose. "Remember that time in the bathroom when you put on deodorant?" she asks.

I was always using deodorant in the girls' room.

"You had them big old hairballs underneath your arms."

"Just leave, Maleeka, okay?"

She check out her watch. Opens the book. "I got twenty more minutes."

"For what."

"To be here."

"JuJu paying you to be with me?"

"No!"

"Then why you here, Maleeka?"

"It stinks in here. You know that?"

She got no business opening my window, letting ice-cold air in here. I tell her that after I run over and slam it shut. I got both fists up when I say, "I never beat you up, but I coulda. I still can."

"Well, I hope you shower first." She squats to pick up a paper cup with moldy, dried-up red Jell-O in it. "Char."

I'm back in bed when I say, "What?"

JuJu told her about Cricket, she says, filling up her arms with some of the mess in here. "I'm sorry."

I tell her that maybe Cricket woulda turned out bad being around me and April. Leaving me might bring her some good luck, I say.

She dropping trash in the can. "My father's mirror brought me good luck."

I remember that mirror.

"So did his poetry."

He could write really good.

"Maybe I'm your good luck charm." I can tell she smiling even with my back her way. "You woulda burned down that whole class-room without me there." She talk about how scared she was that day. How she almost didn't show up at all. I wish I hadn't.

She keep talking, walking, moving, cleaning. In a little while, you can see the floor by my bed. Trash cans from my desk and bath-room sit in the hall now, running over. The can in her hand freshens the air. "My mother was sad a lot." She walks and sprays. "That's how I ended up with those clothes." They was made by hand, ter-rible. I brung Maleeka in clothes that my sister stole. "It don't last always," she tell me.

I sit up on my elbows. "Was she depressed after she got cancer too?"

"Yeah. So was I. Every day. But they say the cancer's gone now."

She spray till I cough. Hits up the bathroom next. Standing over me she say, "I think my mother woulda died if I wasn't there. Sad can do that to you, Char—make you wish you was dead—or want to kill yourself." She talk about the time her mother's chemo got the best of her. She stayed at home all by herself one whole week till her mom came home. "Then I cooked for her, cleaned, helped her get dressed. Just like I done before." Her hands start to shake. Holding 'em behind her back, she breathes, calms herself. "You need somebody, Char, when you get too sad or sick." She smiling. "I'm your somebody, like it or not."

She changes the subject. Asks me about the pictures on my walls and a box of expensive crayons I told her about once. Mr. Bobbie got 'em online. Two hundred crayons, some in colors they don't make no more. "They at Goodwill. Gone."

"My mother sewed. When you going through it, you need something to do with your hands to keep you busy."

"Well, coloring ain't it."

"This is a book from the library at school." She by my bed on her knees. With her elbows digging into me she leans over to show me the jacket. "Maya Angelou. *I Know Why the Caged Bird Sings*." She asks if she can read it to me.

I don't wanna hear nothing about birds. But if I say that, she gonna say or do something else I don't like, so I tell her to go ahead, read. "But keep your elbows off of me."

She read real pretty. Every character got a different sounding voice, even the person she calls the narrator. That's the only reason I start to listen. Her voice is warm as hot tea with honey.

After three pages, she stop and ask me what I think. "She sure is country, I know that. Otherwise I got no thoughts."

She starts up again.

"You think she really wrote that—I mean all them words. Or did she interview some people and write their stories?"

It's autobiographical, she tells me. Then she explain what that word means.

"So, she talking about her own life and the real stuff that happened?"

"Yeah. What did you think?"

"Stamps, Arkansas . . . at least she knew where she was. I ain't know what part of town I lived in till I ran away."

"Oh."

Did my sister tell her not to ask me no questions? To only smile and say nice things? 'Cause that's what she does.

I yawn, then smell something stank—me. I write *put on deodorant* on a list I started my first day back but never did one thing on it. She put her book away. Pulls her phone out her book bag and ask if I wanna see pictures of melon head John-John and other kids from our middle school. I sit up quick. His hair is blond on the tips. He pierced both ears. Got a tat on his neck. I'm not sure what it is.

"He almost look cute," I say.

"He still can't get no girls."

Desda show up on her phone next. She lost weight. There's only half of her now. I can't say that she got cuter 'cause she was always cute. She got a camera hanging round her neck. Maleeka say she's in the photography club at the high school near McClenton. She got a girlfriend now and everything. One picture after the other make me laugh, and wish I was back in middle school.

CHAPTER 81

I JUMP OUT of bed. Run across the room. Turn on the overhead light. "Dang, Char," I say, walking back to my bed. "You peed yourself." I stare down at the dark spot on my spread and sheets. I was asleep, dreaming, on my knees under the bridge. "How come you ain't get up and go to the bathroom?" I touch the front and back of my pajama bottoms—they soaked. Stepping out of 'em, I kick 'em in a corner. And change into more. Grabbing the wet blanket and throwing it on the floor, I shake my head, then yank off the sheets. The mattress gonna take forever to dry.

I don't know how long I'm at the window staring, but when I call her, the sun is almost up. "He wasn't always mean to us."

"Okay, Char."

"Sometimes, he bought us candy and clothes, gave us money."

"What did you say his name was again?"

"I forget."

I ask about school so she don't ask no more about him. She got a twenty-five-page term paper due at the end of the semester. They reading *Anna Karenina*, she say. It's got almost nine hundred pages. Her English teacher is like Miss Saunders. She want to turn their room into a Russian palace, she tells me, like all palaces ain't the same.

Maleeka's quiet a long time before she say, "I ever tell you that I'm in the National Honor Society."

She was always smart, I tell her.

"In middle school, I bet I would have told them no I wasn't joining."

"Why?"

"'Cause I wanted to be like everybody else. And you—" She clears her throat. "Char, you liked me smart but not too smart."

She right. I wanted her smart enough to do my homework, stupid enough to do whatever I told her without asking no questions or thinking she was better than me.

"Are you ever going back to school, Char?"

"Miss Saunders's Saturday school?"

"That too."

"One day."

"Saturday's coming in five days."

"Leave me alone, Maleeka."

"I'm just saying—"

"I slept with a whole bunch of people." Sometimes I try to figure out how many, but it was so many, hundreds, I lose track. Get sick thinking about it.

She say it wasn't my fault, but it was. I ran away from home. And I coulda left that life sooner or tried harder anyway. I don't know why I didn't. "Don't blame him," I say. "Blame me."

She bring up her mother again. Maleeka say she blamed herself a lot back then, and again once she got the cancer.

"Why? You ain't do nothing wrong."

"Sometimes our house was so dirty—" She breathes in and out. "I couldn't clean it like it needed to be cleaned. I couldn't get her into the bathtub every night. She was heavy. Too sad to wanna get in, so she got mad at me for trying. I ran away once. I ever tell you that?"

"No."

"Well, I did. Only for two hours. But I wanted to stay gone forever." I ask why she didn't keep going. "'Cause all my mom had was me. And all I had was her." Clearing her throat, she says, "I write when my brain won't shut up. What you do?"

"Nothing."

"Okay, then, write. Something. Anything. A rap song, a poem. Or I could teach you how to sew like my mom." We laugh. She yawning when she tell me to get a pen or pencil. I dig around in my dresser drawer, my desk. Don't think, just write. Those her words, not mine. I do it 'cause she won't leave me alone if I don't. The words come out quick as snot from a sneeze. I stop to tell her I'm not reading it out loud to her or no one else.

"That's cool, Char. I need to go anyway." Before she hang up, she say she's proud of me.

"Why? You don't even know what I wrote."

"That don't matter. It wasn't for me anyhow."

The Fount Hotel is 2-faced
double-jointed—
a liar that tell you 1 thing when the sun is up
something different when she drinking moonshine.
She like her suits and Nordstrom dresses, sushi too
when it's light out.
Come dark—
she change up on you.
Stealing your babies, spilling milk, she slip and
slide
in dark cars that ride girls to the moon,
no ticket back.

CHAPTER 82

IT'S BEEN TWO months since I got home. The other day, I spent my birthday under the covers, rocking and crying. JuJu don't like how things is going. She walk in my room from one window to the next, pulling up shades, letting in light. "You home, safe. He can't get to you no more."

I focus on all the green crayon-like colors in my room—one's in the rug beside my bed, leaves on my bedspread, different color green markers in a cup on my desk. "I'm fine, JuJu."

I go back to finding colors. She wanna hold me to a deal she made with me. I get another month to get my own self together. If I ain't right in the head after that, she taking me to one of them trauma centers. "I been reading about sex trafficking. And I'm just gonna say it, Char—that's what he done—stole you, raped you, sold you." JuJu wrap her arms around me.

"No, I wasn't. No, he didn't." I shake my head and don't stop. "They paid Daddy."

"He ain't your daddy."

"He paid me. It was business, that's all. Anyhow, he had to teach me a lesson. I'm hardheaded, he said it. You always said it too."

"I was stupid, saying them things. Letting men—come to the house staying day and night drinking and eyeing you."

I lift my hands, and cover her cheeks and mouth. "They never done nothing to me here at home, JuJu. And we had to eat and pay rent. I don't blame you. I never blamed you."

Whatever happened to me out there wasn't my fault, she says. None of it.

"But I feel like it was." I hug her so tight we seem like one person.

"If I had done better by you—"

I wipe her tears with my fingers, dry my fingers on my jeans. "Some girls only learn the hard way." Them Daddy's words, JuJu's sometimes too.

"That's why you got to go see somebody." Her words come out soaking wet with tears. "Because he got in your head. Left his trash there, his evil ways and ideas. Violated you."

I break down when she say that word. I'm not smart, but I know what it means. "If I go to a trauma center or therapist, they'll call the police. They'll lock him up."

"Why you still care about him?"

I yell like she's yelling. "There's other girls there who got nobody else but him! No sisters who want them! No houses to go to! Nothing! And I left 'em, JuJu. It's my fault. Everything is my fault— even Cricket being gone."

Holding me, she remind me that I'm home, hers, and she won't let nothing bad happen to me ever again.

Grown-ups promise you stuff like that, when they shouldn't. 'Cause they can't keep their word with people like him out here. Only they don't know that. So, I promise my sister that I will try harder to get better to be different, and get back to being the old Charlese. It's what she wants to hear.

CHAPTER 83

I GOT IN the shower, wet myself some—no soap. Cried the whole time. I didn't need a towel to dry myself because only my feet got wet. But I at least wanted JuJu to see I was trying.

Maleeka's in my room when I tell her that I showered. "So, you washed up? You sure?" She sniffs around me. "I don't know, Char." She sprays the air. "Want me to comb your hair?"

"No."

"Okay, then." Her eyes bat. "You know it smell like onions in your room?"

I roll my eyes.

In my pajamas, sitting down on my bed, I ask how her day is going. She alway say the same thing. That she's fine. Next, she pull out the book. Reaching into her backpack again she pull out something else. It's flat as paper, wrapped real pretty with a red bow taped in the middle. "Now, before you open it. Let me explain. Oh, I can't do that or you'll know what it is. So, open." She rubbing her hands together, happy.

"Really, Maleeka. A coloring book." She sit down on the floor close to me.

"Don't get mad, look?" She take it from me, turns the pages. It's a coloring book full of famous people, women. They all doing whatever they was good at that made 'em famous, seem like. Maleeka stops on page twenty-six. "There she is. Maya." She's at a desk writing. Out the window is a small town and a sign that says Stamps, Arkansas. That's where she's from.

She flips more pages. "Here's my favorite famous old person. Hattie McDaniel from the *Gone with the Wind* movie," she say like I ever heard of either one.

"Why you like her? She ain't even pretty."

Maleeka making a face at me. "She's dark . . . I'm dark. People thought less of her because she played maids and slaves in the movies. You thought less of me, Char. Most everybody at our school did."

She sits herself on my bed, then get under the covers with me. When I yell for her to get out, she ignores me. Tickling under my arms, on my belly, behind my neck, she try to get me to agree to change my mind about coloring. I laugh until I spit like I done a lot at the house. Then I'm sad again. So sad I could cry. Her fingers find mine, then hold them up toward the light. "What if I color with you?"

"No, Maleeka."

"Why'd you quit anyhow?"

'Cause crayons shouldn't be in a place like that, kids either, I think to myself. But I lie and tell her I don't know. "Why you care if I color or not?"

"My mother sewed and she stopped being sad. If you color—"

"No."

She goes in her backpack and pulls out a pack of crayons this time. Opening the box, she sit a bunch of 'em in the middle of my hand. I see Anthony breaking and stomping 'em. Breaking and stomping me too. But I pick some of 'em up anyhow—just to make her be quiet.

CHAPTER 84

IT WAS MALEEKA that got me to come downstairs. The stuff she said about her mom helped. "It wasn't till she got back to her old ways and habits that things started to change for her for real for real." That's why she think I should color, she said, wash up every day, put on my lip gloss, get my hair did. I ain't do none of that. But I am downstairs in my robe and pajamas sitting at the dining room table between JuJu and Maleeka, where I can keep my eyes on the front door.

JuJu puts another bowl on the table. "Glad to see you out your room." She goes back to the kitchen for a pitcher of Kool-Aid and my favorite cheese biscuits. I'm smiling when she get back. So is Maleeka. They reach for my hands and we pray, like we did that Christmas at the house. I don't tell them I can smell Carolina's chitterlings cooking on the stove. JuJu might say it's me stinking up the place, which is true, kind of. She got a can of Febreze sitting by her napkin just in case.

My sister passes me the green beans and potato salad. I hand her the bowl of fried chicken and a bottle of hot sauce. Maleeka puts peas on both our plates. I ain't hungry. I don't know how much I can eat, I say. Seem like I lost ten pounds since I been home. I can see it in my bony fingers and skinny arms. My old clothes don't fit, so JuJu brought me new ones—paid with cash. Now that I'm down here, she plan to fatten me up, she say. But I got no appetite.

I look around the dining room like I'm new here. My eyes go from my mother and father's picture over the mantel, to me and JuJu's pictures—taken every year at school till our parents passed. We ate dinner together every night in here, even when my father's favorite sports teams played. He bought a small television once. Put it on the mantel. Momma made him return it. The year before he died, Dad seem to always have a business meeting right around suppertime. Mom ain't like it, rolled her eyes. He kept it up anyhow.

JuJu ask Maleeka if she is ready for Charlese Jones Academy of Excellence. It starts tomorrow. Once she done swallowing food, Maleeka say, "I'm ready. You ready?"

"Maybe next week."

"Char—"

"I'm downstairs, JuJu. Why can't you be happy about that?"

"I'm glad about that, but what about school? What about therapy?"

I throw the fork past her head. "Okay! I'll be in class tomorrow!"

"Showered?" She pick up the can and sprays over her shoulder.

I tell her what she want to hear, but I'm not washing. I can't.

She and I don't talk the rest of the meal. We look at everything except each other. Then Maleeka asks my sister if she ever heard of Maya Angelou. She surprise me and Maleeka both when she say yes, and spits some words from one of her poems:

You can write me down in history
With your bitter, twisted lies,
You may trod me in the very dirt
But still, like dust, I'll rise.

Reaching to pinch my cheek, my sister says, "You rising, Char, not dirty and dusty while you doing it either."

I feel dirty, I wanna tell her. Dirty as a fly in garbage, seeds underground. So, maybe Anthony is right. I'll always be one of them, belong to him. Saturday school and a shower can't change that.

CHAPTER 85

"MISS E LET me talk to Cricket the other day." I chew my bot-tom lip like gum. "She sound happy."

Maleeka asks if I'm happy, like she don't know. Then she ask what would make me happy. Before I get to think about that she telling me all the things that make her happy. Caleb, being a student scholar, making the gymnastics team—belonging to different clubs. She asks if I'd ever join a club. I think about the one next door to the Starfleet. That's not the kind she means, I know. Gem and us sort of belonged to a club. We did everything as a group until it was time to work.

I tell her about our house, all them trees, snow under our shoes, sitting around in our underwear playing cards, telling jokes, how glad we was to be family, friends. She don't need to know nothing about what happened after we got in the van.

I turn the light off. Make the room pitch black. Lie down on the floor and stare up at the ceiling. "You know how they find girls, Maleeka? Men like him, I mean?"

"No, Char. How?"

I tell her how he found me, where. Then I talk about how he went after a girl pumping gas at the station. I stayed in the car, while Daddy talked to her. "It's easy . . . getting kids to come with you."

"Did she come?"

"No."

"Why?"

"Some don't, that's all."

"Would I?"

I think on it some. "No. Not without kicking and scratching and screaming." How come I didn't do that? I wonder. Even at the house, I never tried to leave. Maybe 'cause I needed some stuff Maleeka ain't need, like money, somebody to take care of me, a Daddy and a baby.

I'm up, nervous. Turning on the light, I start walking the room. She fanning her nose when I go by. "Was Hattie McDaniel a slave before she was in that movie?"

"Really, Char?"

"I'm serious."

"Slavery ended in 1865. *Gone with the Wind* came out in the thirties."

"Oh."

She asking why I wanted to know. I don't say. I get my list out my desk drawer. I add more things to it every day. Today it was try not to think about them. I do all the time, anyhow. Having it on the list makes me check myself, slow down inside. Comb and detangle my hair got crossed off today, finally. But take a shower never does. This afternoon, I sat on the side of the bathtub with both my feet inside. The shower ran, turned cold. The water was black as mud. My feet are clean anyhow.

"Woulda boy go out with me smelling like this?"

"No."

"Good."

She passes by me. Digs around in her backpack hung on the hook on my door. Out comes a coloring book and crayons. Maleeka's at my desk when she say I can watch if I want. I go watch her color. "I'm glad they killed him."

She stops. "Killed who?"

"The man who raped Sister. You know, Miss Maya when she was young."

"Oh."

"Sister was only a little kid. She couldn't say yes or no—just go along with what he wanted or made her do. He was older. He knew better." I ask if anything like that ever happened to her. Guess she telling the truth when she say it didn't.

"What about you?" she ask.

"No, my father woulda killed him."

"But, Char, didn't Anthony—"

"I wasn't no kid! Plus, it was my decision to go with him or not."

She bring up girls who been trafficked, like JuJu said. I try to explain the difference between me and them. But my words come out all mixed up. They make it sound like me and them been through the same things—and that ain't true.

Seem like her eyes see things I colored over since I got home. With my head low, I whisper, "Sometimes they put Amber Alerts out on girls like them. My sister never put one out on me, so—I can't be one of them—trafficked girls, you know. I just can't."

She picks up a crayon, navy blue with sparkles. On a sheet of loose-leaf paper, she draw a big old circle. Inside, she put eyes, a nose, and lips that frown. I take a hunter-green crayon and draw tears running down her face. "That's me, Maleeka—inside anyhow."

Who start hugging first? I ain't sure. But we both holding on tight. "Char."

"Yeah, Maleeka."

"I miss my father every day. I don't tell anybody though."

I write it down on the paper in crayon. *I miss my mom and my dad.*

At her new school, she tell me, things ain't going as good as she lets on. "I'm there. I'm smart. Working super hard. But I don't always feel like I fit in."

I ask why she didn't tell me that before.

"I don't know, Char. Guess that's because you got it worse than me."

"What that mean? Nothing. Anyhow, if you keep your bad stuff to yourself and only let me talk about mine—that mean you think you better than me."

"No. I don't. It's just—"

"Come out and say it, Maleeka."

She bust out crying. Next thing I know, she hurrying over to the door. I step in front of it, though. "Tell me, Maleeka."

"It's back, Char."

"What's back?"

"Her cancer."

"Oh wow."

"But I don't want to talk about it."

I step aside. She opens the door. Just like that, she's down the steps, slamming our front door. I ain't mad. I understand. Sometime you just can't find the words.

CHAPTER 86

I LAUGH WHEN I see them bangles on her arms. "You still wear those, Miss Saunders, dang."

She smiling. On her way to the kitchen carrying her briefcase, she says, "Are we ready, ladies?"

Maleeka came early. Me and her rearranged the furniture. Me and JuJu painted the kitchen walls peach on Thursday. We ain't talk or say a word. It was nice being quiet together. It was Miss Saunders's idea to paint one of the walls black. To use it for a chalkboard. Our computer broke. Maleeka don't got her own. So, Miss Saunders's idea was a good one.

"We have four hours together, ladies. Let's make them count." She sits a package of papers at the table in front of each one of us. "I will be covering your major courses."

"You mean math, history, and everything?" I flip through the papers.

Maleeka say I owe her one, then apologizes. "I was only joking."

I do owe her. And I pray for her every night now—for myself too—'cause men like Anthony is everywhere. Plus, I don't want her mother to die.

"Char?" Miss Saunders bends down low. "Are you okay?"

I nod.

"If you want to talk or—"

"Shut up! Leave me alone! Why everybody treating me like I'm crazy in the head?" Before I know it, I'm crying.

Her eyes go from mine to Maleeka's. She ask her to take a break and step out of the room for a little while. She in her seat when she say for me to breathe in deep. "That's it. One more time."

I sit back, do like she say, catch my breath, finally calm down. "This the first time I ever listened to you, huh?"

"Probably."

"Miss Saunders. I know you want to help but—"

"Do you mind if I take your hand, touch you?"

JuJu asks my permission a lot now. "It's okay."

My hand is a sandwich in between hers. She asks if I know anything about mindfulness. I don't. She say it just means that you try your best to think on what is happening right now, right in front of you, not what happened to you yesterday, or what you might do tomorrow.

"Oh."

She not asking me to forget what I went through, she says. Just to try to focus on what I'm doing and thinking one minute, one hour at a time. "If you feel stressed, overwhelmed, or upset, take a deep breath. If that doesn't work, tell me. This is all for you. We will move at the pace that seems comfortable for you."

I stare at her. Into her eyes. 'Cause she ain't nothing like she was in school: loud, clapping her hands to get our attention, shoving assignments at you. Her voice is soft as water rolling over rocks, the wind in trees. "Miss Saunders. Anything this bad ever happen to you before?"

She don't say. Standing up, she tell me that she the teacher, but I will be teaching her too.

"Teaching you?"

"Yes—you aren't the only person to go through this sort of trauma. I want to be a good teacher to all my students, not just the ones who make As, have both parents, or sit quietly in the back of the class."

Maleeka hollers from the other room. "Y'all ready? Can I come back in?"

It's our first day. We work the whole four hours. After that, we have lunch. My sister made it. We eat, talk, and laugh. It's the most fun I had since I been back home.

CHAPTER 87

ONCE WE DONE eating dinner, somebody knocks at the door. "Answer it," my sister says.

I shake my head no. Stay exactly where I am, at my seat in the dining room, facing the door.

"Go on. It's her."

My heart speeds up, and I freeze at the same time. "Her?"

"Cricket."

I move fast as a train. Like I got wings. Knocking over a chair, tripping when I get to the ottoman in the living room, I yell, "I'm coming!" The dead bolt won't work with me. I turn it left and right more times than I can count. Finally, JuJu step in. After she opens the door wide, I scream. Just like that—she in my arms soft and sweet-smelling, pulling my hair, grabbing at my lips. "Cricket. You got so big!" I can't stop hugging her. Lifting her high, I step on the porch—freeze—hurry back in. She can't stop talking to me, drooling. "She getting teeth?" I ask my sister's friend.

She on her way down the steps when she say, "Watch out for the drool."

I lift Cricket's legs and each arm, then check behind her neck. JuJu look like she feel sorry for me, then says for me to take her on the back porch. I'm out there before I remember I don't go out there no more either.

We both sit on the floor, on a shag rug that my father put down.

The room is full of windows, so I look around a lot. Feel happy that the sun know where we at. Trees in the yard remind me of them from the house, but I don't let it bother me none. I'm out here, the closest I been to outside since I came home. Progress, Maleeka would say.

"Do you remember me?"

She give me the biggest grin. Then on her knees she go, crawling. I get sad 'cause I wanted to teach her to crawl, and video her along the way. And tell her when she was grown and I was old what age she was when she figured it out.

Checking her baby bag, I yell to my sister, "Miss E ain't bring her no toys!"

JuJu tell me this will be a short visit. No more than an hour. I carry her on my hip, run up to my room to get things I got JuJu to buy Cricket soon as we came home: keys, a Binky, a cloth baby block, a teething ring, and books. She ain't interested though. "Here." She snatch it out my hand. "You remember?" Up to her mouth it goes, until I explain that crayons ain't for eating. When I first got her, I let her hold one and she did the same thing I tell her. "This is what they do." I can't find clean paper. So, I walk her over to my desk and take out the coloring book Maleeka brung me. "See." We both get down on the floor. "Stay inside the lines." I let her think on that some. "If you do, you won't turn out like me."

I clear my throat. Tell her I'm not really sad. Then I get back to the crayons. "Don't use boring crayons like white, light-light pink, beige. And remember, I was the first person to teach you how to do this." I lift her hand. Hold it, help it outline Maya's face. "She is brown like you, so that's why we using this color." She don't care. I turn her hand loose and she throw the crayon. Fifteen minutes later, we on our way downstairs, when I remember she just had a birthday.

I apologize to her for not remembering sooner, or buying a present. In the kitchen, I take a donut out of the box. Sit a candle in it. And sing to her, crying some. "Your momma loves you."

She squeezes the donut, eats the pieces. I remind myself to tell Miss E to get Cricket a candle with a one on it, and to buy her a birthday cake.

A hour later she in the car in her seat leaving me. I wave good-bye from the window seat. JuJu wraps her arms around my waist and rocks me. "Do you think she know I smell?" I ask.

"Char, I bet Jesus knows how bad you stink."

"Miss Saunders didn't notice all that much."

"She was being polite. People do that when you going through it."

I ask her when she think I'll be done going through it.

"I don't know, Char. It take some people years to get to the other side. And most need help to make it. But you got to want it." For the ninety-ninth time she ask if I'm ready for therapy, to see someone or just talk with them on the phone.

"I'm cool, JuJu. Fine."

When I go to the bathroom and stand in the shower, it's because I do not want Cricket to remember me stinking like this. Only, I still don't wash or wet nothing except my feet. I wish I knew why.

CHAPTER 88

SHE SURPRISE ME showing up on a Sunday. We in my room. She at my desk coloring. I'm standing over her shoulder, watching. "Not that one. This. And this—Sunglow Yellow."

"Sooo—" she says, using the crayon I told her to use. "I have a date tomorrow night."

I run to the front of the desk. "With who? What you wearing?"

Pulling out her phone she shows me the outfit she gonna wear, how she wants her hair to look. But nerds don't know nothing but books and numbers. Which is why I hook her up with one of my hair combs and a real silver choker with a bracelet to match. I'm digging in my top drawer for more stuff, when I mention perfume. She never wear it. Never has. But perfume is like a back rub, holding hands, magic. The right smell get a boy to remember you long after you gone. I walk a bottle over to her. "Here, sniff."

Her eyes close. She smiling. Telling me what I already know. It smell like flowers, gets warm in your nose, makes you want to hug yourself. Might even get you kissed. "You can keep it."

"For real for real? The whole bottle?"

"Do I look like I need perfume?"

"You smell like you do." She opens it. Splashes me. "I had to, Char."

I chase her around the room, past the closets, around my bed twice, behind my desk—until I get my hand on the broom my sister left when she cleaned in here the other day. Maleeka ends up in the bathroom with the door closed. Sitting on the other side, resting my back against the door, I catch my breath. Inside, I feel warm as that perfume.

"Char."

"Yeah, Maleeka?"

"You're like her, you know."

"Like who?"

"Sister."

She say that me and Sister are the same because we both quit talking. That's stupid. I talk every day, all day, I tell her. I even talk in my sleep, JuJu say. "Who's Carolina?" she asked once. I pretended not to know what she was talking about.

Sister quit talking because she thought her words got somebody killed and she didn't want to hurt nobody else, Maleeka say. "You think your words will hurt people too."

Their names stay in my head when I say them: Roxanne, Earle, Kate, Gem, Kianna, Katrina, Rosalie, Cricket—JuJu too. If I tell, they'll die. He killed April, didn't he?

"Would you tell?" I ask. "No, you wouldn't. You think you would 'cause you don't know everything. Don't know what he could do, would do, did do to me."

"You're right, Char. I don't know. You could tell me one day. I'll listen. Swear."

"You ever tell your new friends what we done in that classroom?"

"No, but—"

"Some things you keep to yourself. 'Cause what's the point anyhow? What's done is done. You can't put the milk back in the bottle after it spills."

"The cancer spread."

I get to my feet.

"She didn't tell me. I found the papers from the hospital. A couple of weeks ago."

The knob is slippery in my hand, hard to turn.

"She got—" Maleeka stands upright when I walk in. "It's in her lymph nodes now. Stage three. That's bad."

In the bathroom, I take her hands—hold on like forever it seem. "You okay?"

"I'm okay."

"I guess everybody goes through something, huh?"

"The chemo took out her hair again."

"She bald?"

"Real bald."

I don't know why that makes me laugh a little, but it do. Then an idea come in my head, so I decide to do it. Like Maleeka is doing Saturday class for me. Like April and Roxanne helped save me. I run to my desk before I change my mind.

The scissors is sharp. They cut off my hair easy, quick, fast. Knots and string, matted hair and curls drop on the floor, get brushed off my shoulders, pile up by my feet.

Her eyes dance. Her lips curl up. Her hand goes out. "I did this once."

I hand over the scissors. Our hair ends up in a bag together. It'll stay together forever like her and me. Standing behind me, with her chin digging into my shoulder, she say, "You ain't have to do it, Char."

"I know."

"We look—terrible."

"I know. But I'm in the house. Nobody will see me. You—"

"Hair grows back."

I was gonna say she might get bullied, teased for how she looking. But she ain't the same Maleeka. She may not care. Might even kick their asses if they come for her.

Facing her, I say his name. "Anthony. He smart. Bet he was in the honor society like you. He killed a girl. April. Cricket's mom. If I stay in the house. If I keep my mouth closed. He'll leave me alone, I think."

"But what about them—your friends?"

I don't say nothing.

"And what about you?"

"What about me?"

"Sister freed her own self when she opened her mouth and spoke."

CHAPTER 89

PEOPLE DON'T PLAY jacks no more, I tell Miss Saunders. But she never done things the way other people did. She switching things up, she tell us. "Going old-school."

That cracks me and Maleeka up. For a minute, I wish John-John and Caleb was here. They wouldn't recognize her sitting on the floor wide-legged. Throwing the ball in the air, Miss Saunders snatches up six jacks. Then puts them down to grab more. She in the lead. I tell her it's 'cause she the oldest, and this is a old, behind game. After I win, she say it's because I catch on quick.

When it wasn't our turn, we had to keep track on paper of how many jacks the person picked up each time. Our job was to take them numbers and make up our own algebra problem. "Solve for x," she told us, "and x to the second power." Next week, she making us come up with our own word problems—two each.

"What did you think?" she said when class was over.

"It was fun."

"Learning should be fun." She asks us to collect materials and bring them over to where she is. JuJu studies at the kitchen table. Does her homework there too. I asked her once if she was still friends with Miss Saunders or talked to her on the phone. She told me no. It's because of me, I know it.

"Next time I'll bring a jump rope." Miss Saunders packs up her briefcase.

I laugh. "Like you can jump."

She hops a few times. The floor shaking. Maleeka tell her she overweight, might put a hole in the floor. I like that 'cause it's something Maleeka woulda said in seventh grade—even without me making her.

It's like Miss Saunders to profile, strut her stuff across the room like she did that one day at school, like she a model, pretty or something. I remember all the things I said about her face back then. It was because of the birthmark on her cheek. Seem like what I said to her just made her like herself more. Now, that birthmark on her face don't bother me at all.

I clap. With her hands on her hips, Maleeka follow Miss Saunders, who got both arms in the air, snapping her fingers. I join 'em the next time. I'm making moves, doing a cartwheel that lands me on my back. Maleeka pulls me up. We laughing when Miss Saunders start a Soul Train line.

"Okay. You, you two win." Out of breath, Miss Saunders sit at the table. After she take a sip of water, she say it's Tai time. Tai is our old math teacher. She weird, does yoga right there at the board. Arm stretches, leg stand poses. Miss Saunders got a yoga routine from her. We end our day doing that, plus quiet breathing.

"Told you she ain't the same," Maleeka whispers.

Miss Saunders told us she wanted us to have all kinds of tools in our box. Different ways to heal ourselves, calm ourselves, take care of ourselves, and learn. It's weird how she be talking now, like she fixed something inside herself.

I'm almost asleep when I say, "Miss Saunders. You changed."

"I hope so."

"You did too, Maleeka."

"So did you," they both say at once.

"No. I didn't." I tear up because it's a lie what I just said. I changed but in all the worse ways. Wish I had an eraser and could do away with the trip to Alabama that wasn't. Then I'd start all over again, sit myself down in class and do what I was told no matter what they asked of me.

"The old Char was too scared to try anything new," Miss Saunders says softly.

"She was mean too." Maleeka apologize for that, but she meant it. "I guess sometimes I was mean to Caleb."

"Girls—quiet."

"Miss Saunders. You like our hair?" Maleeka asks.

We not bald, just wearing our hair extra short, natural. I even let her wash my hair. It was so dirty I half expected worms to crawl out. Her massaging my scalp, oiling it, almost made me cry. My mother used to do that for me.

"I noticed. You two look beautiful."

I sniff under my arms. Miss Saunders notices that. I wonder what make her speak up about some things and not others? I don't ask. She just told us to get quiet again. We close our eyes and breathe.

By the time I wake up, they gone.

CHAPTER 90

IT'S AN OLD list. I never did much on it, but at least I planned to. Sitting in the shower with the water running, I read it over.

MONDAY: Take a shower. Sterilize Cricket's bottles

TUESDAY: Cook yourself something

WEDNESDAY: Give Cricket a bath, wash her things

THURSDAY: Try to eat

FRIDAY: Do not put your fingers down your throat

SATURDAY: Quit looking out the window for him

SUNDAY: Stop dreaming about him

MONDAY: Call the county and tell 'em to come get her if things still the same

I rip it up. Make a new one. The steam wets the paper, makes it hard to write. But I get it done.

MONDAY: Shower. 4 real this time.

CHAPTER 91

I'M ON THE back porch for the first time since me and Cricket was here. Maleeka got her back to the door, not me. She almost done reading Maya's book. I get to pick the next one. No reading out loud, we both agree. I wouldn't do as good a job with the voices anyhow. Sometime I wonder will I ever be as smart as her or Sister.

"You like words? Anthony did." I tell her about his dictionaries, that he went to college.

"Pimps that smart?"

I jump up, mad. "He wasn't no pimp. He was—" I can't pull the word up in my head. "He was—"

She apologizes. Backs down. Says let's get back to the book. Only, I don't wanna listen to her read now. "You messed it up, Maleeka. And what you know anyhow? Anthony was good to me."

That word keep coming in my head, pimp. Them the guys with girls on the street. I knew that before I knew him. But Anthony, he different. I look down at her, wish I could smack her. "If he was a pimp, what do that make me?" I go over to one of the windows and stare past the trees, houses on hills, buildings downtown. I think about them in the house. Carolina marching us through the woods. Having more clothes than I could ever wear. Good food. "Daddy—" I bite my bottom lip. "He"—I try to find the right name to call him, but I can only come up with one—"Daddy was Daddy, that's all I know."

How I know JuJu standing there. "Men like him prey on young girls like you and Maleeka."

Bet I got fire in my eyes.

"I don't care if you call him a pimp, Daddy, or the man next door. It's wrong, a crime, Char, what he done to you and the other girls."

I try to get past her. She blocks me. Stops me. Forces me to go back the other way past the windows to the door with the lock with the dead bolt that always got the key in it. I hear her say sex trafficking, bring up abuse, rape, yell that people who do them things should be locked up for life—put on death row. Finally, she screams, "If you only listen sometimes!"

The lock turns.

Maleeka calls my name.

JuJu say something about the police, I ain't sure exactly what 'cause I'm out the door, running in the rain barefooted like the night I escaped. My tears mix with the rain, making it hard to see. But I hear them both. They behind me, not far back, yelling my name. It ain't Charlie, either. Not even Char. "Charlese Katherine Jones!" I hear my sister say. "You ain't getting away from me never no more!"

CHAPTER 92

THE RAIN WASHED me. Tried to clean me. But didn't finish the job. JuJu did. She walked me upstairs and undressed me. Told Maleeka to run my bath. Getting in the tub I felt broken, in pieces, not myself at all but me for sure. Sitting down, hugging my legs, I listened to JuJu for once. "We going to the police station and filing a report. You will give them that man's full name and address and tell 'em about them other girls. They got female police officers that say they will meet with us, give you as much time as you need. Listen and not judge. I saw a trauma center, Char, downtown. I looked it up soon as you came home. They got groups. They will speak to you alone. We did this thing your way, now we need to take a different road."

I watched the water turn black, the tub empty out, the next tub of water turn brown, the next batch end up light gray till it was clear as the rain that I ran in. The water was colder every time the tub got refilled. So in between, JuJu brung scalding hot water she boiled on the stove.

When Maleeka left, it was dark. Her mother drives now, has a car, so she came and took her home. I got put to bed by my sister, who spent the night beside me just like when we was younger and my parents first died. Every once in a while, I thought about Sister, plus me and the girls in the house. Wasn't none of us safe. Couldn't nobody protect us. How's it any different now?

CHAPTER 93

SHE CALLED THE police first. Wouldn't give her name or mine, just put me on the phone. But I ain't say a word. Couldn't. They can't make me talk or report what happened if I won't even tell 'em what happened, they told JuJu once I gave her back her cell. The next day, one of Miss E's friends came by the house. She old. Retired. Used to be a prison nurse or something like that. I sat there, listened, cried—but at least I ain't stink. JuJu say I will if I stay out the tub that long again. It's been two weeks. No bath. I just can't. That lady told her why. "She's putting up a barrier, keeping people at a distance, reclaiming her body, hiding in plain sight." JuJu and her was in the kitchen, but I heard 'em. "This happens often when girls have been violated. Some girls put on enormous amounts of weight. Some dress in huge baggy clothes to appear less attractive, to keep unwanted attention away. Then there are girls like your sister, who may use their hygiene as sort of a weapon and a form of protection at the same time."

What should she do? my sister asked her.

"Give her time."

CHAPTER 94

WE HAVING A test. We get to take as much time as we need. It don't make sense to me. We only had six Saturday classes, and I ain't finish some of the homework. Miss Saunders say we can use our notes and textbooks. McClenton Middle's stamped in the book she brung to me. In between looking at the written assignment on the board, I wonder what she know. How much JuJu told her? Or if she told her anything at all.

Our math test comes first. For once, I'm done when Maleeka is done. I take longer on the history part. For English, we get to write a poem about anything we want. She only gave us three rules.

1. Use metaphors and/or similes. (What's them again? I ask.)

2. Draw on nature for inspiration. Use plenty of imagery.

3. Use a dictionary. Spelling errors will cost you points.

It's like that poem been sitting inside me since that night I ran into Anthony. Using a pencil, I write it down fast, erase some lines, cross out others, rewrite the whole thing, then ball up the paper I made a mess of. I turn it into a basketball that I shoot in the can by my desk. And start the whole thing again.

> Night time
> is a lake
> filled with snakes,
> hard to see but still there

waiting to bite
strike
swallow up
kids
too slow
or dumb
to know
this ain't the
kind of place
where lily pads and frogs be—
God neither.

CHAPTER 95

MY SISTER GOT me a book from the library. I asked for it by name. It's more up to date than Maya's, but I won't never forget Sister and Bailey. If I had a brother, I'd want one just like him. I say that out loud to Maleeka. Usually she would agree. Today it's like she got stones for feet. Since she got in ten minutes ago, she still in the same place, staring out the window, spaced out.

"Sit on my bed. I'll take the floor."

She flop down on the floor right where she is. Drops her book bag. I go to her this time. "You sad?" The look on her face don't change. "You mad? At me? What I do? I always do something, so I'll just say it up front. I'm sorry."

"It wasn't you." Her head goes down.

"Caleb. It was him. What he do? Break up with you?"

She shake her head no.

Opening the book, I read out loud even though we said we wouldn't. In between my sentences, Maleeka whispers, "I thought it was stage three. It's stage four."

I hug her like I hug Cricket. "We friends. You my girl. Anything you need—"

She need to cry, I see. To let it out.

"You got a strong mother like I had a strong mother. She gonna be all right." I say what everybody says, but I know people die from cancer . . . all the time. In my mind I ask Roxanne to ask God not to take her.

I take Maleeka's hand. Walk her to the bathroom. I run water in the sink till it's warm. Then I sit a washcloth in it. Cricket taught me how to go slow, be gentle especially around the eyes. Wiping, patting her face, I ask, "You wanna color?"

She nods.

I got her by the hand again when we walk in my room over to my closet. On my toes, I reach for my mother's hatbox. It was empty when I got it. But I liked the pretty color—fuchsia. Emptying it out on my bed, I watch crayons roll around, happy. "Take your pick."

I hid them before I left. 'Cause they're extra special to me. Left over from when I was little, from her trips to the store with me, some never used.

Side by side, on our stomachs with our legs up, we not saying a word. I draw a heart. Put dark lines all through it. Then make different kinds of boxes that I fill in with my favorite colors. I never go outside the lines. I color faster than usual. Maleeka take her time. Moves in slow motion. Starts with a sun in the sky, Caribbean-blue clouds. Her stick people look like they on stilts. But I know that's supposed to be her and her mother. They on the sand on the beach, holding hands.

Our crayons move over the page smooth as skates on ice. Our elbows touch. The sun making me squint sometimes when I look up at it. My fingers is happy though. Hers too. They pick up crayons. Move 'em fast and slow, leaving something pretty behind. She slow down, her breathing anyhow. Says I'm lucky to have a sister. "If something happened to my mom—" Maleeka reaching for the light pink one. Then the Pearl Gray. Her next picture is a house with them colors inside on the walls and furniture. "My mom says it's not as bad as I think it is. But parents lie."

"Don't they." I draw the ribbon. The symbol for breast cancer. It take up the whole page. She help me fill it in. We make it hot pink. After we done, I sign it.

On our backs, watching the moon come out, we talk about our mothers. Not about them being dead or dying. About the kinds of things we done with them when we was little. I run downstairs. Come up fast as I can. Flip through a photo album. She get to see me with my mom and dad. See how much I look like her and him, the clothes I wore, my hairdos back then. Out of nowhere, she take both my hands and squeezes.

"You scared?" I ask.

She shake her head yes.

"I stay scared now. All the time."

"Momma does too. She try not to show it. But I see." Her mother won't talk about her treatments. She comes home. Gets sick. Loses her hair. Bought a wig. Says she's okay when Maleeka asks if everything is all right. "But now—" Her legs shaking so hard it sounds like a dog's tail hitting the floor. "Should I quit coming here, Char? Stop my after-school activities?"

"Did your mother ask you to do that?"

"No, but—" It's the right thing to do, she say after a while.

I know. But I don't want her to quit coming. Bet she don't want that either. What I say is way different from that. "She your mother, Maleeka. Do what you gotta."

CHAPTER 96

SHE AIN'T COME today. It's only me and Miss Saunders here. I got a B on both my tests, B- on the math part. She wants to go over things I might not have understood well. I don't know about her and me with nobody else around. We might turn into who we used to be, argue and fight, I say to her.

"Well, let's give it a try anyhow."

She go over my tests one line at a time. I chew my lip, wonder when this gonna be over—and if she think I'm still as dumb I used to be. She get up on her feet, puts one of our test problems on the board, asks me to work it out. Standing beside her, I write the answer in neon-pink chalk. Step by step she show me where I made my mistakes, and how not to make 'em again. Later she move on to nouns, verbs, predicates. It take a while, but she help me see how they work and that they don't all do the same job in a sentence. It's almost an hour before we finish covering the test. She had to make certain, she said, that I understood the errors I made and that I know way more than I thought I knew. I do see how I can improve. How much I have improved. When I thank her for her help, I ain't lying. I mean it, for once.

She erasing the fake blackboard when I ask, "Do you think I'll earn my GED one day?"

"I'd like to see you in school full-time. With kids your own age. Going to the prom one day."

I'm already three years behind other kids at school. Grown up in ways I hope they'll never be. If I was in class now, what would we talk about, anyhow? How to do it in the alley? What position old men like? I wish I could ask her that. But teachers never understand what kids be going through.

She compliments me on my poetry, then goes in her briefcase. It's on the chair at the table. Like always, she keep the locks on. Out comes a purple journal tied with a silver see-through ribbon wide as my phone. She want me to continue my writings, she say.

"Just like Maleeka?"

"Writing can be cathartic."

"Ka—what?"

Miss Saunders ask my permission to go to the stove and start up the kettle. While she doing that, I get the cups and tea out the cabinet beside the sink. At the table, she pour steaming hot water over green tea bags shaped like triangles. JuJu bought them for me. I need to heal inside and out, she be saying.

In her seat, stirring her tea, she real quiet for a while. Me too. I add more sugar. Look out the window past her head. Right then Maleeka calls. Tells me she just couldn't make it. I ask about next week, she ain't sure about that either. "My mom needs me."

Miss Saunders asking what I wanna do. Finish our tea? Discuss how Maleeka's absence is affecting me? How her mother's cancer may change things for her? Her eyes shine when she say, "We can talk about anything at all."

I cross my legs, notice dirt on my left ankle when I bring up Maleeka's mom. "She was always nice. Why something bad like that had to happen to her?"

Miss Saunders saying what grown-ups always say. "The world can be a terrible place."

I ask what she know about bad things happening, besides what she see on the news. She stay quiet. I think about Cricket being taken from me, the friends I left behind. And him. "Anthony said it was my fault."

She don't know who he is or ask who he is. "What did he think was your fault?"

"Everything." I pick at the dust in my hair. Smell my stank fingers. "Never mind. You wouldn't understand."

"I see." Her hands is folded on the table like she the student not the teacher. The steam in her tea is gone after a while. I go to the stove to pour more hot water in my cup, then add too much sugar and wish she would leave. Miss Saunders sit her cup and saucer in the sink. Takes the seat beside me. Licks her lips. Clears her throat. Blinks and blinks like there's something in her eye she wants out. "If I tell you something personal do you think you can keep it to yourself?"

I got so many secrets I'm all full up. I say sure anyhow.

"I was a little younger than you when someone in my family—" She stops, fills her cup again, and puts three teaspoons of brown sugar in, stirring. "I've always been a big girl, Charlese. Tall, you know. Overweight." She pats her stomach. "And of course I was born with this." She touches the birthmark on her face. I laughed about it, talked about it at school. What I said was mean. Back then, I ain't think she liked me. I wanted her to know we felt the same way about each other.

She tell me what I heard before. That when she was little, she studied extra hard. Always was first in her class. Did anything she could to stand out for being excellent, so people would focus on something other than how she looked. But they bullied her anyhow. The way I done Maleeka.

"The first person to tell me that I was pretty was twenty years older." It made her feel pretty and special, she say. The next thing she knew he was treating her to lunch, asking to hold her hand. "It didn't feel right because it wasn't right. Adults should protect young people, but some—" She smiles but her eyes say what she won't. That she still think about what happened. Clearing her throat, she says that what he did to her wasn't her fault. "I was fifteen. He was—" She got both my hands in hers when she tell me, "It wasn't your fault either. Anthony knows that. Do you understand?"

I shake my head yes.

She don't talk long, but once she's done, I see that some parts of her story match me and Sister's story. A grown-up done something to her. He didn't steal her or beat her, but he did rape her, molest her, change her life forever. Them kind of people always make you think it's your fault, she say. "It's how they keep their hand on your shoulder, over your mouth. But if you stay silent, Charlese, they win."

My legs swing sideways like a door opening wide, but it's the opposite inside. I feel small, ashamed of what I done. Dirty. I turn my face away from her. "It's different with me. Not the same thing that happened to you at all. That wasn't your fault."

She slide her cup close to mine. Stands up, doesn't ask permission to go in our cabinets this time. Opening one after the other, she come back carrying a soup cup—wide and fat, a China teacup that never had a match, mugs, and cups with North Carolina, Maryland, Philadelphia, Dominica, and Pittsburgh written across the middle. She put 'em all on the table in a line. "Are these cups one and the same?"

"They the same but not the same."

"Right. Some hold eight ounces." She lifts the teacup. "Looks like this holds less." Some are plastic, she points out, then there's the mugs, and the ones with names of the places my parents visited before I was born. "They are similar, not the same."

Standing close to me she ask permission to touch me. Her soft fingers lift my chin. Her eyes and mine see each other for once. It may be that we ain't have the same exact experiences, she says. "But in many ways, it was similar, which does not make what you went through any less tragic, horrific, or abusive than what happened to me or any other child that has been sexually abused."

I pick up a cup and sit it in the palm of my hand. "It's the same, but it's not."

"That's all I'm saying."

I put my mother's China teacup back where it was. "And you told . . . what he done to you?"

"Yes, I did."

She ain't stay quiet. And she did something good with her life after a while. JuJu say I can too, but first I have to get out this house. I walk over to the stove. Turn the fire on under the kettle. After I fill our cups, I tell her a little more and a little more after that till she know the kind of work I did, where and who with. I feel dirtier than I look, cleaner at the same time, full, not empty like I been all these months.

CHAPTER 97

IT'S LIKE I got sunshine in my bones. Good ideas coming to me quick as Cheerios falling out the box and onto the floor. JuJu say this is the happiest she seen me since I been home. I took a shower. Washed myself from head to toe. She so proud of me she asked her friend to let me visit with Cricket. She'll drop her off this morning. Said she could spend the afternoon with me while she take her grandmother to the doctor. It's a lot to manage old people and babies at the same time, she said.

Lying on my bed, I call Maleeka and she does to me what I'd do to her—ignore the call, hang up. Yesterday I got JuJu to mail her a letter, plus a picture of her and me together. It was taken at McClenton Middle. I cut the twins out. Glued it on white paper, right in the middle. Then I drew a star around us, big enough to fill the rest of the page. All of my favorite crayon colors filled up that space. Made it look like rockets or fireworks was going off. Before I put it in the envelope, I wrote on the back for her to hang in there. Her mother too. She woulda done it for me.

CHAPTER 98

JUJU SAID THAT I might want to take it slow, just go up the block, around the corner, and back. But since my conversation with Miss Saunders, I know I can't sit still no longer. I woulda went out yesterday, but Miss E had everything all wrong. Her grandma's appointment was today. So, I waited. I wanted company, Cricket with me, in case I lost my nerve.

At the window, with her on my hip, I look out the blinds, then dig in my pocket for her Binky. It's in her mouth when I look down at the jeans I got on. You could fit two people in 'em. It's the same with my shirt. On my way out my bedroom, I untie my night scarf and sit it on the bed; slide a baseball cap on my head. Downstairs, I feel my stomach drop, my throat drying out. But I keep walking, thinking that if Miss Saunders's life could turn out okay, so could mine.

Cricket's strapped to my belly, faced out, when I shut the door, jiggle the knob. She coos, kicks, leans her head back—don't mind me kissing her sweet brown lips. We a team again. Maybe if I get myself together, I can get her back. Be her mother like April woulda wanted.

I look up and down the block, double-check every car I see. In the middle of the street I stop to let a school bus pass. My heart beats double time. So, I breathe in and out the way JuJu and Miss Saunders taught me. But I still feel like running home.

Maleeka live ten blocks from here. No big deal at all. Bet after I show up, she'll want to color or get her nails painted. I got everything in my backpack, plus a dozen glazed donuts. Swallowing spit, I hurry up, but don't get far. A block away my feet feel heavy as buckets. Inside, I'm turning sad. That's why I stop in front a daycare center. Me and Cricket get as close to the wall as the paint. "Go ahead." I take her by the hand. "It's okay." She touch the green circle. Her little fingers slide over the yellow triangle and red apples. I name all the colors for her. Look back over my shoulder. Point out the seals and walruses, polar bear and penguins, and then look over my other shoulder again. I help Cricket trace a few numbers: three, five, ten, eight. "My mother was good at math. Maybe you are too." I face the street 'cause I ain't comfortable with my back to people behind us. I smack my forehead for letting Anthony get all up in my head.

CHAPTER 99

I PUSH HER higher. Watch her feet kick. Listen to her giggle. When I can, I walk two swings over and do like she doing—swinging with my head back, laughing at the sky. Not for long though, 'cause she don't like sitting still. Jumping up again, I run and push her, tickle and kiss her. Tell her how much I miss being with her.

A hour is gone by the time I carry her over to the bench to give her a bottle of juice and Cheerios. Cricket couldn't eat nothing like that when we was together. She was too young. Now she got rolls behind her knees, a double chin. "You remember our place?" She don't, I know, but I wish she could. Shutting my eyes, I go back to the Starfleet Motel. We're on the floor playing with her blocks, reading *Goodnight Moon*. "Cricket." I open my eyes while I bounce her on my knees. "If it happens to you, tell somebody."

I pack her up and walk as fast as I can. Using a pencil, I scratch *take her to the park* off my list. If I wasn't doing that, I woulda seen them girls coming this way. Today ain't my best day clothes-wise, so I turn around and walk the other way.

"Char? That you?"

I look back. She catches up. Her eyes got question marks in 'em.

"Hey. What's up, India?" I say.

She with a girl who don't look up from her phone at first.

India and me was never close friends. But we would walk to elementary school together and go to the park sometimes. She ask how I been. After I say fine, her lips curl up, like she smelling something foul. Don't know why. I took a bath.

I'm walking when she ask about Cricket. I lie. And tell her she mine. She lies. And says she look exactly like me. Then she reaches over and pinches Cricket's chubby cheek. Right then, I let my guard down and ask how she been doing, what she been up to?

"You ran away, right?"

"What?"

She look at her friend, then Cricket, then me. "I heard you in that life."

"Huh?"

"You got a pimp, right?"

I start backing up.

"Ain't nobody surprised, Charlese Jones."

I turn around and run.

"Hope you came back rich!"

CHAPTER 100

I TURN ON the TV in the living room, open a bottle of gin, and sit down with my feet up. The more I drink, the more I think about him. With the bottle in my hand, I go upstairs. Taking a swig, I stare at my parents' door. I drink out the bottle, wasting gin on my shirt and my arm. Laughing, I go in their room.

His pictures are everywhere. So are hers. Their bed still the same way they left it—with the spread on and the sheets tucked under. On my way to his closet, I try to remember Anthony's number. It popped up on JuJu's cell when I first got home. She cussed him out and changed her number the next day. Then three times since then. He quit calling after she said she would give the FBI his number.

The door to my father's closet always opened extra easy. He only had three suits, but he owned a lot of shirts, all white. I bury my nose in 'em one at a time. Then, sitting on the bed, I drink until my throat and belly burn. In the hall, I take out my new cell, and dial his number. He don't answer right off, on purpose I know it. So, I call again, begging this time. That's when he pick up. "Daddy—"

"Apologize."

"I'm sorry, Daddy."

"I told you, nobody wants you. Loves you. Just me."

He orders my bus ticket without me asking. He gonna meet me at the Greyhound station tomorrow night. But I gotta leave now so I can make the last bus. "If you mention anything to any-body, I'll—"

"I know, Daddy. I don't wanna come back here no more any-how." I look around the room. Think about India and her friend. "Everybody know what I done."

"And, Charlie—this is your last chance."

CALL ME BY MY NAME

CHAPTER 101

I DROP HER off at Miss E's next-door neighbor's house. She an extra set of hands, I heard Miss E say once. The only other adult she trust to take care of her foster kids. She shakes her head but take Cricket just the same. Right after I hug and kiss her, I'm in the car again.

I got one last stop. If she ain't home, at least I know I tried. And at least I'll have everything checked off my list for today. When the driver turn the corner my head spins. I ain't drunk, but I'm not all the way sober either. I stuck my fingers down my throat and threw up what I could. Then took aspirins and drank two gallons of water before I showered.

He don't complain. He stop the car in front of Maleeka's house. "Maleeka!" I bang on her front door a bunch of times. I'm taking too long for him I guess, 'cause he already blowing his horn. I put up one finger and tell him to wait. Then run around to the side of the house where the kitchen is. They got sheer curtains at the windows, so she can't hide from me. "Maleeka! Girl, open this door."

It's around three. She still in a robe and slippers. Her hair don't look dirty, but it still messed up. This time, I use my fist on the door.

"Char! Stop it." Soon as it's open, she says, "I saw you, you know."

"You okay?"

She give me that look like I give people who ask stupid

questions. I pass by her, walk really fast into the living room, then the dining room. Some people get sad and so do their houses. Other people get sad and their houses lie, look all neat and happy, smell like good perfume. That's Maleeka's house, most of her room too when we get upstairs. I ask if she got the mail I sent to her. She sit on the side of her bed not saying a word.

"Talk to me. Say something."

The car horn beeps. Next, the driver bangs on the door. I don't answer 'cause she crying in my arms. Looking out the window, I see him put my suitcase on the curb. "Don't leave!" I say like he can hear me. "Maleeka, I gotta go."

I leave her. Run down the steps and out the front door. But he already gone. I smack myself upside the head. "Stupid, stupid, stupid." When my phone ring this time, I answer. He calling me out my name. Telling me what he's gonna do to me when I get back. Then he say something he already told me, "This is your last chance, Char."

His words turn to ice in my blood. 'Cause what if I'm already out of chances? And my last chance to get away from him was the last time I got away?

"Charlie? Charlie? Answer me."

I take the battery out my phone. Grabbing my suitcase, I run into Maleeka's house. Dumping my things on her floor, I tell her to pack. Fast.

"Why?"

"You coming home with me and JuJu."

"But, Char—"

"Hurry up. Sometimes you only get one chance."

Maleeka hug me so long it hurts. "It's always been me and Momma. Whenever something go wrong—"

She can't finish her words because she all choked up. But I think

I know what she was gonna say. Whenever something goes wrong, it's just her here to help her mother out.

I open her closet door. And ask her which clothes she wanna take. She in her drawer ready to pack everything, it seem like. "Maleeka."

"Yeah."

"I'm scared."

"Me too."

"What if he drive here and make me come back with him?"

She keeps packing.

"Nobody can stop him if he do."

Sitting on her bed shaking, I watch her fill up the suitcase. She's almost done when I take my cell out. Twice, I put the battery in wrong. Then I accidentally drop my cell on the floor. Picking it up, I look till I find the number to a place that helps kids like me. Three times I dial the number. The fourth time I get it right. I whisper, "Can I come and see somebody—right now?"

Maleeka says she'll go with me. So, we headed for the bus, even though JuJu said she'd meet us here at the house. No, I told her. I gotta go right now. While I still got the nerve. Otherwise, maybe I won't never go. And I'll end up back where I started or like April or Earle.

"The Roberta Henry Trauma Center," I whisper to the driver. I watch the door close, and don't hardly breathe full out until we walking up the steps to the center. Then, all of a sudden, I ain't so sure. "I don't wanna go to jail. He made me do those things."

The lady near the front desk hears me. "It wasn't your fault. You understand? None of it. And you're not in trouble. You're brave." She smiling when she walk up to us, introducing herself. "My name is Miss Cassandra. I'm a counselor here."

Maleeka take my hand and squeeze it. I'm staring at the floor when I say Anthony was my pimp. Miss Cassandra stops me to let me know that she is a mandated reporter. "A what?" I look up. When someone under eighteen tells her they have been abused, she has to report it to child protective services, she tells me.

I step back. Then back up some more.

Right then, JuJu runs in. Before I know it, I'm hugging her as hard as she hugging me, talking fast, stepping on my words. Her eyes get big after I repeat what Miss Cassandra just said. "I wanted to talk to you about that, Char, 'cause Miss Saunders is a mandated reporter too."

"She is?"

My sister say she found that out after I talked to Miss Saunders the other day. "She said the law makes teachers report abuse when they learn about it." She hug me tighter. "You was so happy that day, Char. And I thought to myself, if I tell her what Miss Saunders's gonna do, she'll run again."

I think I woulda.

"So, I kept quiet the last few days, hoping . . ."

Miss Cassandra walks up to a door and opens it. After I'm in counseling here, whatever I share will be confidential, she say to me. "That means even the police or a judge can't make us disclose what you've told us, unless you give us permission. That's the law here, too."

I nod. Maleeka take a seat in the lobby. Me and my sister walk slow up the hall far behind Miss Cassandra. "JuJu. How come you never put an Amber Alert out on me? Or sent the police looking for me, even if I ain't want you to?"

She stops, and starts crying, hard. Her shoulders shake, then her whole body. "I wanted to, Char. I wanted to. But I just kept thinking . . . what if they make it worse? Shoot you, instead of him." She done enough wrong by me, she say. "Exposed you to more than a child shoulda seen. So, I figured . . . if I could just get you home, alive . . . I'd make sure you got better, and I'd do better by you too."

I take her hand. "I know you aspire for good things to happen for me, JuJu."

She winks, then whispers, "You think I can get some counseling here too?"

"Maybe." We turn the corner, watch Miss Cassandra walk into a room. "JuJu?" I say.

"Yeah."

"I love you."

"I love you too, Char. And I always have."

BEGINNING OF THE SCHOOL YEAR

CHAPTER 102

"CHARLESE JONES," THE teacher say.

"Here."

A few kids look back at me. They know some of what I been through 'cause pictures of me are getting around. I'm proud of myself anyhow. He in jail because of me, waiting for trial.

"Miss Jones. You're new to our school. Did you know anyone before you came?"

I point to a girl in back of the room. Miss Saunders introduced her to me. Her name is Myra Grace. Her mother is a new teacher at McClenton since last year. She sort of shy, a nerd, reminds me of Maleeka only she ain't tall or dark. It's hard for her to make friends. Miss Saunders figured that since I'm good at that, we gonna be a good match. Since Myra Grace is good at math and English, turning things in on time, and obeying all the rules, Miss Saunders figured she would be a good influence on me. I think so too.

I raise my hand and start talking before the teacher give me permission. "There's another new girl coming," I tell her. She look down at her book. "She's in the office," I say. "With her foster mom. Her paperwork—"

"No problem. I see her name here. She a friend of yours?"

I nod. Kids stare. Guess Roxanne will get the same treatment.

Miss Evans brings up the things I'll need for this class. I write 'em down with the new pen Maleeka gave me. It came in a skinny white box and cost twenty dollars. She bought it with money she earning from tutoring elementary school kids. She's proud of me, she say all the time. I'm proud of her too, glad her mother's doing better. The cancer is in remission 'cause of a new treatment she taking at the university hospital. We both keeping our fingers crossed, saying our prayers. So is JuJu and Miss Saunders.

For a minute, my mind starts drifting. Before I know it, I'm thinking about him. "You're okay," I remind myself. "He ain't win." I close my eyes. "He got what he deserved." It took a while, but they charged Anthony with rape, child abuse, transporting minors across state lines, trafficking, murder, some other stuff too.

"When is the trial?" Mr. Bobbie asked the other day.

"It could be in a year; maybe two. It all depends," I told him.

I'm gonna be in that courtroom for sure. Right there on the witness stand. It won't be easy for me to go through something like that, people say. Anthony's lawyers will try to make me and the other girls look bad, like we wanted those things to happen to us or brought it on ourselves. But I ain't scared to speak up. Not all the time anyhow. Besides, the trauma center gave me a lawyer. A good one. She a district attorney. Her and my counselor gonna practice with me so I'll be prepared and know what to expect in court. I can even write a victim impact statement if I want and read it in court out loud in front of everyone. That way, I get to say in my own words what happened to me, how it made me feel, how it changed my whole life, and what I think they should do to Anthony.

When I first started counseling at the center, they let me draw and color my sadness and break plates when I couldn't find words for what I went through or was feeling. None of this was my fault. They say that a lot at the center. It's what my sister said all the time. Now I know it for myself.

"Charlese Jones."

I look up, hoping the teacher didn't ask a question while my mind was somewhere else. "Yes, ma'am?"

Kids laugh at them words.

"Would you prefer to be called by your first name, a nickname, or something else?"

"Call me by my name! Charlese." I spell it so everyone knows.

A kid behind me say I didn't have to holler it. Only that's not true. Anthony changed my name so I would forget who I was. I almost did, I told Maleeka. Then the other day I apologized to her 'cause I used to call her out her name all the time. I used to do a lot of mean things to her. Now I know how it feel to be disrespected, beat down, broken.

"We're the same, Char," Maleeka told me. "We both been through a lot. But we still here, right? Not standing still either."

She right about that. The other girls at the house ain't standing still neither. Gem is in a group home. Not that she wanted to leave our house. And she still won't squeal or turn on Anthony. Earle is on the street again, I hear. Gemini said she saw her in an alley—dressed in a cat suit—working. I pray for her sometime. Kate, Katrina, and Kianna are back home with their families. Joining clubs in school, dating. Texting me. Carolina is out on bail. She snitched on Anthony, big-time. Told the cops and FBI about April to keep herself out of jail. She still gonna do time, though. I'm glad about that.

I open my new notebook and smile at the note I wrote to myself. Never give up. I wrote that on the first page of every book I got, even my textbooks. It's sort of a promise I'm making to myself. A reminder for when things get hard, or I get scared or depressed. I drew the words too. Put them in a envelope and mailed them to

Cricket. She living with the bus driver. Him and his wife gonna adopt her, but right now they her foster parents. Solomon said he would be her big brother.

Last month, the driver and his wife drove Cricket to our neighborhood. We had a nice ceremony for April at the park. It was my idea. Miss Saunders came, Maleeka and her mom too. My sister asked if I had any words to say. At first, I said no 'cause me and Maleeka done enough work to make this day special, I figured. So, I didn't need to do no more work. But they came out, them words, soft and slow, pretty too. "April was worth something no matter how she looked or dressed or acted. And she ain't deserve what happened to her. No one does. I am glad we was friends for a little while, anyhow."

The driver opened the box in his hand and seven butterflies flew out. One landed on Cricket's hand, and stayed there awhile. The wind blew, and the sign me and Maleeka taped to the fence looked like it might rip. Only, it didn't. It stayed strong and showed off our work. Miss Saunders said, "I'm proud of you, Charlese. You also, Maleeka." We was proud of ourselves too.

I knew I could color, but I ain't know I could draw, till Maleeka told me to try. But right there on the sign was the proof, plus Maleeka's hard work too. All kinds of girls walked and flipped across the paper. They sat at desks in school; played jacks on the floor; jumped rope with friends; went to school in groups; hung out in the bathroom smoking; kissed under the bleachers; crossed against the light—and did all kinds of things that kids do. April was there too. On a bus. Holding Cricket—happy.

Us, it says at the top of the page. I put it there to remind us girls that we need to stick together, fight for one another, look out for each other, and never forget—no matter what people tell us—that don't nobody own us or got the right to beat or abuse us. I looked at Maleeka and almost apologized to her again. But I had done that already. So, my arm went over her shoulder. And her arm went around mine. Quiet as the sun going down, we left the park together, smiling.

Roxanne ain't make it to the ceremony for April 'cause social services didn't have everything worked out with our state and theirs until the other day. JuJu wanted to take her in. Only, she still got her hands full with her new job, and me. That's why I asked Miss Saunders if she would foster her. "She don't belong to nobody," I told her. "And that ain't right." It helped that the judge and the police sort of took a liking to Roxanne. She that kind of girl. You like her even if you can't exactly figure out why.

Walking into Miss Evans's class smiling, Roxanne waves at me. "Hey Char." I wave right back at her. She hand the teacher some paperwork. Then asks her if she can sit beside me for the rest of the year. I stand up when she get to our row. Roxanne squeezes me tight. "I knew God wouldn't let you forget about me," she say. Then she tears up like she might cry.

I almost cry too . . . but then I stop myself. 'Cause all I been doing is crying. And I'm tired . . . ready for good things to happen to me. Like going to school dances and basketball games, joining a art or writing club and going to college one day—Miss Saunders said it could happen, if I work hard enough.

I know I ain't done healing. I know I still need counseling. But I color myself happy anyway, 'cause I am.

MY JOURNEY TO CHAR

I've never liked Charlese Jones very much. As the bully in my first novel, *The Skin I'm In*, she tormented thirteen-year-old Maleeka Madison, the girl in the book who is most like my younger self. So, why write a novel based on such a character? In many ways, it's a no-brainer. Char is unforgettable.

Strong-willed and in need of love and guidance, Char kicks those close to her. Still, educators and students clamor to learn what makes her tick. Their interest in her goes beyond the pages of my book. Has Char's life improved? they ask me, as if she were a real girl. Will she ever go live with her grandparents? Is she still stuck in seventh grade? My answer was always the same. I do not know. As an author, once I've completed writing a novel, I don't continue to communicate with characters or plot out their next moves. But like many readers, I could never completely get Char out of my head.

The Skin I'm In has defined a generation. Readers tell me that it helped them find their voices and feel proud and positive about who they are and how they show up in the world. Before I wrote it, I don't believe I truly understood the power of books to make a difference. Now I know that literature can also be a survival tool. In many cases, it arms and equips us. It can help us untangle the threads of our lives, and better connect us to ourselves as well as the world at large. Young people inherently understand this. Which is why so many teens and tweens read the same book half a dozen times or more. I cannot tell you how many people have read my work. But I can tell you that millions of them are young people.

Today, young people around the world need us more than ever. Which is exactly why I wrote *The Life I'm In*. And why Charlese Jones is the perfect protagonist to tell the story and shine a light on a global pandemic, human trafficking, which disproportionally affects women and children.

Against all odds, Char endures and survives the insidious and inhuman world of human trafficking. As the novel unfolds, readers witness her life spiraling out of control. Char no longer attends school. She continues to grieve for her deceased parents. Her sister insists she leave their family home. Independent, yet naive, Char decides to live on her own. Challenges abound. Money and other resources evaporate. At her wit's end, she encounters an adult who has made hundreds of thousands of dollars preying on children.

This book was a particularly difficult journey for me. For starters, I had to develop a real relationship with Char, to like and empathize with her. Then there was the subject of the book itself. I'll admit—there were weeks I could not read the articles and reports I had tracked down or go over the interviews I had done. Human trafficking is a horrific, immoral crime against some of the most vulnerable people on the planet, especially our young. To tell this story, I could not shy away. To write the novel, I had to step into the lives and minds of these young people, to remind the reader every step of the way that these are our children, worthy human beings, while also showing the brutality and viciousness they are subjected to day and night. It's a delicate but necessary balance. I thank my editor, Andrea Davis Pinkney, who helped me walk it.

In 2000, the United Nations Palermo Protocol to Prevent, Suppress and Punish Trafficking in Persons established a commonly accepted definition of trafficking. In short, human trafficking involves the exploitation of vulnerable individuals for profit, by way of fraud, force, or coercion, in an effort to engage them in commercial sex or to obtain, recruit, harbor, or transport them for labor or services. It is the second most profitable illegal enterprise in the world, after drugs.

Human trafficking may occur in one's neighborhood, in the office, on farms, in factories, in eateries, or near schools, group homes, and other institutions where young people are served. Traffickers may be male or female, our neighbors, strangers, employers, or even relatives. Based on the United Nations Palermo Protocol and the Victims Protection Act, trafficking may not always involve a person being transported from one location to another.

According to Polaris, the organization that operates the National Trafficking Hotline, "human trafficking is a $150 billion global industry that robs 25 million people around the world of their freedom."

Trafficking survivors are among the bravest, most self-determined people on the planet. To work through the trauma they experience may take years. Yet, these individuals serve as a beacon of hope for many. A host of organizations and individuals around the globe stand with them to help combat and eradicate this plague. Some of those groups include survivor advocates, governments and NGOs, trauma-informed centers, child welfare organizations, law enforcement, religious organizations, the United Nations, and everyday citizens like you and me.

No city or town is too small to join in the fight. Conducting research, I learned of a number of initiatives taking place in Erie, Pennsylvania, a city near Pittsburgh. At the time of this writing, the Sisters of St. Joseph of Northwestern Pennsylvania were working to pass legislation that would make it easier for victims in public spaces to find out what trafficking is and how they could get help. The legislation will also educate travelers who may not know what human trafficking is. The Crime Victim Center of Erie offers trauma-informed counseling, prepares survivors for their day in court, works closely with law enforcement, and helped over five thousand victims in 2018. A thirty-eight-member group in Erie has taken a holistic approach to tackling human trafficking by bringing together survivors, social justice experts, law enforcement, government officials, higher education representatives, and others.

If you or someone you know is a victim of human trafficking, please contact the National Human Trafficking Hotline at 1-888-373-7888.

RESEARCH AND RESOURCES

1. "The Hustle: Economics of the Underground Commercial Sex Economy" (accessed from apps.urban.org)

2. "On-Ramps, Intersections, and Exit Routes: A Roadmap for Systems and Industries to Prevent and Disrupt Human Trafficking" (accessed from polarisproject.org)

3. "Safe Harbor: State Efforts to Control Child Trafficking" (accessed from ncsl.org)

4. "Selling Innocence: Human Trafficking Along the 1-90 Corridor" by Jonathan Skinner (accessed from erienewsnow.com)

5. "Selling Innocence: Survival and Recovery" by Jonathan Skinner (accessed from erienewsnow.com)

6. "United Nations Convention Against Transactional Organized Crime and the Protocols Thereto" (accessed from unodc.org)

7. "US Department of Justice National Strategy to Combat Human Trafficking, 2017" (accessed from justice.gov)

8. "US Department of State Trafficking in Persons Report, June 2019" (accessed from state.gov)

ACKNOWLEDGMENTS

There are a number of individuals who proved extremely helpful to me during the process of writing this book. I would especially like to thank Rebecca Mackenzie. A trafficking survivor, Rebecca shared her story, and critiqued my novel, on multiple occasions. She is an advocate who works tirelessly with other survivors as well as the homeless, while maintaining her own family and working full-time in the sciences. Thanks also to Officer Joseph Ryczaj, Narcotics and Vice, City of Pittsburgh Bureau of Police. Detective Ryczaj met with me early on my journey and shared contacts and resources. Lastly, I want to thank Paul Lukach of the Crime Victim Center of Erie and Betsy Wiest, the Social Justice Coordinator with the Sisters of St. Joseph of Northwestern Pennsylvania. They each helped me better understand the important role organizations play in helping survivors work through trauma and getting the help they seek and need.

With much gratitude, I want to thank Amanda Lewis, MSSW, Statewide Community Organizer, Texas Association Against Sexual Assault (TAASA), for her careful reading of the book, and her insights into the world of human trafficking. My love, hugs, and thanks to my daughter, Brittney, and my friends Yolanda Harris, Kathy Payne, and Ty Greenwood. I so appreciate you all reading the manuscript and giving me necessary feedback.

Leah Pileggi, thank you for the title. Leigh Skvarla, you are amazing, thanks. Jennifer Lyons, my agent, well done, my friend, and here's to a long, successful working relationship together.

Tonya Bolden, what can I say? You have meant so much to me as both an author and a friend. You have been a critique buddy, hand holder, and encourager as I struggled to give birth to novels these last years. Watching you flourish, discussing politics with you, and laughing along the way was much needed medicine—thanks. I am truly grateful for our friendship.

Lastly, I want to give a big, loud thank-you to my Scholastic family. You did an incredible job and I appreciate it. Shout-outs especially to my editor, Andrea Davis Pinkney (you rock in so many ways); VP, creative director Elizabeth Parisi, who created such a powerful cover; editorial assistant Jess Harold; production editor Melissa Schirmer; copy editor Holland Baker; and Lizette Serrano, VP, Educational Marketing, for getting this book into so many hands.